MADONNA FROM RUSSIA

By the same author

Angels on the Head of a Pin (published by Peter Owen)
Contemporary Myths: A Skeptical View of the Literary Past
Informer 101
Passport to Yesterday (published by Peter Owen)
Prisoner of Russia

MADONNA
FROM
RUSSIA

YURI DRUZHNIKOV

Translated from the Russian by
Thomas Moore

PETER OWEN
LONDON AND CHESTER SPRINGS

PETER OWEN PUBLISHERS
73 Kenway Road, London SW5 0RE

Peter Owen books are distributed in the USA by
Dufour Editions Inc., Chester Springs, PA 19425-0007

Translated from the Russian *Superzhenshchina*

First published in Great Britain 2006 by
Peter Owen Publishers

ISBN 0 7206 1255 1

PART ONE
LOVE'S TATTERED SAIL

'There are just three things worth writing about:
love, death, and money.'
— *Ernest Hemingway*

I

Pulling the auditorium door closed behind me, I went to the blackboard, wrote out the day's topic and began speaking, when I noticed that this old man was once again sitting right in front of my lectern. Sprawled in his seat, he was looking me straight in the mouth, drawing in everything I was saying with his noisy breath through a nose that looked like a worn-out baby bootee. It's not every day that you come across such enthusiastic students.

These lectures of mine, on Russian poetry of the Silver Age, were at eight o'clock in the morning, in conformity with a schedule drawn up by some mindless computer, indisposed to differentiation between poem and theorem. The students came in late and sat there sleepily, slowly coming round. Even worse was that the lectures were mainly in Russian. Comprehension among my American listeners was never the best, and when they were half asleep it was even worse than later in the day. If a question came up, a short clarification in simple English was always necessary.

Today's class was on the sources of symbolism, specifically three collections of Bryusov's that exemplified this emotional topic. I myself hadn't become emotional about it for a long time. I can emote on the subject, true enough, but it's just superficial, out of habit. I talk away entirely automatically, without any notes – something that comes from years of well-worked-out professionalism. Slowly, somewhat histrionically, I read out Bryusov, with pauses in between:

> I am bothered by a single dream:
> To die, my dreams unbelieved in,
> But before death to press a kiss
> To your dear, pale lips.

An old, sprawling fig tree was taking in the class as well. It grew right outside the window, and it pressed its fretted, clammy leaves against the window's panes so as to hear better. Under the tree shone a bronze memorial tablet saying that some lady had planted this fig as a gift to the University of California. Because the fig tree grew as high as the roof, sunlight never penetrated into the auditorium, but I had no wish to turn on the lights: they were neon lights, and one of them, the one directly over my head, always buzzed.

I had several well-rehearsed witticisms in readiness. The students – except those who were sleeping off a night's boozing – would always laugh whenever I came out with the next joke from my bag just to see if they had their wits about them. To keep from getting bored myself, I would scrutinize my seated students one after the other.

I could tell by some of my students' eyes that my words were burbling in their ears like bubbles in a boiling kettle or hissing like the surf on the Pacific Ocean not so far away. Two-thirds of the class were girls, some of them attractive, with cute knees and that sort of thing, but even those weren't in the best of form that early in the morning. They brought their breakfast with them and ate it there, sucking up their coffee through straws from paper cups, and then combing their hair. One of them half reclined, draping her legs over the back of the chairs in front of her like someone on a gynaecologist's couch. To my left a young single mother took out her breast and put her nipple into her infant's mouth. The mother was white, the little baby was black. He made a face, spat it out and squinted his eyes at me: evidently the baby was more interested in the problems of Russian symbolism than he was in milk.

Right beside the nursing student – now I was slowing down my gaze again – sat the elderly man with a thin goatee and a mane of bright-ginger hair round his bald, tanned pate. His bronzed face was weatherbeaten and fissured with deep wrinkles, his skin peeling. Like everyone else, he was dressed in shorts and a tank top, and his seriously hairy legs terminated in sandals without socks. His tank top had a picture of a cow on it, a speech-balloon with the words '*Non-fat only!*' emanating from its mouth.

In general the various students' ages had ceased to give me pause a long time before. People of middle years would suddenly decide to change their profession and showed up at the university. An ageing woman, escaping into retirement after smiling herself nearly to death for twenty years at her bank cashier's window, would dream of spending her time at something more romantic, like ceramics.

I remember a seventy-year-old former Marine who had sailed into Murmansk during World War II. This guy had come to some lectures of mine several years ago on the history of censorship. He'd been tormented all his life, he explained, by some expressions that he'd heard from Russian sailors but had been unable to find anything like them in the dictionaries. These expressions were something that I understood, as you might suppose, but there was no way I could have translated them properly into English.

A postman by the name of Bob had registered for a seminar for young writers the previous year. For twenty-seven years he'd gone from house to house delivering mail, with a high-frequency sound generator around his neck to scare off dogs. In order to make the time go by faster, he'd taken to mumbling to himself, and he'd managed to rhyme himself into thinking that he should take up poetry in his retirement. Unfortunately, according to his ID, his name was Robert Frost, and that was something of a trap, as you can appreciate. Not long ago an Alexander Pushkin published some of his poems in the New York magazine *Novy Zhurnal*, but he was a real-live descendant, at least. At first he proudly signed himself Alexander A. Pushkin, but then he gradually came to the sensible conclusion that it was quieter to live life under a pseudonym, one that I have no right to divulge.

In a word, the pressing advice for my older-than-he-should-be student Robert Frost was simple enough: to adopt a pseudonym of his own, even if it had to be something like 'Bob Postman'. Not long ago I ran across some verses in *The Potomac Review*, the prestigious literary magazine, with the signature 'Bob Postman' underneath. So the postman hadn't been mumbling in vain while delivering his letters.

The symbolism of the Russian Silver Age meanwhile continued its exposition, partially flying off into nowhere, partially being drawn in by the ears of my students and the nostrils of the elderly gent sitting in front of me. He howled like a vacuum cleaner! How old *was* he, anyway?

The calendar stops entirely for some Americans of a certain age. Surely he was over seventy-five, though. But he looked to be in thoroughly good health, his eyes weren't closing with fatigue and he laughed when everyone else did, although with a little restraint. He got to the lectures in good time, in order to get a nice spot, fresh as a daisy from his shower. He would sit with his bicycle helmet strapped on, hugging his knapsack on his knees, and his lips would move, as I soon understood, muttering everything I was saying to himself word for word, like a prayer. Devotion like that to Russian symbolism isn't often come across among students.

In California there's a vast multitude of things more diverting, pleasant and – most important – more practically useful than these lectures of mine, anyway. What the hell did he need the Silver Age for? But even this question just fleeted by me while I was coming out with my closing remarks. An hour and a half had passed; the gaunt figure of Prof. Pete Hayter, the Hemingway specialist, was already looming in the doorway.

Coming outside I found myself in an anthill. From all sides and in every direction students were tearing along on their bicycles. Alongside me someone braked sharply, asked me something, disappeared. On the way I lingered a moment at the snack stall to get a cup of coffee – caffeineless, sugarless, tasteless. Sucking the slop through a straw as I walked, I hurried back to my room for office hours.

Students were already sitting expectantly in a line along the corridor to one side of my door; I'd been trudging along on foot, while they were on their bikes. The red-haired elderly man was sitting on the floor as well, at the very end of the queue. Everyone came in by turns. Briskly sorting out all their problems, I managed to gulp some of my coffee. Now the old man leaned against my door jamb and froze.

'I'm not interrupting anything?' he asked hoarsely. 'I really like your lectures, sir. They're most diverting!'

It was obvious that this dutiful praise wasn't what had brought him. After shaking his hand, I gestured towards the chair. He introduced himself.

'My name is Ken. Ken Stemp.'

And he sat down, snuffling, putting his helmet down on the floor and squeezing his knapsack to his belly with both hands. What had earlier seemed to me to be a cross hanging from a string around his neck was actually, when I looked at it, the key to his bicycle lock.

'How can I help you?' I asked mechanically, picking up some letters that needed responding to from the heap on my desk.

'I have to learn Russian right away.'

Dear Lord, how often you get to hear that 'right away'! And not from stupid people either. How come they always came to me and not the linguists?

'The language?' I elaborated. 'Easy as pie! For that, it's not even necessary to be a student at the university. Check out the campus bookstore: I just recently came across a textbook called *Russian in 15 Minutes*. Open it up, and . . .'

'I did open it, sir,' he said disappointedly, wrinkling his nose. 'It didn't work in fifteen minutes.'

'What's the date you need the Russian by?'

The joke went over his head.

'It has to be as quick as possible.'

I sighed. The conversation was proceeding entirely in English. However, the lectures that inspired him so much were in Russian. In class his reactions were entirely animated, though; so, naturally, I had to be curious:

'Isn't it hard for you when the lectures are in Russian?'

'Quite the opposite – it's really easy,' he said, smiling politely. 'Since I don't understand a thing.'

'Well, why don't you ask me to translate the parts you don't understand?'

'You still don't get it,' he amplified. 'Except for what gets said in English, I have *absolutely* no idea what you're on about.'

At this point, if not surprised, I did have to look on him with a certain curiosity.

'Not a single word?'

'How could I?' he'd taken offence. 'I know *pee-rosh-kee*, *toh-vah-reesh*, *nee-yew ladnah* . . . and *toap-toap*. *Toap-toap* is what my mom used to say to me when I was little. She spoke Polish and Russian. But for some reason you don't use any of these words.'

'Listen, my dear Ken! I'm giving this very same course in English, only it's next quarter. Why don't you come to that one?'

'Not a chance! I'm drinking in the music!'

'What music?'

'The music of the Russian language. Not a word of which I can catch, yet, unfortunately. However, there is one thing: who's that Katory? You keep coming back to that fellow. Is he some famous Symbolist poet?'

He wasn't being modest about the level of his understanding; that much was clear.

'It's a pronoun,' I squeezed out, gloomily.

Ken looked sad.

Why some Americans suddenly take an interest in Russian things is always a mystery: their motives are as various as from big-business necessity all the way down to sheer boredom. One of my female students crammed Russian proverbs for two whole years and would spout them out whenever she got the chance. And why did she bother with them, considering that no one these days expresses himself in these folksy sayings? 'It's so when I'm at a disco I can rattle things off that nobody understands,' she explained. 'It blows the guys' minds.'

We don't ask why students want to take Russian. Sooner or later all of them come to explain their craving themselves, in the hope of getting some advice. Even Ken was bound to crack some day. Not some day, as it turned out, but right here and now.

'I need your language right away, sir – it's vital to me,' Ken repeated. 'My new girlfriend is Russian, doesn't know any English at all. I need to be able to talk to her.'

'And how do you propose to tackle Russian?'

He gave it a moment's thought.

'Do you know how children pick up a language? From the air.'

'Forgive my rudeness. How old are you?'

'Eighty-four.' Ken looked himself over and smoothed his goatee. 'So what?'

'Well, you're no longer a child.'

'But I'm in great shape!'

'I don't doubt that for a second. So here's the thing: we have good instructors here and wonderful programs to use on talking computers. You'll have to cram away at vocabulary, grammar, dialogue, translation and all the rest, like someone at hard labour. Then in three years . . .'

'Three years! Yeah, but I'm in love with her right now, and I can't tell her about it.'

'Hire an interpreter, then, damn it!'

'I've already thought about it. But it wouldn't be very convenient: in bed with my girlfriend, and the interpreter underneath the bed.'

'That's true . . .'

'And that's why I've decided to kill two birds with one stone at your lectures: drink in the language and the poetry at the same time!' He demonstrated his method by drawing in the air through his two huge nostrils. 'In the situation I'm in, a knowledge of Russian poetry is exceptionally important, even drastically necessary!'

Since I was worried about several urgent things that I had to do right away, his last phrase didn't register, to my regret. Everything in this sublunary world repeats itself, surprising us less and less. Even young Americans spend years of boring labour at the acquisition of this foreign language, with the intention of making it their profession: they travel to the Russian heartland for experience, where they learn how to drink vodka in order to understand the local lexical irregu-*larities. And this eighty-four-year-old Ken Stemp wanted to gain command of the language on the fly, out of thin air. He had to be able to chat up his new girlfriend, you see.

'So she's a recent émigré,' I said, stating it more than asking it, looking at him and trying to estimate her possible age.

'Good guess!'

In this modern day and age this Russian woman could even be an eighteen-year-old – nothing strange about that. Or even younger – but in America you get put in gaol right away if you mess with a nymphet, and you don't get out again until she's retired. Russian émigré girls, though, in contrast to American ones, hardly ever run off to the police after the deed is done.

'Of course, she's only just here from Russia!' Ken exclaimed, proudly. 'And, by the way, she's the most outstanding poet of the twentieth century as well.'

Oops! The fellow had managed to surprise me after all.

'A distinguished poetess? What's her surname?'

'I don't remember,' he said, embarrassed. 'My memory's worn out from all the work I've done, so names don't stick so easily. Her first name's Lily. She r-r-really looks sexy! A genius of pure beauty, as one of your poets said. Which one, if you have to know, I'll try to remember later. But the most important thing, of course, is that she's the girl of my dreams!'

'I have no doubt, since you've taken to her so quickly.'

'Taken to her? Hey, if you want to know, I've flipped my lid over her! I've even decided to give my sailboat to my eldest son, so it doesn't distract me from Lily. I feel like I'm getting younger by the day.

Pretty soon I'll be able to chuck my diet. But I'm going to speak the language – I'm digging my heels in!'

Throwing his knapsack over one shoulder and his helmet over the other, the old man made his way out of my office, disappointed at my scepticism. I honestly didn't know how to help him. Maybe you do?

2

Nope, Ken Stemp not only didn't take offence, he came back for more. Everyone has the right to come see you during office hours with whatever rubbish they have for you, and you're required to lend them a benevolent ear. Students, with their entirely practical questions, crowded into my corridor. Having waited his turn in line, Ken now sprawled hugely in the chair, and no hints of any sort could drive him out of my office. He was radiant. He had to have someone to listen to him. He couldn't wait to share his surfeit of happiness. Like all successful Americans, he adored talking about himself.

'I was around three years old when my parents sailed to California from Poland . . .'

The Stempowskis, father and mother, considered themselves socialists even before they had left their homeland, but their homeland had no wish to hurry them into any radiant future. Someone had given them the idea that the time was ripe for this in America, so they crossed over the ocean. To simplify their life the tailor Stempowski snipped off exactly fifty per cent of the letters of their surname, tailoring the name down to its first half, Stemp, and then sewed the simple American name Ken on to his son. All that was left was to realize the cherished goal of theirs that America was ripe for.

'Everything would have been fine in the United States if there'd only been socialism here,' Ken said. 'World War I ate away at Europe, but there wasn't a whiff of the good life here in the western USA, either. And the harder my parents worked, the more they dreamed of the workers' paradise.'

'And where are they now?' I asked, not thinking of his age.

'Heaven,' Ken answered simply.

He had completely forgotten the Polish language, or maybe he had never actually known it very well. The new European war clattered him into military intelligence in Germany, and he spent a while in ravaged Poland, from which he extracted the English-teacher daughter of a former neighbour and married her, after which she bore him two sons. His wife had died fifteen years ago.

'I've got five grandsons now,' – he raised his hand, showing me five fingers – 'but I don't want to play with them. I got worn out at my government job, and now I've got my pension and I'm taking it easy. Or, more properly, three pensions: my military one, my California pension, and my social security. So I'm insured against any need or medical expenses. Since I retired I've realized how boring it was to be an official.'

'What kind of official were you?' I was getting interested.

'I served in the Collection Agency.'

It was hard for me to imagine what kind of service that could have been. The Lord has so far preserved me from contact with that office. I've merely heard that this is the agency that goes after debtors.

'What did you do there, if it's not a secret?'

'Sat at the telephone morning till night, squeezing money out of deadbeats. People who wilfully don't pay and then try to hide it. People who owe alimony, for instance. Or drunks who've been fined for drinking on the street or driving under the influence. Or from parents, if their kid has been up to something. I'd winkle them out via the police and call them. They say that the only thing that's free is the cheese in a mousetrap, but not even that is, in America; you've got to pay for everything here. For example, when somebody gets out of gaol, after his stay behind bars, by law he has to pay for it – just like in a hotel. Not much, but he owes it: forty-one dollars for every month locked up.'

'No kidding? Boy, I didn't know that!'

'That's because you've never been in gaol. If you had been, you'd know.'

'But what if the fellow refuses to pay?'

'Heh! That's how I earned my salary! One gaolbird refused point-blank: "Gaol wasn't so hot," he objected, "so I'm not paying for it." So I put a hold on his bank account. I go to his employer to garnishee his wages. "Your child," I say to a kid's parents, "broke a park streetlamp with a rock and has to pay a fifteen-dollar fine. But to process the fine on the computer is going to cost forty-seven dollars. You choose, OK?" Or, here you go: they catch some guy who's been peeking through girls' windows in the dorm. Every night towards the time the girls would be undressing, taking showers, and all that sort of thing, this peeping Tom would haul out his folding chair and his beer and set himself up on the little hillock out in the trees and get his kicks.'

'But what did you have to do with it?'

'It was the chair and the beer that bothered the judge the most. He said, "*Nee-yew ladnah!*" and fined him one million dollars.'

'How was the guy supposed to come up with a million bucks? Rob a bank?'

'Once again, that's what I was there for. He was directed to pay thirty dollars a month to the treasury. Whenever the peeping Tom forgot to send in his little sum, I'd call him up and ask, "Have you suddenly gotten a desire to sit behind bars?" And the agency would get its regular check.'

'Hang on! He'd have six hundred years to pay the whole thing off in?'

'In six hundred and forty-one years. Of course, the clerks in the Collection Agency are never left with nothing to do. That's how I worked my four hundred people a month, replenishing the California state budget. I'll give it to you straight: that was good practice in the study of bad people. My own Silver Age! But the work was exhausting: the norm was to make up to two hundred calls a day. Of course my military discipline came in handy, but all I did at home was sleep. Maybe that's why I never found myself a girlfriend after my wife died. My kids all went their various ways, and I was just left on my own. And now . . . at last!'

'Well, how is your true love?' I asked, imagining that he'd go away once he'd told me about his girlfriend.

Ken was thirsting for the question and was overjoyed at the chance to shift from business to feelings.

'We're getting closer all the time,' he pronounced solemnly, in a whisper. 'Now we're on an ideological basis.'

'How do you mean?' I gave Ken a quick, suspicious glance, since the thought that he might have some psychological trouble had sprung back into my head.

'How do you feel about' – he paused to stare me fixedly in the eye – 'socialist ideals?'

Our Russian past has developed in us a certain irony towards this sort of people. Of course, Western pluralism has now influenced this scepticism even more. But it's more than that.

'You see . . . that's a very good question,' I mumbled, so as not to impose my own orientation.

But it turned out that Ken hadn't needed my answer at all.

'You have a convinced socialist in front of you, just like my parents. And Lily and I will never stray from that path!'

Losing all hope of salvation, I was crestfallen: 'Surely there's some kind of alternative?'

'Don't you doubt it! It's only a question of time. I'm not just sitting on my hands.'

'Are you starting a revolution?'

'Not one like the Bolsheviks'. A slow one. I'm writing letters of protest to imperialists like McDonald's, Soros and Gates. I'm protesting against . . . well, against everything! McDonald's sells fried meat and therefore increases the cholesterol level in our blood. Soros throws his money away, while simple folk just need some. While Gates, that snot-nose, wants to establish total computer control over mankind!'

'And have the imperialists answered your letters?'

'They have! Not personally, for some reason. Their secretaries have thanked me for the constructive criticism. But nothing ever changes! I'm not giving up, though. I've bought myself a new computer, and I write and write and write . . . Do you drink Coca-Cola?'

'These youngsters swill it down, but I never touch it at all.'

'Very sensible! That means you're preparing for life under socialism.'

He was frightening me again. 'In what sense?'

'Well, after all, with its overabundance of sugar, Coca-Cola is turning us all into diabetics, so that we'll suffer in the radiant future.'

'Well, what do you know!'

'Of course, I've been writing to protest, but chances of success are small. When Russia and Poland flipped upside down, I really caught fire. That's where socialism with a human face will be! They can do it. They just have to put right the cash flow into their treasury. And I've decided to help them open their own Collection Agency. After all, it's even more necessary there than here in the States!'

'Have they opened one yet?'

'Just imagine, now – yes, they have. In Moscow. I've opened a channel to their Communists, with Lily's help. They demanded the loan of some money to develop the idea. I gave them what I could. They've put together a list of deadbeat defaulters who're hiding from the law.'

'And have they started calling them up?'

'That's the thing, they've only made one call. The very first debtor said that if they called him one more time, he'd hire a hit man.'

'And what about the money you lent them?'

'I write them and ask, but there hasn't been any answer, for some reason.'

'You know what they say in Russia: you borrow for a while, but you lend for ever.'

'Hah! Let me write that expression down. After all, I need to try to open a collection agency in Warsaw. The failure of the attempt has convinced me even more of the expediency of your Communist ideals.'

'Mine? But I ran away from them . . .'

'Too bad! McDonald's, and Soros, and Gates, and your New Russians there, digging themselves a capitalist pit, would behave a lot differently under a socialist planned economy. That's where the future of mankind is. And that's just the thing that's bringing me and my dear Lily closer. She's a real *toh-vah-reesh*!'

'Oh, Lord! You're soul mates!' I exclaimed in delight. 'At long last our country is going to get its own little Party organization!'

Ken had problems with humour, possibly from the unhealthy nature of his work at the Collection Agency.

'No doubt about it!' he nodded. 'Lily and I need a common language, though, not just for conducting Party meetings . . .'

I wanted to utter some sort of sarcasm like 'What else for, then?' but the telephone rang. The auditorium was filling up with people coming to hear a lecture by a Czech writer, and I'd been asked to introduce him to the assembly.

'Maybe I'm holding you up?' Ken thought suddenly.

'Not at all! It's been very nice.'

After shaking his hairy hand, I ran off.

On Saturday morning my wife and I went to Wilbur Hot Springs to treat my old bones. Valerie had telephoned ahead in advance to reserve two places.

A standard sunny autumn day had begun. The cool breeze blowing from the ocean had weakened considerably after crossing the mountain range and had warmed up enough for us to open our car's sunroof. Rice fields grew green along both sides of Interstate Five, leading to Canada, but we weren't heading there for now: it was only an hour and a bit from our house to Wilbur Hot Springs.

Getting off Interstate Five at Route Twenty, we started winding back and forth on the switchback that rises higher and higher into the mountains, and then, at a mountain brook, we turned on to a narrow ledge, our wheels bouncing over the rocks between bent trees, catching on dried-out bushes.

After five miles we had to stop to open an iron gate, then stop again to close it – it's self-service for all the guests there. There was still another mile of bumpy road, and then here was untended Wilbur Park. There's a little wicket gate on the left leading to the baths and an old-fashioned wooden mansion to the right. At the entrance the girl at the cash office, the daughter of the lady who owns the place, charges twenty-five bucks a head per visit, plus California state tax.

Everything here is like you're at home: you even have to take off your shoes on the porch. Electricity, television, music – there's nothing like that at Wilbur Park. Someone was clattering pots in the kitchen, another person was asleep on the couch in the living-room, face covered by a magazine. The most important thing is the peace and quiet – I would even say liberation from conventionality. They say that life at Wilbur has remained the same as it was in the middle of the last century, when Indians came here to treat themselves for all manner of diseases.

Leaving your car in the driveway for very long is prohibited, so as not to spoil the innocence of the landscape. I had to drive over to the parking lot and spend the next fifteen minutes walking back on foot. When I got back, Valerie had already undressed and was sitting in the stone tub; to be precise, in the second tub, since there are three. The first one is way too scalding, the third is barely warm. Hot water from the sulphur spring, bursting its way from underground, runs from one carved-out-of-the-cliff stone tub into another, cooling down as it finds its way to the swimming pool, so that people can choose whatever temperature suits them.

The peculiar smell of sulphur – rather pleasant, actually – hung beneath the wide roof. The stone tubs are elongated, each of them accommodating up to fifteen people or more. Despite the fact that it was a weekend, there weren't many people here.

Several middle-aged men and women (evidently in one group) were sitting in the hot water up to their necks, occasionally exchanging words in the clouds of steam. Two young people – probably here for the first time – reclined on sunbeds, feasting their eyes in amazement on the crowd of naked women. Three very young adolescent-looking Japanese girls, not hiding their curiosity, were scrutinizing the normally hidden parts of passing men, and, although it was prohibited here, were snapping photos – but only of themselves.

The rest of the ladies and gentlemen were indifferent to one another. Or at very least they were pretending to be. They would flop into the tubs and hold themselves motionless as crocodiles, then they would crawl out, walk over to the pool or the brook, lie on the sunbeds in the shadow of the trees, toss rejoinders back and forth or just read.

Since I was the only one left dressed I had to get like the rest, which is what I did. The water was scalding at first, but my body quickly adapted, and all that was left was pure pleasure. Around us the mountains, covered with low trees, dozed in a light haze. Visible through the spaces in the roof above the tubs, little clouds floated unhurriedly, casting a sleepy spell.

I don't know how much sulphur baths can heal you, but all manner of pains subside, stresses soak away, cares vanish, and you find your ease. Bliss! There comes a moment when it seems you're about to ascend to heaven. But then you see the abundance of feminine charms around you and you realize that it would be better not to rush the ascent. Rodin should have come here along with the French Impressionists – they wouldn't have had to hire their nude models.

Valerie tugged on my hand so that I wouldn't lie too long in the tub, and we headed off for the shade, to cool off and dry off in the shadow of a spreading oak.

'Sdrass-vooey-tay,' someone exclaimed almost in Russian, and then right away switched to regular English. 'Are you treating your arthritis, too?'

Sighing, I nodded, at a loss: 'And all my other ailments as well . . .'

He sprang up heartily from his bench and spread out his arms, blocking our way past.

'Arthritis brings souls closer,' he laughed, pleased with his joke, and addressed my wife: 'It looks like your husband is too surprised to recognize me. I'm his student, Ken Stemp.'

Stepping back a pace, he looked Valerie over from head to toe and, noisily sucking in air through his nose, smacked his lips and declared: 'You look marvellous, madame.' The compliment sounded somewhat frivolous, since everyone was unclothed.

Naked, Ken didn't look like such a buff student but reminded one more of elderly nude males painted by classical artists. He eagerly explained why he had remained unrecognized.

'I was dyeing my hair red before, but now I've got to look a bit older.'

'Why so suddenly?' I failed to understand. 'After all, you've only just fallen in love.'

'That's precisely it! I can't go looking younger than my girl, and

26

now, as you can see, I'm dyeing my hair black with a touch of grey.'

He giggled, turned, and called out: 'Lily! *Delly toap-toap zdess . . .*'

His Russian had without any doubt improved, but as far as his choice of women went, between you and me, I had serious doubts.

An old woman of indeterminate age leapt up cheerfully from her bench; she was as long as a pole, with yellow breasts sticking to her stomach and a necklace of amber beads as big as ripe grapes hanging between them – her only clothing, unless you took into account her red high-heeled shoes. Everyone here normally went around barefoot – the heels made her nakedness in some definite sense inappropriate: naked women in high heels walk around in a different sort of place, as everyone knows.

Closer up, though, she turned out to be better-looking. Obviously, her face, because of the makeup on it, differed strikingly in colour from the rest of her body. Her high forehead, pale with powder, and her rouged cheeks, were almost smooth – only her neck, breasts and stomach were wrinkled. Her chocolate hair seemed to be – or maybe was – a wig, close-cropped and arranged into a multitude of curls organized geometrically around her forehead, her large, slightly tinted glasses, and her sunburnt ears. Her age, as Maupassant has already noted, was given away by her hands, the kind that elderly Frenchwomen used to hide in long, elbow-length gloves. Her nails were painted a bright red. The number of rings she wore exceeded the number of her slightly crooked fingers. Her dried-up knees stuck forward, as though she was about to sprint off the starters' blocks.

After attentively looking my wife over, she stepped back a bit to avoid any comparison. Unnecessarily. She was beautiful, in her own way.

For the first time in my life it occurred to me that the female body is so perfect that age can change it but can't ruin it. Something remains of the perfection of line and even – I swear, since this occurred to me while standing next to my wife – sexual attractiveness gets preserved. Plus there's something that obtains, something you could call *veterancy*, for lack of a better word. The same way scars suit an old soldier. The body becomes something eternal. Naked old ladies are gorgeous – I say this on good grounds: you won't be able to shake my conviction. Were I a painter, I'd have begged this woman to pose for me.

'And here's Lily, my girlfriend! I've told you all about her,' Ken said proudly, gazing enraptured at her. 'I've told you all about her. You can chat away with her in Russian. After all, you do know that it's purely a musical pleasure for me.'

I bowed to her: 'Can we speak in Russian?'

'You've got to speak Russian!' she nodded. 'Since I don't understand the teeniest bit of this double-Dutch here.'

Lily was a whole head taller than Ken, and he feasted his upward-cast eyes on her the whole time. I liked the fact that she wasn't the slightest bit embarrassed either by her nudity or her age, unlike many elderly women.

'Tell her that you're that professor whose lectures I go to,' interrupted Ken. 'Explain to her that I'm going to be talking Russian real soon, so she won't be bored with me any more.'

My wife raised her eyes in alarm, instantly feeling that he wasn't just making me repeat someone else's thoughts but was forcing me into the position of bearing false witness.

'Your friend Ken,' I paraphrased, 'is passionate about acquainting himself with Russian poetry and is striving to acquire the language.'

'What could he possibly understand about poetry?' she said exasperatedly, and imitated him. '*Pee-roash-key* . . . his Russian is just awful!'

She suddenly recalled that she was carrying on a public discussion stark naked, and, covering her pendulous breasts with one arm and the other place with her free hand, she reminded me of the Venus de Milo, if the statue had had any arms. Or, more accurately, a parody of the Venus. Incidentally, Lily's shoulder lines were still beautiful, balletic, like Maya Plisetskaya's. It wasn't her face, and of course not in any way her figure, but her low, velvety voice that seemed somehow familiar to me. Surely I'd heard that voice before, but God help me if I could remember where or when.

'Maybe you can translate for me what I've finally decided to tell her,' Ken importuned again, not even giving us the opportunity to exchange a couple of insignificant words – he'd suggested himself that we converse with her a bit.

'What, precisely?' I asked.

'Tell her that I love her madly, like your Lensky loves Tatyana – or is it Olga? That not a single woman in the world has ever had as profound an effect on me as she has, and I've known a few, before and after my own wife . . . well, let's say, several dozen. Explain to her that I brought her here to Wilbur Hot Springs because I wanted to see her, so to speak, *au naturel*. You can't get married, damn it, without having a look. Here at Wilbur I've understood that she's lovelier than Marilyn Monroe and Julia Roberts put together. And I'm asking for her hand. *Nee-yew lad-nuh?*'

He looked at her adoringly, undressing her with his eyes, as they say, which has to sound funny in so far as there wasn't anything left to take off. Then he asked me if she understood.

It's not that I was at a loss for words, I was just taking my time. It seemed to me that Lily already understood what he was on about, even without any translation. But I was mistaken.

'That's the way it always is,' she sighed. 'He mumbles some kind of rubbish and thinks that it's interesting to everyone. What does he want from me now?'

The woman's frankness – counting on the fact that Ken didn't understand – was somewhat embarrassing. But Lily had pronounced her boorish words softly, almost tenderly, as if with a smile. And, on the whole, there was something about her of our native Muscovite *beau monde*.

Weird coincidences do happen, as has long been noticed. Here, near the fence, some lilies were in flower – I've seen them in various places in California. These are startling, violet blossoms on long, shapely stems, completely without leaves. The flower is called locally a 'naked woman' – I haven't got a clue which romantic it was who thought of that.

Ken twiddled his fingers in the air as a reminder to interpret. I looked to my wife in the hope that she would do it. Valerie shook her head negatively and whispered: 'Do it yourself. Proposing is a man's business.'

So I had to propose hand and heart in marriage to Lily, even though not my own.

There isn't a woman in the world who wouldn't at least shut up when she's being proposed to. I had barely uttered Ken's foregoing monologue – leaving out his sexual-relations statistics, just in case – when Lily fell silent. Only her gaze switched back and forth from Ken to me.

She was at a loss, most probably because she couldn't decide if what she was hearing was serious or a well-thought-out practical joke. The situation was extraordinary, you would agree. Out of the stress of it, tears were welling in Lily's eyes. I felt sorry for her.

Ken, a little out of sorts himself now at her hesitation and the distress on her face, decided to put forward new and weighty proofs of the seriousness of his intentions.

'Why does she have to live in an old folks' home? Tell her – we don't have to buy a house, I already have one in Sacramento, on the riverside. It's not a new one, but it's just been remodelled, and it's really spacious: four bedrooms. A tile roof, with new window frames and drains. It's sited high enough that the garden won't get flooded. I gave my boat to my son, but now I'll get it back, and we'll have fun sailing around on the Pacific. Just along the coast, without any heroic crossings. We'll hoist the sail of our love!'

Apparently Russian Silver-Age poetry had had some effect on him after all. I had to go ahead and translate the second half of his proposition, too. Lily flapped her thickly mascaraed eyelashes, wiped the tears away from under them with a finger, twisted her mouth into something like a grin, and suddenly asked, after yet another long pause: 'He's making fun of me or what?'

'Of course not! Ken's absolutely serious.'

'Well, if he's serious, why is he talking such nonsense? I've already been married eighteen times, officially, and for real – I've lost count. He's just an idiot!' Here she reduced her volume and muttered sternly and emotionlessly: 'You don't have to translate that, young man. Translate this, instead . . .'

Her eyes flashed spiritedly, and a smile of revived happiness lit up her face, momentarily grown young again. Glancing at Ken, she coquettishly batted her eyes and whispered: 'Yes, my darling! If you insist, I'll do it.'

Ken hopped up and down like a little boy who's just been promised he can sit behind the wheel.

'Yes, *ya ponimat!*' he yelled with joy.

His shoulders spread, his sunken chest, filling with air, began to swell. He took a step back, putting some distance between us and himself, snorted in some air just like he did my lectures and suddenly burst into song:

> The fire of love within me burning,
> You touched so deeply this soul of mine,
> Please kiss me more, oh kiss me, darling,
> Each kiss as sweet as chrism or wine!
> Kisses as sweet as chrism or wine . . .

I hurriedly propped myself against the back of the bench with one arm – just in case, so that I wouldn't topple into the hot water. The translation was his own. Ken had come into my office dozens of times to get advice, now about the rhythm, now about the sense of it, but it would never have entered my head to think that he'd be singing this *romance*. If you knew the original, you'd understand why I was so surprised. The Silver Age wasn't enough for him, he had to go and stick his nose into the Golden one!

In the silence that was broken only by the gurgling of the water running from one tub into another, the stark-naked singer had attracted everyone's attention. The youngsters flirting in the gazebo broke into applause. The women surfaced from the swimming pool and, propping their breasts on the stone ledge, stared at us. Someone shouted: 'Bravo!'

The singer bowed elegantly all around. Ken's baritone had turned out to be pretty good, if a bit husky.

'What was he singing about?' Lily asked my wife. 'That tune seems a bit familiar.'

'About his love for you.'

'He sings like a nightingale,' Lily responded, 'and him older than the hills.'

'That's my wedding gift for my fiancée,' said Ken somewhat guiltily, flashing his ideally snow-white porcelain teeth. 'I sing a bit in operettas. And nobody's kicked me out yet . . .'

He pointed at the mountains, behind which the sun was setting, and switched to his Russian: 'Lily, darling – *Delly toap toap nah ow-toe-moe-beel.*'

He whacked her resoundingly on the butt like a little girl, and she coquettishly wagged an arthritically crooked finger at him.

Twilight was coming on swiftly, the way it always does there in the mountains. They were lighting candles in the main house. Ken and I got dressed and walked together out to the parking lot, leaving the ladies more time to put themselves in order. On the way Ken sang arias from his operettas, joyful as a child. He was a happy man.

Coming back, I got out to say goodbye. Lily seemed less attractive to me now in her old-fashioned, expensive, raspberry-coloured dress. Nature had better taste than she had, apparently. But dressed as she was, now, her more characteristic appearance convinced me that I *had* seen her on some occasion before. Surely I'd seen her! Should I ask what her surname was, anyway? I should have done it earlier, but it hadn't occurred to me.

While I was mulling it over, Ken seated Lily in his truck, slammed the door and, nodding to us, climbed in behind the wheel. Lily spoke sadly from her window: 'What has my life come to? I've always had my own chauffeur, and first my *Emka*, then my *Pobeda*, then my *Volga*. But nobody in my life ever took me anywhere in a truck before!'

She acted as if the whole world knew who she was.

Waving goodbye, Ken drove off, and the truck disappeared into the dust. Valerie and I climbed into our seats as well, and I began the careful descent down the stony, dusty switchback into the valley and Highway 20.

And there it was, under the monotonous whirring of the air-conditioner, that the dam of my memory finally burst.

5

I hadn't recognized her at Wilbur Hot Springs. But even if I had remembered her I wouldn't have shown it. When you've got used to it general nudity doesn't impede conversation, but Lily was there for the first time. Maybe she wouldn't have wanted to introduce herself in such peculiar circumstances. And who knows if you want to have your past brought up to you? What if, owing to some circumstance, you'd rather have the past forgotten? It was weird, though, that I hadn't recognized her. I recalled the woman in nothing other than formal clothes, anyway.

Once, long before I left Russia, I was an accidental witness to the following scene: on a Moscow winter's evening a drunken woman was reeling down the middle of Gorky Street, tossing off articles of her clothing. Her hair was blowing free in the frosty wind. Behind her a man shuffled along like someone doomed, picking up her clothes. A policeman was all ready to blow his whistle when she, in nothing but her stockings, grabbed him by the hand. The cop, in a panic, barely managed to pull away and ran off to the nearest hidey-hole, while the woman kept on walking, the crowd jostling along behind her on both pavements, until an ambulance summoned by somebody drove up, its siren warbling. The husky attendants bundled the good-looking woman into the ambulance and climbed in behind her, hurriedly pulling the doors to. Someone in the crowd cackled: 'There's going to be a orgy on the way now!'

Memory is a queer thing: there was no connection with what was happening now. Or maybe there were hidden associations? Because right away I imagined an official assembly at the Writers' Union: the important poetess Lily Bourbon heads for the stage, straight for the podium, taking her clothes off on the way, and, as completely naked as she was at Wilbur, starts prophesying.

The audience is frozen in anticipation of a scandal, while the Party bigwigs onstage, at a loss, do not know what to do with her: pack her off to the loony bin, expel her from the Party for amorality or, pretending to see nothing, quietly hush the whole thing up.

I giggled. Valerie had been dozing, her seat reclined. Hearing me laugh, she half opened her eyes, but I said nothing and she went back to sleep. All around us lay the impenetrable darkness. I would have to speed up to join the traffic on Interstate Five, and I switched on my high beams. A swathe of gnats clattered against my windscreen.

Of course, I knew Ken's new girlfriend from the Soviet half of my life: from editorial offices, from the Authors' House, from sitting around in people's kitchens. In fact, several generations of us had all known Lily Bourbon, from childhood.

Little books with her little poems for children flooded the whole of *Rus* the Great in editions of millions and, not only that, but the whole of the Soviet camp. I had seen her a multitude of times, mainly on the television screen, but I had met her in the flesh, too. But meet or not, I'd never been introduced. Lily Bourbon belonged to the Secretariat elite, the dizziest heights of society, and walked around without even noticing anybody but *apparatchiks*. No, she didn't walk around – she *carried* herself.

Her low, velvet voice echoed down to us from the podium at writers' conferences held for glorifying or unmasking someone or another. You could hear it fairly frequently over the radio. Wake me up in the middle of the night, now, in the quiet California desert, and I'd be able to shout out her burning lines, reproduce all of her intonations. Shall we recite them now, all of us at once?

We'll speak them with feeling – sonorous, loud enough for us to be heard in the Kremlin. And three, and four:

> We, children of this great Soviet land,
> Want there to be no war in the world, today.
> But if enemies attack our Motherland,
> Stalin the Great will lead us to the fray!

In later editions Lenin replaced Stalin and then, for some reason, Pushkin did, while it seems that Brezhnev was never vouchsafed the honour. But she did have some witty verses, all kinds of catchy rhymes about slobs, lazybones, stick-in-the-muds or, as the critics put it, about certain deficiencies in the bringing up of children that needed eliminating.

She got medals for all this singing out and eliminating. Doubtless, her position and her prizes – both the Stalin and the Lenin – obliged her to do it. She travelled abroad to take part in forums championing peace and the happiness of children – and always in the company of interpreters and consultants. Whenever the latest campaign for the rights of Soviet Jewry would flare up in the West, she would speak out in its refutation.

'Take me, for instance,' she would announce with a smile. 'I'm a deputy and a prize laureate, and a woman – am I being persecuted? On the contrary! All these conditions have been created for me by our Party and our government. Only under a Soviet regime could I have become who I am . . .'

The strangest thing was that this was the absolute truth.

Probably she had her human side as well, but her laurels were an obligation. Then came a time when she stood up for somebody she liked personally, I think it was Galich, who was about to get kicked out of the Writers' Union. She was called in by her superiors and threatened with the loss of her shiny medals and her summer house and the cutting of her books from the publishers' lists. After recanting, she never again stuck her neck out.

Lily Bourbon would periodically rejuvenate herself, but gradually it came to everyone's notice that she was the same age as the twentieth century itself, and the century then was about two-thirds of the way through. I was young when she was considered an old woman, and now I myself wouldn't mind buying myself a good age somewhere – but that's not for sale anywhere, not even in America.

There was tons of gossip about her, and the more official Lily's defences became, the more tell-tale were the stories doing the rounds. What in them was the truth, and what was made up by wags on the literary scene? I can recall some of the details even now.

Old writers in their cups would tell stories about how they used to see her in the evening on the streets of Petrograd: she had just arrived there from the provinces and stood on Nevsky Prospect in expectation of clients. Then the Bolsheviks began their machinations and recruited this category of working woman into their Party. Lily reinforced the ranks of these fighters. Now she was working for free, servicing the activists in the Party cells.

These stories seemed to me to be mere malevolence, but one day in the beer hall at Journalists' House an elderly intelligent-looking fellow with a bloated face and bags under his eyes sat down next to me. He was already slightly drunk. It would have been impossible not to recognize him, so I immediately said to him: 'Don't deny it: you're Andrey Bourbon.'

'That's right! In the flesh,' he chuckled, flattered.

I still had his books for children at home, the ones that Granny read to my daughter. His photo was on them. But now I was looking at him up close. He was neatly dressed, although his blue suit was worn, and he had on a floral waistcoat and a purple bow tie with polka dots. A bow tie in those days was a challenge, almost a political statement.

The young Andrey Bourbon had hung out with the Futurist and Egofuturist groups, drawn cubes and cirdes *à la* Malevich, been friends and at odds with Burliuk, Mayakovsky, Benedict Lifshits. An avalanche of writers was abandoning their homeland, but him – it's not that he had any faith in the new regime, quite the opposite: absolutely indifferent to any form of politics, he had stayed behind for some reason. But he – with his ways so in tune with the times – was one who should have hitched up his trousers and scuttled off, ahead of everybody else, when the time came.

Time passed, and, like many another, he found his niche: he

started publishing verse about birdies and furry animals for children's magazines and stories about toddlers. Children's books were coming out in editions of millions, and it was possible to subsist on the royalties.

He had met Lily at the tram stop at Nikitskiye Gates. Just having made it from Petrograd to Moscow, she had started taking a stenotypist course; she was staying in a communal apartment with a friend of hers and walked around in a trendy, coquettish hat. She was twenty-three years old, and she was in great form.

Lily came to his place to type his manuscripts, and soon enough took to hanging around after her typing was done. She would boil potatoes for him and more and more often stay the night. Within half a year he was married to her.

'I had a splendid room on Kamergorsky Lane, young fellow,' Bourbon said dreamily, sipping his beer, 'the pitiful remnant of the six-storey house that my parents owned before the complications. If it hadn't been for my loathsome origins, I might have done well at this new literature. But is this really *belles-lettres*? It stinks of the dung heap, *cher ami*. Like certain other people, I am opposed to the prostitution of art. I, my man, am an *a-ris-to-crat . . .*'

Bourbon would compose verses about birdies and beasties, and Lily would help him: she would type them out and take them off to the publishers. She tried her hand at composing some herself, but he would just make fun of her opuses, finish them for her, rewrite them.

And then one day Andrey took her poems over to the official children's newspaper *Pionerskaya Pravda*. At the behest of the editors, he made up a proper revolutionary biography for Lily. It seemed now that, in the years of the armed struggle for what was right, she stood shoulder to shoulder with the best of the best in the workers' vanguard.

She didn't so much *stand* shoulder to shoulder as lie there, of course, and not with the best but with all of them. But this page of her biography no longer existed. The proletarian children's poetess, Lily Bourbon, had appeared to the world. She showed up just in time, in fact, because the purges were starting up, and Andrey himself was soon to be unmasked in the press as an alien bourgeois element.

Now his poems were published under her name. Lily Bourbon quickly became popular among children's magazines and publishing houses. She made the acquaintance of editors and writers and took to sleeping with them. She made appearances at schools, clubs, orphanages. Now she was made an honorary Pioneer, now an honorary Octobrist. In newspaper photographs the red Pioneer scarf fluttered around her neck. It even seems to me that in some ways she surpassed her husband and teacher, turning out to be more talented and definitely more practical.

Stalin's army commander Berdichevsky caught sight of her at the Writers' Club. Soon they had moved in together, at Government House on the embankment. She got a divorce from Bourbon. Where did I get this from? Berdichevsky's son from his first marriage was studying with me at the philological faculty, and he wasn't very keen on his stepmother, Lily. One day he revealed a family secret to me:

'When they came to our place to arrest my father, my stepmother hid him between the fire doors and offered herself to the three NKVD men. They couldn't resist. My father meanwhile slipped into the neighbouring apartment and phoned Stalin, who apparently decided to hold off on the arrest for a while.'

'But that was a heroic thing to do!' I remember saying at the time.

'You idiot!' my classmate rounded on me. 'My father got taken away, anyway.'

They arrested his father later on, after Lily had begun an affair with Yagoda, and Yagoda decided to get rid of her army-commander husband so that he couldn't interfere. They didn't touch her.

When the Purge came to an end, Andrey Bourbon once more began writing for the children's magazines, but his verses only squeaked through now and were getting rejected with greater and greater frequency. On one occasion he had gone to Detgiz, the State children's publishing house, in the hope of getting a contract for a book. The director, an old-fashioned man, and therefore with some conscience left, had hummed and hawed for a long time.

'I don't frankly know how to deal with you . . . Our list already has contracts for five books with the *lady* writer Bourbon, whose approval comes from on high, and now you, yet another Bourbon! They're going to be asking, "What is this, the Bourbonization of children's literature?" They won't be giving me a pat on the head. You know that I get along fine with you personally. So there's only one possible way out . . .' There and then in Journalists' House, Bourbon wrathfully told me about his only way out.

'Just think! How can this be? I, Andrey Bourbon, a blueblood, the descendant of French kings, a Russian nobleman!' – his eyes filled with blood, and he hit the table with his fist so hard that our beermugs leapt in the air and conversation at the neighbouring tables came to a halt. 'I took this stray slut, Lily Shapiro, for a wife, gave her my ancestral name, made her into somebody – introduced her into literature, understand? – and now they're telling me, "Get yourself a pen-name"!'

After his confession I ran into him many times in that buffet at Journalists' House. Andrey Bourbon didn't talk a lot; he would borrow money and wouldn't ever return it. He changed his bow tie for a regular one with a greasy knot, then stopped wearing any tie at all; he drank, got carted off to the loony bin (not without the cooperation of his former wife, they said) and dropped dead on a subway escalator.

The stream of cars grew larger the closer we got to the city. I had to force myself to suppress my sad recollections and concentrate: I switched on my windshield wipers to clean off the bugs that were stuck to it. My wife woke up and telephoned our son. Our offspring had promised to visit us with his girlfriend, and, just in case, Valerie informed him that we were already approaching the house. I began to think about my affairs in the coming week. Life was moving on, even though nobody knew where to exactly.

5

Naturally I didn't give Ken the slightest inkling of what I had remembered, even if I should have, out of masculine solidarity. He'd gaily informed me that Lily was older than him, but he hadn't said by how much. Men should generally marry women older than them: our lives are shorter, we die younger. But that logic never works for some reason, and the younger the wife is, the happier we are. But Ken – he was in ecstasy at the contrariety of it all. Her seniority was merely an inspiration to him.

'We were strolling around the market yesterday,' he informed me, coming up after class, 'and this Russian guy generously helped me and Lily chat. This is really hard for her. Over there, she says, she was famous as hell, but here – nobody knows.'

'Does she have any children?' I asked, pulling on my jacket, which I had taken off in the middle of the lecture.

'No, she thinks that children would have gotten in the way of her literary glory.'

'Then why did she leave, exactly?'

'Oh, she'd flourished under socialism: a huge account in the bank, a summer house, a personal chauffeur, free resort vacations. But afterwards they'd started persecuting her.'

'For what?'

'What do you mean, for what? For her convictions! By the way – ' Ken grabbed me by the arm, since I was about to walk out. 'Did you know Lenin personally? Lily is sure that he had to suffer emigration, too.'

His questions always turned out to be interesting.

'I never had the chance,' I answered. 'So?'

'Lily told me that she had intimate relations with Lenin. Apparently his wife was fat and ugly. But Lily, as you can tell, is elegant: she even studied ballet. Her idol was Isadora Duncan, from San Francisco. See? My fiancée has close connections with California. True, later on she and Isadora had a fight out of jealousy over some alcoholic. Seems his name was Yesenin . . .'

He was proud of her intimate relations.

Several hectic days passed.

We had been asked earlier on to come to their wedding ceremony and not entirely unselfishly, you understand: Ken might have need of an interpreter. The newlyweds (I'm embarrassed at having to use this word, but what else is there?) were getting ready for the ceremony on an American scale, something that Lily was going to have to master.

Ken telephoned his sons to inform them that he'd decided to get married and told them to come and meet his new girlfriend. His sons were delighted and immediately began discussing all the nuances, guilelessly.

'But then why get married at all, Pop?' said the youngest Stemp, George, a computer geek in Silicon Valley. 'Just live together, like me and Casey. What do you want to get stuck in all that legal hurly-burly for?'

'The youngsters don't understand how we can be in love,' Ken remarked to me.

The wedding preparations took nearly two months of intense labour. It reminded me of a wedding in Samarkand that a friend had invited us to once. An entire block had been closed to traffic by the police. Tables for seven hundred people had been set up in the street. At the crosswalks at either end were sentries in red armbands collecting the presents – money in envelopes. The richer you were, the more money you had to put into it; that was the whole ritual. And this hadn't come to my mind accidentally. There is something of this Oriental tradition in an American wedding, even if it is computerized.

The invitation that came in the mail was formal, with a request to respond as to whether or not we would be taking part. The bride and groom had meanwhile gone off to Macy's department store, where with expert help they had compiled a list of things that guests could give them as wedding presents. My wife went there to buy them one.

She entered the name Ken Stemp on to the computer at Macy's wedding department and got back a long list of presents that the guests were supposed to buy, selected by the newlyweds-to-be. The list started with china and ended with bed linen and towels. Alongside every item was the brand, the pattern, the price and two further numbers: the required quantity and the quantity purchased by other guests who had already bought their presents. The salesgirl was curious as to how much Valerie was prepared to spend. 'Non-relatives', she elaborated, 'usually spend from fifty to a hundred dollars.'

My wife paid for an electric waffle iron but never saw the actual present – they have centralized delivery of all gifts for newlyweds.

There were only a few people at the Catholic church on Fourteenth Street, mostly gawpers and accidental tourists. The organ played. When it fell silent, the young priest – tall and epicene, with a flat and colourless face – addressed Ken and Lily with the standard words in the name of the Lord.

'Marriage is a reflection of the love of Christ for His church,' said the holy father. 'Will you, Ken, take this woman for better or for worse, for richer or for poorer, in sickness and in health?'

'I will,' Ken nodded.

'Will you promise to love her as long as you both shall live?'

'I will,' repeated Ken, adding as instructed: 'And all that is mine will be yours.'

Then the priest addressed Lily with the very same questions. From her appearance, it seemed that the bride understood the whole ritual. But she didn't answer for a long while – not because she was having second thoughts but because she was going to have to pronounce it in English, all on her own.

'I will,' Ken whispered in her ear.

'Eye you eel,' she repeated.

The priest placed his slim, bony hands on their shoulders and, gazing up somewhere on the ceiling, said through his nose: 'I now pronounce you man and wife.'

After asking Ken in a whisper whether they had purchased the rings, he loudly addressed each of the newlyweds in turn as he slipped the gold rings on their fingers: 'With this ring I thee wed, in the name of the Father, and the Son, and the Holy Ghost. Amen! Seal your love with a kiss.'

The church fell silent. Ken raised himself up on tiptoe and pursed his lips. Lily understood. She squatted slightly and bent her neck so that her bridegroom could reach her. There was a sound like someone loudly sucking hot soup out of a spoon, and their lips met. Ken's children and grandchildren, sitting in the front row, raised their cameras. Their bulbs flashed.

Friends of the family surrounded the newlyweds, dressed like him in black tuxedos, as if all they did their whole lives was either get married or go from wedding to wedding. Lily, in a snow-white gown, rented and slightly oversized, looked like (I can't come up with a better comparison) the elderly countess in Pushkin's *The Queen of Spades* who had found herself here by mistake. I'm just being malicious again – it wasn't easy for her. Nobody had asked her if she was a Catholic or not, but that wasn't bothering her. She was worriedly looking around her to see if there was anyone to have a word with in Russian.

'After the wedding,' Ken announced to me, 'we're heading straight off on our trip up the Pacific Ocean to Canada. I've already renamed my boat: it was the *Bluebird*, but now it's going to be the *Lily*.'

'Lily's going to be sailing on the *Lily*,' I joked, wretchedly.

'I'm the captain, and she's my ordinary seaman,' he giggled. 'I could ask you and your wife along, too . . .'

Well, of course they'd need an interpreter. 'You'd stick me under your bed?'

'Not at all! It's got a saloon plus three cabins. If you like, we can go down tomorrow and you can inspect my sailboat. She's gorgeous, that sweet thing . . .'

He was talking about his boat with the same enthusiasm as about his new wife. He had already acquainted me with one of them. I wasn't up for meeting yet another.

'A minute of your attention, ladies and gentlemen!' yelled Ken. 'Lily and I invite you all to the Port Rouge restaurant on Del Paso Boulevard. The cuisine there is finger-lickin' good! Dinner is already on the tables. *Proszu, pane!*'

Wow! He could manage Polish, too. Making our excuses, I pleaded that work was forcing us to take our leave and walked over to Madame Bourbon to say goodbye.

I kissed her hand. 'Congratulations.'

'What *is* this urge of his to marry me?' she whispered, bending towards me as if we were conspirators. 'He's a decrepit old fart! Maybe I shouldn't have given in. True, they do say he's rich. Out of my natural modesty I haven't found out anything about our finances. But I would like to clear it up anyway. You don't know how much my new spouse is worth, do you? Find out from him, sweetie!'

I took fright. 'Oh, no – it isn't done in this country to ask about someone's money.'

I'd long ago grown accustomed to the brutal frankness of Russian émigrés. It's possible that it could be explained by the lack of close, old friends – you've got to share things with somebody. This is why you sometimes get to hear revelations that you don't really want to know anything about at all.

'Just think,' she continued. 'He wants me to take his name. I'm the world-famous poet Lily Bourbon, and who the hell is he? Let him take mine!'

I blew out my cheeks so I wouldn't crack up. Here it was, in truth, history repeating itself as farce.

6

I started my lecture at eight o'clock as usual, and the students sitting there weren't any sleepier than they normally were. But there was no one right in front of me snorting and snuffling – his seat remained empty. At first I even chuckled a bit to myself on this account: our newlywed was sleeping late after his wedding night. And then I remembered: they had sailed off to Canada aboard his boat, hadn't they?

A day later, just after beginning my lecture and somewhat to my surprise, I discovered sitting in Ken Stemp's seat – he who had almost become Ken Bourbon – herself, Madame Bourbon. Without breaking off, I nodded to her and continued talking about early Mayakovsky and Lily Brik. I had known Lily Brik, I'd met her several times, we'd had tea together and even a thing or two stronger than tea. It suddenly came into my head now that these two Lilys had something in common.

At first Lily listened to me with a stony face, except for a contemptuous twist of her lips when I made a joke. Dissatisfaction with everyone else on earth is the conspicuous characteristic of the majority of know-it-all Russian émigrés, never mind what they're looking at or listening to. You don't interest them. Even when they have everything going for them they pay no attention to you at all. They come to life only when they can complain about something, so as to make everybody else around feel guilty.

Gradually Lily began looking around her at the young girls in the class, now adjusting her necklace, now her earrings, now touching her hair, as if trying to keep up with them. But these girls weren't wearing any jewellery: they were in shorts and tank tops, with carelessly combed hair and no makeup whatsoever – that's the style these days.

She was dressed up as if for a ball, in an elegant and tight lilac dress, with an immoderate quantity of gold in her ears and on her hands, while from her neck hung a cross – actually, not a cross; it was in fact a little bicycle-lock key on a string.

I had barely finished my lecture when she walked up to me.

'Where's my best student, Ken?' I asked cheerfully. 'Busy with the boat?'

Lily looked at me disapprovingly from behind her glasses. 'He's dead.'

Very strange sense of humour. But her eyes filled up with tears.

'What do you mean – dead?' I said, at a loss. 'When?'

'After the wedding,' she finally replied, sniffling, 'he . . . he didn't take me home from the restaurant in his truck; he took me to the harbour. He wanted to show me the boat. "*Toot me boodyum bye-bye,*" he said and started to hoist the sail.'

'Well, sure! He was going to take you sailing straight after the wedding ceremony,' I recollected.

'I was horrified, but he'd just renamed the boat in my honour, after all, so I shut up. The rope jammed. Ken pulled with all his might, but the sail wouldn't go up. He strained his hardest, and then suddenly snorted and sat down. He wiped the sweat off his brow, closed his eyes, and said, "*Nee-yew ladnah.*" I could see that he'd stopped breathing. I rushed ashore and stopped a police car. When the ambulance showed up, he was already cold. It's hard for me just to sit at home alone, so I came here . . .'

She fell silent and pressed a tissue to her eyes. Then she added: 'My lawyer informed me that Ken left me all his savings.'

'Well, that's some sort of consolation in your grief.'

'And how! Blood from the turnip, after all. Only I have to give the sailboat to his eldest son. What does he need it for? What, can't he buy one himself?'

'When's the funeral?' I asked, even though I wanted to ask: 'What do you need a sailboat for?'

'Funeral? What's he to you?'

'He was my student.'

'Today at four.'

It was easy enough to find an open spot in the parking lot next to that same church on Fourteenth Street where their wedding had taken place two days before. Going into the church I sat down in a pew at the back and looked around. An oak casket with decorative carvings was in the middle of the church on a high pedestal. Candles guttered the same way. There were fewer people than at the wedding. On that occasion I hadn't paid any attention to the fact that the modern building was more reminiscent of a youth club than a church. A portrait of the Saviour just down from the cross hung on a basketball backboard and jazz instruments were stacked in one corner.

The same pale young priest went through the ritual, periodically dwelling on the positive qualities of the dear departed and then walked around the coffin with his censer. The smell of the incense carried down to the pews in the back. The organ started playing.

The hereditary knight of socialism has died, I thought to myself. *He's up and gone* toap-toap *off to nowhere.* There was now one less chance for the hope of constructing a radiant future in America. Surely his widow wasn't going to continue the struggle for his life's goal?

Lily was sitting in the front row, next to Ken's sons and their girlfriends. She was wearing a black hat with a veil – God only knows at what garage sale she had picked it up. Of course in that particular situation it was a sin to carp. Suddenly Madame Bourbon-Stemp stood up and started looking around for somebody. Catching sight of me, she took several steps in my direction, gesticulating for me to come to her.

'Tell the priest to open the coffin.'

'That isn't done,' I objected after a pause, 'among Catholics.'

'That's none of your business! Translate for me . . . I demand that they open up his coffin! I want to make sure that it's him lying there.'

It would have been stupid to argue. Stepping over to the priest, I leaned towards his ear and relayed the widow's request. Without hearing me to the end, he shook his head. Lily was standing next to us.

'My daughter,' he said, in fright – something that made him sound ridiculous, since he was young enough to be her grandson – 'that's totally impossible! It's – against the rules . . .'

'Madame insists,' I whispered. 'She's a world-renowned celebrity – a star, so to speak. Wouldn't it be better to open up the casket – just this once – to avoid a scene?'

The priest, dithering, finally made a sign to the sacristan, who froze in shock but didn't dare contradict him. They raised the upper half of the coffin lid, and the deceased became visible to the waist.

Ken lay in the coffin in his black wedding suit, black-haired with a noble dab of grey, with a smirk on his face, if it's not inappropriate to say so. Maybe it just seemed that way to me because the atmosphere at the funeral was typically Californian – less than solemn.

His widow stepped up to the open coffin, stood as if spellbound, then kissed the brow of the deceased and suddenly burst into sobs, the way they do in Russia but not in any way, shape or form in America. The people there waited patiently. The priest made the sign of the cross over Lily, muttered 'God bless you', and quietly shifted her away from the coffin, while the sacristan hurriedly closed the lid.

Nothing awful happened, the heavens didn't open, thunder didn't roll. The widow went back to her seat. The ceremony went back on track.

At the other end of the hall a choir was lining up – around twenty of them, the men dressed in tuxedos and the women looking like nuns. There was the barely audible sound of a tuning fork striking. Gaily and as one, the choir suddenly launched *a capella* into:

> What good is sitting alone in your room?
> Come, hear the music play.
> Life is a cabaret, old chum – Come to the cabaret!

Nobody in the hall was the least surprised, except probably Lily, because here the usual thing is to send people off to their graves in the same manner as they preferred to live. The dear departed himself had sung in this choir, in the operetta *Silva* put on by the local amateur theatre company. And now his colleagues were singing for him.

When the choir fell silent, a parishioner – a neighbour of Ken's who didn't sing – said that as a deeply religious person he was happy to see Ken Stemp here, in the church, where the dear departed, a Catholic by birth, was finding himself for only the second time. The speaker thought a little more and added: 'It's a pity that this is the last time, but it's a good thing that this time it's for ever . . .'

Several days passed, and Lily again showed up at my class. She arrived in a white tank top and shorts, almost identical to the other female students. 'Lily Bourbon' was printed in a half-circle on the front of her shirt, and in the oval below was her own portrait, done at the beginning of the century, probably. After the lecture she came up and, noticing me looking at the photo, said: 'This was knocked up for me in a studio. Pretty, isn't it? But I hope you don't think that I came here just to show you this tank top.'

'Something on your mind?'

She looked at the flocks of students around us. 'I would prefer to have a chat away from passing ears.'

'Then come to my office.'

She kept quiet on the way. Stopping at the snack stall, I got her and myself a cup of decaffeinated coffee. In my office I sat Lily down on the chair and drew a question mark in the air with a finger.

'Show me the list of the people you study here,' she requested.

I began ticking them off on my fingers: 'Bely, Gumilev, Khlebnikov, Mayakovsky, Voloshin, Mandelstam, Pasternak – '

'They were all bad poets!' she declared, categorically. 'Nobodies! Dreadful lovers!'

'Why do you think that?'

'Well, they all slept with me. All of them! Except Khlebnikov, of course, who took his last bath before the Revolution and only met me afterwards. And they all recited their own poems to me, instead of listening to mine. Mayakovsky dedicated heaps of poems to me.'

'And the ones to Lily Brik?'

'When I went to live with Pasternak in 1932, Mayakovsky rededicated them to Brik. He didn't even have to change the name. And his poem "About This" was written for me. It has the dedication: "To her and to me." Well, all right! All that's water under the bridge. Properly speaking, I have come here to remonstrate: how come you don't study me at your university? I'm going to go to the administration and demand it.'

'There's a thought!'

'Are you being sarcastic, young man? Surely you know that I have endured my own horrors, too. More than that! Now I can admit' – she looked around at the open door to see if anyone could hear and lowered her voice – 'I'm the niece once removed of Leon himself.'

'Trotsky?'

'Naturally! And my uncle loved to pat me on the head. I used to have photos – I burned every last one of them, of course. But at any moment they could have discovered who my relatives were.'

I looked at Lily, and suddenly the penny dropped. After all, with some other roll of the dice the lines in her poems could entirely possibly have sounded thus:

> . . . But if enemies attack our Motherland,
> Trotsky the Great will lead us to the fray!

Fate nevertheless toys with us all. Think about it for a minute. Change the historical construction of the time – and the founder of socialist realism could have been the proletarian poetess Lily Bourbon instead of Gorky and Mayakovsky. Then it would have been her and not Gorky that they gave the Ryabushinsky mansion to. She would have been designated the best, the most talented poet of our Soviet epoch. Indifference to her in particular would have become a crime.

So, she would have been the one studied in schools and colleges. There would have been marble bas-reliefs, they would have put plaster busts of her and bronze monuments to her on pedestals here, there and everywhere. And, everywhere, memorial plaques: 'In this house on such-and-such a date, Lily Bourbon sneezed twice.' Libraries and schools would have been renamed in her honour. Did anybody ever count how many streets Russia has with their names on them? There are thousands of them throughout all Russia. In the final analysis, does 'Lily Bourbon Avenue' sound any worse? And Nizhny Novgorod would have been renamed Bourbon and not Gorky. And it would have been in Bourbonskaya province.

But . . . these things never came to pass, ladies and gentlemen, and now things probably never will come to that.

'Slavicists, or whatever they're called here,' Lily broke into my inappropriate fantasies, 'should have been studying me in the Silver Age for a long time already. In essence, I *am* the Silver Age!'

Under the force of the argument so passionately adduced by Lily, and under the sheer weight of imagination, I had to admit that, however stupid it was, in some way this woman was right yet again.

'Hmmm . . . the difficulty', I objected softly, 'is only that all professors in universities here get to decide for themselves which writers and in what context to offer their students.'

'So you go ahead and decide! I, by the way, went to the library: there are piles of my books in there – not a whit less than that show-off Akhmatova.'

'You see, in German universities there's a rule: an author is never studied until he's been dead for fifty years. Of course, we're in America, and you are a special poetess. But nevertheless . . .'

'Don't call me a poetess! That sounds insulting. I am a *poet*.'

'But it just means the feminine gender, that's all there is to it. You don't deny the fact of your femininity, do you?'

'Honey, I am the *oldest* Russian poet. Nobody else has lived so long. And nobody else has remained young for that long. I've outlived them all. Every one of them! Even Yagoda never knew how old I actually was. And I was never older than my man of the moment. Ken only found out by accident. He volunteered to take me to sign up for social security and saw my documents. As you can guess, they aren't accurate, either: I've forgotten how many times I've knocked years off my age, but, surprisingly enough, he wasn't a bit scared by my ninety-one years.'

'He was a real American,' I agreed.

So she'd turned out to be ninety-one years old – I began to get confused. She was worthy of respect for her boldness of spirit alone. For many years, in essence, without knowing her, I had despised her, while Ken, without understanding a single word of her language, had fallen in love with her at first sight, and for him she'd become a beacon in the dark. Had it really been necessary to see her in the nude, in all her womanly grandeur, in order for me, too, to respect her?

'What a fool I was', she broke into my ruminations, 'to have knocked just five years off when I emigrated! I should have taken off fifty.'

'How's that – take them off?'

'How, how?' she mimicked me, making a childish grimace. 'Remember this, once and for all: women need to be however many years old that it's necessary for them to be at any given moment.'

'Balzac used to say that a duchess is never more than thirty . . .'

'Did he say that? Stuff and nonsense! Even thirty can be too much, sometimes. In a civilized country, the right of a woman to be any age she wants should be written into the constitution. But, for now, it has to be done for money. You don't know anybody who takes care of that sort of thing, do you?'

'Do what, exactly?'

'What a dimwit you are! To add on age! It just occurred to me to get the truth written in.'

'They say Mexicans can do that . . . But what sort of truth?'

'Well, sweetie, I'm actually turning ninety-six in a month's time.

That is, there's only four years to go till I'm a hundred. Everybody who lives to a hundred gets sent personal birthday greetings and an expensive present from the American president himself. To hell with his present: now I can buy myself whatever I feel like. But a card from the president . . . Can you imagine? Fame all over America.'

'Maybe you could go confess, Lily? Repent?'

'What are you talking about? They can take away your rights to American citizenship for cheating. True, I do have a German passport, an Israeli one, a Canadian one and one more I can't remember, to say nothing of my Soviet passport. But the American one is the best – that's plain as the nose on your face! Oh! I nearly forgot – explain to me what this means, would you, sweetie?'

She rooted around in her purse and then handed me an official document. I had to glance at it. Judging by its title, 'Last Will and Testament of Ken Stamp', it was his bequest to her.

'No, no,' I refused, hurriedly. 'You have to see your lawyer. I don't know anything about this sort of thing.'

'Nobody's asking you to figure it out,' she objected. 'My lawyer, Tony Gobetti – a real Italian, by the way, even though his grandmother's from Odessa – declared that all my husband's fortune belongs to me.'

'Splendid! So what's the problem?'

'But then he made a proviso about some sort of restriction. But the interpreter mumbled something – I couldn't understand a word of it. Translate this, sweetheart, this teeny bit here. Here it is, somewhere . . .'

Sighing, I put my finger on the spot she was pointing out to me. 'Personal and real property, bank accounts, and securities', I read to myself, 'in case of my death become the property of my wife, Lily Bourbon-Stemp, who, sharing my political views, should use all these resources for the construction of socialism.'

I scratched the back of my head.

'Well, what is it there? What?' she asked impatiently.

I translated it as accurately as I could.

'What socialism, goddammit?' she exclaimed. 'I won't have anything to live on.' She bit her lip.

'That's what's written here, Lily . . .'

'Well, they're not going to get anything out of me! I'll think of something. I'm not handing over any money for crap like that! I'm telling you – me, Lily Bourbon!'

Her eyes filled with tears, and she didn't wipe them dry. The bicycle-lock key that looked like a cross hung from her neck on its string.

'Do you ride to the university on your bike, like Ken did?' I asked, to change the topic.

'What am I, nuts?' She pulled out a tissue and pressed it carefully to her eyes. 'I hired a car and driver, a Russian boy of seventy, as simple-minded as a donkey. Do you think it's easy to keep a personal chauffeur on such a small pension? True, I am getting a German pension and a Canadian one – they just don't know yet where I'm living. What have I come down to? I don't even have a masseur come to me at home! Now I'm going to have to sell the things I got for my wedding.'

'Return the presents to Macy's and get your money back.'

It was obvious that she didn't believe the simplicity of it, but she didn't object.

My gaze again rested on the bicycle key hanging from her neck.

'I sold his bicycle to the neighbours. But the key . . .' she pinched the string around her neck with two fingers and fell silent. 'Ken always wore it. You won't believe it, but I did manage to fall in love with him. Men don't understand any of this. I fell in love for real for the first time in my life, and now . . .'

What was there here to object to? Maybe for the first time in her life she had fulfilled her promise to be true to her husband till the end of his life: the marriage had lasted for nine hours, after all.

Flashing a barely noticeable smile, Lily quietly added, as if adjuring herself: 'I'll wear this key in memory of my last husband . . .'

With a sudden shudder she jerked back.

'What are you scared of?'

'There's someone there!'

'Where?'

'Outside the window!' She pointed in that direction with both hands.

'But this is the fourth floor. Who could look in here from the street?'

'What do you mean, who? Him! Ken has come here!'

I stuck my head out of the top half of the open window. Beneath the trees below I could see the brightly painted roof of the box-like drama theatre and to the left of it the windows of the Music Department, from which the sounds of a piano carried across. Bicyclists moved like ants along both pavements, while between them crept the double-decker student bus. Nothing else. I attempted to convince Lily.

'There's nobody there.'

'I'm not surprised by your naivety any more,' she observed contemptuously, looking round at me. 'After all, Ken flies around everywhere after me – he follows what I do, and he's particularly jealous of other men.'

She wandered around a little longer in the office, inspecting the portraits of the Silver Age authors and murmuring something under her breath that sounded like poetry. Finally she slung her bag over her shoulder and walked to the door. Taking hold of the door handle, she suddenly turned round and with a certain ardour asked: 'By the way, would you know of any man around here who would be worthy of me? Only not someone as old as Ken. And one who speaks Russian. I'm not accustomed to living alone.'

Part Two
TANGOING WITH THE PRESIDENT

'"Just draw it the way you see it, and to hell with it," wrote
Hemingway. He asserted the truthfulness of his stories,
important to the writer. But he strayed a long way from
the truth, something Michiganders won't forgive him for.'
          – *Pete Hayter, biographer of Hemingway*

I

After a lecture on the novels of Turgenev I was ambling from the class-room to my office, keeping to the shade of trees to avoid the ultraviolet rays. The spring quarter was in full swing. My throat, hoarse despite the microphone clipped to my tie, demanded warm liquid. I stopped to buy a cup of coffee and was sucking at it through a straw on the way, when someone clumped up from behind, overtaking me, and clapped me hard on the shoulder.

It was my colleague from the English Literature Department, Pro-fessor Pete Hayter. The previous quarter his lectures had followed mine, and he would wander back and forth past the window in the door, periodically pressing his nose against it while he waited for me to round things off. Now we were giving our lectures at the same time in neighbouring auditoriums.

His nickname among the students was the Woodpecker. He really does look like a bird: wiry, with a long nose, and, when he speaks, he rocks to and fro slightly, as if he wants to peck you on the shoulder.

It wasn't that Hayter's familiarity surprised me now (in America soon even students will be clapping their professors on the shoulder), it was just strange that it was being done by this fellow, a regular Man in a Suitcase, prim, who distanced himself from the general bustle, was close to nobody and spent his time reading archival papers and micro-films in the library from opening to closing time. To save time he even has his meals in the 800-seater student union cafeteria, where he's always the 801st in the queue.

A biographer of and commentator on Ernest Hemingway, Pete Hayter travelled in his youth to absolutely every place the famous author had ever visited or lived, either in reality or according to rumour. The American press wrote up one of Professor Hayter's outstanding discoveries in the field of Hemingwayiana as something sensational.

Pete made his discovery near the town of Petoskey, Michigan. The young Hemingway had lived in those parts, on Lake Walloon, with his parents at their summer cottage, Windermere. That was where he wrote his book of stories about Nick Adams, someone very like the storyteller himself. There, too, in between fishing and playing tennis, he had chased after Irene Goldstein, the prettiest girl in town, with whom he'd had no luck. But if we're to believe the letter that Professor Hayter obtained from the elderly Irene herself, living in an old folks' home – a letter from fifty-year-old Big Daddy Ernie, as Hem called himself – the writer had loved her all his life.

Hemingway's letters are plentiful and scattered all over the world, and no one is surprised by them. The electricity pole under which the famous writer got engaged for the first time was a sensation when Hayter found it. This is the pole to which the newspaperman Hem – dressed like a soldier in his World War I Italian Red Cross uniform – had squeezed his other girlfriend, Hadley Richardson. Embracing her and the pole, too, Hemingway informed her that he had been wounded in various places by bullets and shrapnel 227 times during the war. But now he was wounded for the 228th time by her, and in his very heart, moreover. Hem kissed her and then proposed.

Unfortunately, there still is no memorial plaque on the pole, although Hayter has been pushing for it for the past ten years with the local authorities there, and nobody has said no to him yet. There's a sign hanging on the outhouse door at his parents' cottage: 'Ernest Hemingway sat here.' But on his connubial pole – so to speak – not a thing! The original pole embraced by the author has already fallen down, though, and the power company has put in a new concrete pylon that will never rot away. Even if everyone is for the idea, there hasn't been any headway made.

But, more seriously, this Hayter has written three books and a hundred and twelve articles, forewords and commentaries enveloping all sides of the author's life. The professor for sure knows more about the great hunter, cat-fancier, drunk, womanizer and Nobel laureate, as well as about his numerous girlfriends and his four wives – Hadley, Pauline, Martha and Mary – than the beardy Hem knew about himself. On top of that, the biographer is the absolute antithesis of the famous writer.

Everyone who has ever wanted to knows that the skinny sixty-four-year-old Hayter, tall as a streetlamp, is a confirmed bachelor. It remains a mystery why he's shunned women all his life. Even with the cute secretaries who treat everyone around as if they are ready this very minute to do anything right there on their desk, Pete remains strictly businesslike, shifting his slightly crossed eyes to the screen of the nearest computer.

Various rumours, principally about Pete's probable gay orientation, make the rounds, like they do of every inveterate bachelor who prefers to chat with men, even at work.

At our university – in the whole of California, in fact – as soon as a person demonstrates membership in the aforementioned group of people that affords certain advantages: the voice of minorities today is louder than the voice of the majority, and America listens eagerly to such voices. If a man doesn't make a big deal out of his homosexual tendencies, then nobody gives a hoot. They even talk behind a man's back with circumspection, so as not to offend him by accident.

So none of this with reference to Professor Hayter arrests anyone's attention in any way. In his ascetic indifference to worldly passions there is something not just academic but almost monastic, even.

Clapping me on the shoulder just now, Hayter, an energetic Irishman by ancestry, was smiling in slight embarrassment.

'Listen, colleague,' he said with an artlessness unnatural to him, 'we cross paths at idiotic committee meetings and assemblies, but why haven't we ever had lunch together?'

Not knowing what to answer, I shrugged my shoulders. Why not, indeed?

'That's always remediable,' I tossed off.

'There, I thought so, too!' he rejoiced, as if afraid that I might have refused. 'There's a nice place that's opened up downtown, where the food's not bad at all, at least now that they've just got going – the Mustard Seed restaurant. Let's go eat there. You'll explain to me what's with the mess going on in Russia, since I don't understand a thing. Let's go today, OK? Maybe even right now?'

Given how busy we all are, lunch together is normally arranged at least a week in advance. What had got into him all of a sudden? Russian issues had never worried Pete before, and if now he'd heard something and become curious, he should just have opened up *The New York Times*. I was up to my ears in work at the department, and I had three unfinished manuscripts lying at home. But if I tried to put lunch off, Hayter would take offence.

So we agreed that he would pick me up in an hour.

2

He appeared at my office forty minutes later and waited, leaning against the door jamb. Some time passed while I untangled myself from appointments with my students, and then we set off downtown on foot.

On the way we talked about trivialities, even about the weather. I didn't rush him, expecting him to get around to revealing the reason for this urgent meal together, but I couldn't keep from trying to work out what he needed from me in such a hurry. Most likely it was support for a vote in the academic senate, for or against some kind of innovation. Or a recommendation for a postgraduate student of his. Or maybe he wanted to publish a translation of his Hemingway biography in Russia.

At the Mustard Seed they sat us face to face over a little table by the fireplace. There was real firewood stacked inside it, but the cold was long past and the fireplace wouldn't be needed until autumn.

'A bottle of Mexican Corona and a Caesar salad with Italian dressing,' Pete demanded resolutely. 'Would you like a beer?'

'A bottle of Saint-Pauli Girl,' I whispered to the waiter.

After ordering myself a bowl of Boston shrimp-and-calamari chowder and a tuna salad in addition to the Bremen beer – which I like a lot – I asked Pete: 'What's the word in your department? Did they slash your budget again?' I was just asking to break the silence.

The waiter set down our bottles of beer. Hayter poured himself some and greedily downed half a glass, wiping his mouth with his napkin.

'Ah, the department can burn in hell, for all I care! Burn up in blue flames! . . . Here's what I wanted to ask you . . .'

He glanced at me searchingly, still doubting whether to trust me, and then turned his eyes aside to the logs in the fireplace. It seemed to me that his right eye was getting crossed a little more, out of nervousness.

'This is strictly between the two of us, right?' Pete knocked back some more beer. 'I noticed a pretty student in your class at the end of the last quarter. Afterwards she disappeared . . . what's her name?'

I bit my lip. It just wasn't done to have an ambiguous conversation on this subject. Periodically, the university administration insistently warns us in confidential letters that flirtations at work in general, and especially between those teaching and those learning, are extremely dangerous for your career. The campaign against sexual solicitation has gone beyond all reasonable bounds. Just glance at a girl student the wrong way and she, offended by a low grade, will sue you for harassment, as if she were some sort of steely, morally steadfast monolith and her poor grade just revenge for her intractability. And you get taken to court . . .

But that wasn't the issue in this case. The confirmed – one could say legendary – bachelor Pete Hayter had turned his ordinarily dismissive gaze to one of my girl students, while he himself had half a hundred in his class – it was enough to drive you schizo. But I had to pretend that everything was as it should be. I kept quiet until I'd thought up an answer.

'Which one of them?' I eventually came out with. 'They were all pretty in my class, not just one.'

Pete apparently concluded that I didn't want to name the girl, out of personal or – so to speak – politico-administrative considerations. 'Right, you don't want to tell me . . . What – did you have your eye on her, too?' he asked, jealously.

The fact that Pete, out of his monkish naivety, thought that the whole world simply could not avoid falling in love with some girl that *his* attention had turned to also made me prick up my ears, not least by its wild seriousness. This Hemingway biographer, devoted to that nonstop womanizer down to the marrow of his bones, hadn't acquired anything of the man's life experience.

'Hey, knock it off!' I said, hurrying to cool him down, understanding that there was no way I could make light of it. 'What do my proclivities have to do with it? It's a big class. What does she look like, at least?'

'Don't put me on! You know very well who I'm – '

'I swear I haven't got a clue! Does she have any distinctive features?

'Eh-h-h, she's a particularly noble-looking lady, stately, with a bead necklace. She's got a real European look. Of course, she's not a girl any more, but, still, she's *something else!*'

And then it struck me. So, standing in the corridor and looking in through the door-window whenever I went on too long with my lecture, he had actually been taking stock of the fact that she wasn't a girl.

'That's got to be Lily Bourbon, most likely.'

'Lily Bourbon? Remarkable name. Is she French?'

'Something like that . . . Figuratively speak – '

He interrupted me: 'Lily! That sweet-smelling flower . . . And a Bourbon, to boot . . . What, does she have royal blood?'

'Not a hundred per cent. But her husband was genuinely of the blood.'

'Was? You mean, now she's not married, your student?'

'She's not a student at all!'

'Well, what is she?'

'She just came a couple of times to my lectures. Is she someone . . . you *seriously* need?'

' "Need" would be putting it too strongly, without finding out,' Pete said pensively. 'Although there's a certain sort of emanation coming from her. Haven't you felt it?'

Oops! Yet another fellow enveloped by her emanations.

My deceased student Ken Stemp, who was obviously not the first to be smitten with her, was turning out not to be the last man enchanted by this remarkable personage either. Ken had married her and died; Pete, of course, was a quarter of a century younger, but . . .

What would you have done in my place? Told my colleague that his darling girl was the same age as Hemingway or kept silent? After all, what business was it of mine?

And indeed, then, there was something mystical about Lily Bourbon, something heavenly or, on the contrary, devilish, some kind of aura that men fall under (I don't know whether that would be all men or just the odd one here and there), ready to lose their independence, to fall down before her on their knees or, more simply put, get stuck to her like flies to flypaper. A straightforward supernatural ability to captivate men.

'Do you know what struck me about her most of all?' Pete broke into my thoughts.

Of course I was curious to find out what, exactly.

'Her back!' he blurted out in delight. 'Straight as a redwood!'

Redwood grows everywhere here in northern California. The tree is undemanding and not afraid of sharp climatic changes. This variety of the sequoia, a kind of gigantic spruce, is an evergreen and constantly drops its dried branches. An enormous redwood grew near my house several years ago, and, tired of cleaning my roof and unplugging my rain gutters, I called up the lumberjacks and had it liquidated.

So Pete liked her back in profile. Let it be her back . . . Why not? Every man finds in a woman something more inspiring than the other parts of her body or soul. I don't know where the composer of this has got to, but I recall this gem of his:

> Look at half the country, mind,
> Even half of Europe 'round,
> The world has no better mounds
> Than my own wife's behind.

But, according to Professor Hayter, the back is more important. The reader is left to pass judgement on Pete's comparison of a woman's back to a tree.

They brought us our food. I broke off a piece of the hot bread and concentrated on my soup.

'If she's not a student,' Pete continued to press me, 'then who is she, your mysterious auditor?'

His pathos was getting irritating. 'She's a recent émigré from Russia.'

'Oh! A Russian!' Pete's countenance suddenly changed.

'Why, does it make any difference?'

I asked this because the local papers in Sacramento were printing various things about Russians, far from always anything good.

Russian thieves, addicts and alcoholics quite successfully manage to get to the States via the same channels as respectable émigrés. Young Russian loafers steal cars, serve time in gaol. One committed a murder, did a bunk to the Ukraine and is now in gaol there, not without a little prompting from the American police. I read in the newspaper that three Russians are in gaol now for using someone else's credit card in a store.

They still let long-suffering Baptists and Pentecostals into the country quite easily, but a lot of other Russians, getting letters from their relatives about how money gets handed out for free here, just pretend to be one. It's got to the point where the American consulates in Moscow and Kiev open their Bibles and hold a little exam before handing out visas. But not even that will save the day, sometimes.

'So it turns out she's a Russian!' Pete slowly repeated. '*Bowl-shoy tee-at-rr*. Oh, yeah, I saw *Swan Lake* at the Metropolitan Opera . . . *Tschay-koff-skee*.'

He'd unequivocally stunned me with his erudition, mentioning *Swan Lake* and Tchaikovsky. But what did it have to do with Lily Bourbon?

'I don't think she has anything to do with the Bolshoi . . .'

'But for sure,' he contradicted me, 'she knows how to cook that – whatsit – *borshchhhhhh* . . .'

A certain involuntary surprise must have shown in my eyes, because he now tried to explain: 'That's the sort of soup that's made from cabbage and beets, finger-licking good . . . I ate it once at a Russian restaurant in San Francisco. I'm absolutely positive: a Russian lady will know how to make *borshchhhhh*!'

'Maybe she can, but I won't vouch for it,' I said. 'Do you need a cook?'

'Why a cook? I'm not a bad cook myself . . . If you want to know, I have a whole library of cookbooks from all over the world. Don't you see, I'm choosing a *part-nerrr*.'

Of course he was choosing a partner. What else?

Pete asked: 'Does she like Hemingway?'

Putting down my spoon, I stared at him. 'Why Hemingway?'

'How else am I supposed to get acquainted with her? In the Soviet Union, I heard, old Hem was really popular. Maybe you could invite her to one of my lectures.'

'First I'll have to find this passion of yours – '

'Think of something that'll make our paths cross.'

In his excitement Pete hadn't even touched his salad.

Leaving the little restaurant, we went in different directions. But then he suddenly called after me: 'Listen, is her heart in good shape?'

What was he doing – picking out a horse? I'm not a vet after all . . . To hell with him, this Hayter – he's nuts.

'You'll have to find that out from her doctor, if he'll let you in on his physician's secrets. Do you want her to have your child?'

Finally Hayter put on a smile, waved a hand to me and marched off. Russian issues, something Hayter wouldn't have a clue about, were just as untouched-upon as I had expected.

Who would have thought that the Woodpecker would get so stirred up? But I was feeling sorry for myself. Even without all this I grumble incessantly about all the idiocies that drag me away from my writer's desk. And now Hayter was demanding my attention, as well.

Invite her to his lectures, when she doesn't understand English? Anyway, it didn't have anything to do with Hemingway . . .

In a word, for the first time in my life, I was going to have to be a matchmaker.

3

Finding Lily wasn't terribly hard.

More than 70,000 Russians are now living in Sacramento, and the local television news channel recently announced proudly that the California capital was becoming a Little Moscow. This is nonsense, of course, since it's Pentecostals and Baptists from Siberia and the Ukraine who come here. However, lots of émigrés do know lots of others, they settle down near one another, and even the most insignificantly famous personalities are in the public eye – known, if not by one person, then by someone else. Besides, you can open a telephone directory and find practically any person by their surname, unless they're a movie star who's paid the local telephone company to block off their number with a secret code.

In short, your obedient servant – now a matchmaker – was going to have to call Lily Bourbon. I resisted this uncharacteristic-for-me occupation by every means, and Pete Hayter's mission fell to my wife.

Lily Bourbon was actually in the Sacramento phone book. After several standard phrases of greeting and more about the difficulties of the émigré's life, Valerie got to the point of the call: 'Lily, you asked my husband to hunt you out a boyfriend. It looks like there is such a man, and he would like to meet you. Of course, nothing is definite, but what if it works out?'

'Whose friend is he?' Madame Bourbon elaborated. 'Yours or your husband's?'

After establishing that the friend was mine, Lily wanted to talk only to me, and, however much I resisted, I had to pick up the phone. With the phone in my hand, I went for a walk in the nearest park, so as to compensate in some fashion for the waste of time.

The luxuriant spring vegetation that I hadn't noticed before, because I had been so incredibly busy, the colours and the smells of the April-blooming flowers distracted and relaxed me. Otherwise I would have lost my temper. What could be simpler, it seemed to me, than just saying yes, she'd meet him personally and make up her mind. Or say no and never meet him. Any other woman would have done that but not this one.

Lily asked: 'Is he black or white?'

'White, not even sun-tanned . . .'

Various questions were asked and re-asked even, several times, until she'd had her fill of answers. Aside from my sessions with that well-known organization that has a place in the Moscow part of my life, nobody else has ever interrogated me like that. Fortunately, this time there was no risk of my incarceration. But I didn't know enough about Hayter to satisfy Lily's curiosity. And I ended up dodging the questions, just as I'd done with that aforementioned organization.

'Describe how he looks.'

'He looks all right.'

'Is he up to my intellectual level?'

'I think he'll be able to keep you on your toes.'

'Well, that's something, anyway . . . But is he well bred?'

'Utterly.'

'How old is he? I don't need him to be any older than sixty.'

'But, hey – ' escaped from my lips, and I shut up.

What a fantastic woman: she herself was ninety-six.

'I know what you were about to say!' Her voice grew stern. 'Damn me for letting the cat out of the bag, anyway. I hope you haven't given anything away, have you? Keep this in mind: I am now fifty-nine years old. Got that? Fifty-nine and not a day more!'

'But, Lily, forgive my indiscretion – how are you going to get away with that?'

'You're the one who heard that Mexicans do this sort of thing, aren't you? My chauffeur drove me down to Mexico, to Tijuana – you know it?'

Did I ever know Tijuana . . . We sometimes bought souvenirs there. It's a couple of hours from Los Angeles, south down Interstate Five. You pass through the border control without a hitch. There's never anyone in the exit windows. A minute later and you're in Mexico. A dirty little town of street hawkers and brothel keepers, Tijuana is painted in poisonous colours (for some reason they love their walls there to be painted blue and orange).

Swarthy women of tender years – some even possibly underage – stand around the little restaurants and shops; if you're alone, they indicate with their eyes their second-floor windows, hung with red curtains. Moonlighting garage mechanics hawk their services, and dentists of the same class, and everywhere wheeler-dealers dart in and out, offering their services in various spheres but tending towards the illicit.

It's no trouble getting back into the States in a car with American plates. The road widens out to twenty lanes. Little placards hang on all the booths: 'Show your driver's licence.' The first time I stopped, I asked the American border guard: 'Show my licence?'

He wearily wiped his forehead: 'Well, show it if you want to.'

I haven't bothered showing it since.

'So what were you doing in Tijuana, Lily?'

'What do you mean, what? Got myself a new birthdate, for a modest price. Now I'm fifty-nine. Slick as a whistle!'

'How much did they hit you up for, if it's not a secret?'

'Oh! Mexicans are real men! Rodrigo, the dentist who'd been recommended to me by some Russian acquaintances in San Diego, said to me, "Madame, you look so great that I'll do everything for you for fifty per cent off."'

'Do what?' I didn't understand. 'Your teeth?'

'What do teeth have to do with this? A new birth certificate.'

Knowing that she didn't get around in English, I asked her: 'So in what language did he say this to you?'

'In Russian, of course! I understand Spanish about as well as I do

English. First he explained that he'd graduated from the medical institute in Omsk or Tomsk or somewhere. Then he chuckled and made it clear that what he'd learned was how to have sex with the girls at the medical institute in Omsk-Tomsk – but he'd forged his Russian dentist's diploma himself in Tijuana, and now, under his dentist's sign, what he did was improve on documents.'

'So, he "improves" on things . . . "I'll do it for fifty per cent off" . . . of what?' I was trying to understand.

'What do you mean, off what?' Lily fell silent, figuring it out. 'Evidently, off some kind of accepted fee down there. But you're distracting me from my point. So what, actually, does this fiancé of mine make himself out to be?'

'Well, he's hardly your fiancé yet . . .'

She ignored this. 'Does he speak good Russian?'

It swam back to my mind how indignant she'd been that her deceased husband, Ken Stemp, scarcely spoke a word of Russian, and how she had made fun of his accent.

'Yes, he does!' I announced with confidence. 'He knows four words: *Bolshoy teatr*, *borshch* and *Tchaikovsky*.'

'Are you serious, or kidding me?' she asked, after a pause.

I kept quiet. For some reason that was incomprehensible and exasperating to Lily Bourbon, people in America continued to speak English despite the fact that she had arrived. It had taken her a long time to come to a realization of this bleak truth. But now something had evidently given way inside her. Perhaps for the first time in her life here she was feeling what it was like to run into a brick wall: the American people were obstinately resistant to switching over to her native language. And now, understanding the dead end of her situation, after thinking and vacillating over it, she added without the slightest irony: 'Four words – that's something, already. By the way, does he know that I'm a famous Russian poet?'

'I think he doesn't know yet.'

'Why didn't you enlighten him right away? I'm a poet first of all and only then a woman! But where does he live?'

'That's a difficult question. Most of the time in the university library.'

'What does he do?'

'He's a professor of contemporary American literature.'

'Hmmm. And he knows the word *borshch*? But he'd better not count on my making any for him.'

'You can tell him about that yourself, if the necessity arises, OK? And in the meantime, can I say hello to him from you? For instance, can I tell him you wouldn't mind meeting him?'

'What for?'

'Well, as a gesture of goodwill . . .'

'Don't you dare! He might decide that I'm easy, and that's completely unacceptable. Men think like jackasses. You always have to hold the carrot in front of them at a distance. Here's what: I'll meet him completely by accident. So, here, get this . . .'

And she proceeded to elaborate a whole scenario, and my role in it, over the telephone. That way I didn't have to wrack my own brains. I myself would never have come up with a plan like hers. My orders were to act strictly within the bounds of her instructions.

5

At the end of the working day, when it was already growing dark, I entered the university library. It was two hours before closing time, exams were a long way off, and there were almost no visitors to be encountered in its rooms. I took down several books from the shelves in the Slavonic Department, chose a desk not far from the exit, hung my jacket over the back of a neighbouring chair and sat down to leaf through the pages, taking notes as they occurred to me. At least it wasn't a total waste of time. But how much longer I would have to sit there was completely unclear, and I was angry with Lily and even more so with myself for getting drawn into this stupid situation, something I needed like a wolf needs a waistcoat.

I hadn't leafed through more than a hundred pages when somebody hit me painfully on the shoulder from behind.

'By God, how lucky I am to run into you! You're just the man I need!'

It was Pete Hayter, bent double.

'What's happened?' I said in surprise, according to my instructions.

His nose was sticking into my very ear, his face was florid, his eyes, always staring in different directions, shone tenderly. Why didn't he just get a simple operation to uncross them?

'She's here!' he whispered, even though there was no one around.

'Who?'

'Lily, of course!'

'Sorry, I don't get you at all. Who do you mean?'

'Lord – your student with the beautiful back. Or not your student, whatever . . . It seems that she's working on some big project, and she's reading microfilms in the archives, as well. As soon as I noticed her, this afternoon, I straight away shifted my seat to the projector next to hers. She and I have spent a half a day together, like comrades in arms.'

'What does this have to do with me?'

'I was actually on my way to the reference section for an English–Russian dictionary when I caught sight of you here. Today's my lucky day! Can you help me? I don't understand everything she says, and it's really essential that I do.' He was nervously clenching and unclenching his fingers.

'Well, listen, Pete, I'm actually finishing up already. My wife is coming home in half an hour, and we're going to have dinner . . .'

It's possible that I was coming on too strong, getting into my role, but Hayter didn't notice.

'Come with me, please!' he begged. 'It won't take long.'

All I had to do was heave a deep and slow sigh, put on my jacket, and . . . in a nutshell, we stepped into the lift.

'See, you didn't have to work at getting us acquainted,' Pete proudly declared. 'I accomplished the whole thing myself!'

Cutting through the basement, I nodded to Lucretia behind the counter, a plump black lady, the bibliographer of the Photocopy and Microfilm Department, and she waved back to me.

In the semi-darkness of the reading room I didn't recognize Lily right away, but when Pete brought me up to her I couldn't help appreciating her taste. Madame's body was swathed in elegant, snow-white dotted figure-hugging trousers, a bright-red blouse accentuating her ample bosom and, mark this, a bead necklace wound around her neck in an inconceivable number of turns. There was something of ancient Egypt lurking in these beads, and they hid her wrinkles at the same time. She sat there without slouching at all – a redwood, indeed.

'I'm almost certain that you know each other,' said Pete, radiant, striking his version of a diplomatic pose.

'Oh, what an unexpected and pleasant *meetink*,' Lily pronounced artistically, smiling charmingly and stretching out her hand to me. 'We haven't seen each other *for ay longue time*. It seems that you and Pete are *frents* . . .'

The percentage of her English interspersions had increased.

'Of course!' Pete cried out, pathetically, once more clapping me on the shoulder in his excitement. 'We're not just colleagues but old friends, even. And we'll both be your friends, if you don't object. I would like to take this happy opportunity, Lily, and tell you that there's some hidden passion in you. You remind me of a fairy-tale princess . . .'

That was why he needed me so urgently! We're born to make fairy-tales by means of flirtation.

Lily heard out the translation and pretended to be surprised, but she was clearly satisfied with the compliment.

'Did you really notice that, Pete? It's far from every man who can do that . . .'

She glanced at him briefly and straight away cast down her dark eyes. Her rouged cheeks (what a lady friend from New York once termed 'painting on the fresh country air') blushed even pinker.

It looked to me as if Pete was about to fly off and hover under the ceiling. But it didn't happen. He remained on the parquet floor and only bowed, rocking back and forth on his heels, his long nose almost touching the nearby projector. But what about his chief compliment – her straight-as-a-redwood back? What, was he going to keep that in reserve? Her long, fan-like violet eyelashes – thickly mascaraed or, more likely, glued on – fluttered, screening the mysterious looks that she was throwing him. With looks like that and a complete absence of backbone, you'd soon find yourself on your knees.

The three of us left the library together. Pete found out that Lily had no car and volunteered to give her a lift home. She answered that she had her own chauffeur she'd just have to call him and he would come and get her. But she playfully added: 'If you insist, though – I give in . . .'

At the parking lot, before we went variously to our cars, Lily winked at me. I felt a little sorry for Pete, although nobody was roping him into the affair. Seating her, he purred solicitously: 'I'll move the seat so that your splendid back will be more comfortable.'

There it was! Thank God he hadn't forgotten about her back.

Once again I translated, and Lily nodded in satisfaction, arching her back like a cat being stroked. She was nearly purring.

'It's a bit hard for émigrés in America,' Pete continued sympathetically. 'We're all born behind the wheel here.'

'Of course I wouldn't mind driving a *carr*, too,' Lily fantasized, pouting like an aggrieved child. 'What am I, dumber than American women?'

The seed fell on fertile soil. Pete quickly offered to instruct her in this uncomplicated art.

'There couldn't be a greater pleasure for me!' he cried out, with excessive emotion.

There's the way to get closer, I thought. I translated to her what the lovestruck Hemingwayist had said, went to my Toyota, slammed the door and pulled out on to the street.

It never occurred to me that events would unfold with such speed.

A couple of weeks later, Pete and I found ourselves sitting next to each other at a committee meeting to examine student petitions. Once a month a group of professors would meet and go over students' complaints about their low grades. If there were any documents supporting the fact that someone wasn't able to pass an exam owing to serious illness or the death of a relative, for example, the grade would be passed on to their teacher for review. More often the students would complain that their professors hadn't taken into consideration their participation in a baseball match or their late arrival at the exam because of a traffic jam.

During a break in the proceedings, while they brought in tea, Pete informed me confidentially that Lily, under his tactful guidance, was already learning to drive.

'She's making colossal progress,' he said, thinking positively, like the majority of Americans. 'Only she still doesn't always keep the wheel straight. When she's driving, the car wags its tail like a Montmartre prostitute. Because of the language barrier I can't explain it to her properly, and sign language isn't always intelligible. I beg you to do me the small service of sitting alongside her and explaining how to hold the wheel.'

Towards evening we met at the parking lot next to the university's drama theatre. The lot was nearly deserted. The sun was going behind the mountains and the grey shadows of the trees had grown long. Lily winked at me and got behind the wheel of Pete's white Honda, and I got in next to her, in the front seat. Pete settled into the back, slinging his long legs crossways on the seat. Pressing the button, he moved her seat forward.

Lily determinedly started up the engine, and the Honda moved down the lane running around the lot. 'The most important thing is to learn how to stop' was what came surfacing in my memory, the precept of the experienced Moscow taxi driver who had taught your obedient servant how to drive some forty years before in the quiet lanes near the Garden Ring.

'See?' Pete pecked at my ear with his long nose. 'We're not doing badly, eh?'

But he was nervous just the same. The Honda was moving forward, strangely enough, but swerving now left, then right.

'How am I doing?' Lily asked, looking at me like a triumphant jockey who'd just taken the lead in a race.

'Concentrate on the road,' I noted carefully. 'And if you want my advice, don't rock the wheel back and forth. The car will go straight ahead by itself as long as you don't interfere.'

'By itself?' she countered, seizing the wheel more firmly.

'By itself. You only have to make minor adjustments . . .'

A certain alarming acceleration became noticeable. It grew rapidly.

'Don't hurry!' barked Pete from the back seat. 'Learn how to drive slow.'

In any other circumstance I would have burst out laughing to hear such international advice. But now I had to translate it as quickly as I could.

'It's speeding up by itself, though,' Lily objected. 'What am I supposed to do now?'

'Step on the brake!' I yelled. 'Quick!'

'But where is the brake? I remember it was somewhere, but it's slipped out from underfoot . . .'

Lily brought all her weight to bear on the steering wheel. We tore around the parking lot in a tight circle.

'Brake! Brake!' Pete yelled hoarsely.

'Brake!' I screamed, simultaneously trying in vain to shift her foot, now stuck to the accelerator, to the left, on to the brake, with my own. It was as if Lily had turned to stone. I wasn't able in any way to get my hand in and straighten the wheel, on which she had as deathly a grip as someone would have on a lifebelt. The Honda tore on headlong towards the only car that was left in the huge parking lot. Every other parking space in the place was empty, but Lily was heading straight for this powder-blue Buick.

Finally Pete thought to pull up the hand brake, sticking his arm between the two front seats. Careening slightly to one side, we slammed into the rear fender of the Buick, knocking it to one side, which softened the blow.

The hood in front of our noses squealed and flew open unbidden. I looked at Pete: he'd turned white. Drops of sweat were running down his forehead and hanging from his eyebrows. I surely looked no better.

'I never thought that American cars were such stupid creatures. Dumber than a man, even,' Lily said, looking at me, back on her favourite hobbyhorse. 'Only don't translate that last bit . . .'

'The Honda is a Japanese car,' said Pete, his national pride inappropriately awakened.

'Dumb anyway! It doesn't understand what I want – brake or go.'

We slowly regained our composure. Lily was still sitting with the wheel tight in her grasp. Pete reached over and pulled a telephone out of the glove compartment, dialled 911 and gave them the number of our parking lot.

'Probably,' he said, 'in your case, Lily, in the interests of safety it's preferable to have a chauffeur. I, too, am always ready to give you a lift, of course, whenever I've got the time . . .'

A university policeman drove up, a man as thin and long-nosed as Pete. The guardian of order shook our hands and glanced at the smashed front end of the Honda.

He shook his head. 'It's hot today,' he soothed us. 'That's why . . .'

He tossed his hat on to the seat and grasped Lily around the waist as tenderly as a child, lifted her from behind the wheel and carried her over to the back seat of his car. Hayter jealously followed his movements. The policeman started filling out forms. Lily suddenly burst into tears. Pete consoled her: 'The insurance will cover everything . . .'

The degree of his tenderness had grown.

But I kept silent, taking pleasure in the fact that all three of us were still alive. Right next to the Buick grew a huge 300-year-old oak tree. The local paper had even printed a piece about how criminals had been hanged from the tree's lower branches two hundred years ago. In contrast to the Buick, the oak wouldn't have budged from its spot after getting hit.

6

The devil only knows what went on between Pete and Lily, but one day Hayter sat down next to me at a table in the student union. I was hurriedly munching a pizza between two lectures, washing it down with a *caffè latte*. I always drink it there: there's little coffee in it but a lot of frothed skim milk.

'It's none of my business to interfere in your programme, old pal,' said Pete, slurping chilli from a plastic spoon, 'but, purely as a friend, why are you opposed to broadening your syllabus?'

'In what sense?'

'Your Poetry of the Twentieth Century is a survey course, but the most distinguished Russian poetess of modern times is left unmentioned.'

Intrusion into someone else's teaching plan is an unprecedented effrontery. Nobody has ever done it: neither the deans, nor the chancellor of the university. The fact that Pete had even brought it up proved to what an extent he'd fallen under her influence.

'You, too?' I exclaimed in exasperation. 'And who told you, man, that she was the "most"? She herself?'

'She did,' Pete admitted imperturbably. 'There's going to be a library named after her in Moscow soon.' Incidentally, that was evidence that she'd acquired a feel for America fairly quickly: here we call it 'blowing your own horn'. And Lily was blowing with all her might.

'Pete, do you know even one of her poems?'

'Not yet, but – '

'If you want, I'll recite you one that I remember from childhood. We all had to knock this one into our heads at school. Just have a listen:

I want to sing your praises, social-ISM!
Where can a rhyme for this festive word be found?
That rhyme would be – commun-ISM.
There's where I'd surely like to fly right now.

Of course, this was an impromptu translation into English that I gave to Pete, so the effect wasn't quite right. But I tried not to get too far away from the original and to demonstrate the whole magnificence of this twentieth-century masterpiece.

'Do you like that?' I asked, after giving him a chance to mull over the text.

'Not bad!' Pete retorted with sang-froid. 'The poet sees herself as a bird, flying into tomorrow . . . By the way, Hem in his old age also considered himself a lefty and hugged Fidel Castro, didn't he? So what? Nobody except Russians and Vietnamese are fearful about ideas like these. Lefties impart a certain aroma to life.'

'Aroma or smell?'

'OK, smell. What's the difference?'

'The difference is, as you can see, that she actually came here, where there's quite a different aroma!'

'How to put it . . . these ideas haven't yet been officially approved here.'

That's the last thing that needs to be approved, here. Where would I emigrate to again, then? It was useless explaining it. 'Pete, do you know where you can go?'

'Where?' he asked, with placid curiosity.

'To He . . . mingway . . .'

He took me literally. 'OK! Lily, even though she's young at heart,' Hayter started speculatively, 'is from that same lost generation as Uncle Hem.'

'That's an interesting thought,' I said.

'Yes, I'd barely turned twenty when I met Hem. I'd dreamed of becoming a famous journalist, like him. But whenever I saw him he was always hiccupping, pumped full of whisky and always talking utter nonsense about "universal brotherhood", something that he and the likewise-bearded Marx imagined as a community of wives for him and people of the same mind. Now I understand: it was discontent with the cruelty and hypocrisy of life around him.'

'Somehow I can't quite grasp the connection, Pete. What does this have to do with Lily?'

'You'll get it now . . . Just like Hem, in the face of this cruel world, Lily steadfastly preserves her dignity. She complained to me that she bears a grudge against the whole wide world. Or maybe the whole universe.'

'A grudge? What for?'

'Madame Bourbon was considered the greatest poet of the Soviet Union, and she was never even nominated for the Nobel Prize!'

'She's in good company,' I said, 'since neither Tolstoy nor Nabokov ever got the prize.'

'But it's still not too late for her. I used to have a friend on the Nobel committee: he personally shook Hemingway's hand when he was awarded the prize in 1954, and I interviewed him later on. I'll try to find out if he's still alive. Lily tells me that her entire body is imbued and boiling with creative ideas. Hemingway's archives still have unpublished material. Maybe there's something she has to publish in America?'

'Publish all Hemingway's stuff first, Pete.'

'I don't have any time to spend on Hem,' he answered. 'And generally speaking, I'm fed up to the gills with that fly-fishing tosspot.'

For someone as methodical as Hayter, this was a paradoxical announcement. Was he just imitating the logic of his Russian girlfriend? Could it be that he would now even take up the study of her Soviet output and become her biographer – that is, if you'll pardon the phrase, a Bourbonist? The worn-out old Russian actor Yevstigneyev would sadly say: 'What surprises me is people.'

7

Lily phoned and said she had to see me urgently.

'Has anything happened?'

'I can't say over the telephone.'

My God! Here, in America, where even international Mafiosi boldly and openly chatter on the phone about their narcotics deliveries across whole continents and order murders over the phone, this Soviet Madame Bourbon felt that she couldn't discuss her problems over the phone. Maybe it was something more terrible than narcotics or terrorism.

Opening the door to my office she looked at me sternly and, after a pause, aggressively asked me from the threshold: 'What was your purpose in introducing me to him?'

I felt embarrassed. Indeed, what was the purpose of a man and a woman becoming acquainted? One could suppose that there are various purposes. It could also be supposed that more often than not they become acquainted precisely because he's a man and she's a woman. Although, of course, there could be other variants.

'Your friend has dishonoured me,' she announced reproachfully, nailing me to my chair with her gaze, as if I was the one who'd stripped her of her honour and not Hayter.

'In the first place, he's not a friend, he's a colleague,' I elaborated just in case, so as not to be drawn into yet another scandal in the capacity of witness to sexual harassment. 'In the second place, Pete is an intelligent man, that is, a decent man.'

I felt an urge to do something, like when an audience yells, 'Give us the details!' But I restrained myself and simply asked: 'What's he gotten up to, the smart aleck?'

'He asked if I had a healthy heart.'

'What's criminal about asking that?'

'My heart's up to scratch, but that's just shameful, asking a woman about her organs.'

'Pete was asking out of courtesy.'

'Not a bit! He had a mercenary motive. He asked me out to dance.'

'Where?'

'Don't pretend you don't know! This was a planned provocation. He's a maniac, a tangoist!'

'A who?'

'A tango dancer! He can't live without the tango . . .'

'Really? I've never noticed, even though I've known him ever since I made it to America . . .'

'You men,' she sneered, 'you never notice what's going on around you. But you surely blabbed to him about the fact that, in the first flush of my youth, I used to dance with Isadora Duncan and that we had one and the same lover, Sergei Yesenin?'

'Merciful heavens! He caught sight of you, fell in love like a boy and asked to be introduced to you. That's all.'

'That was naughty! You should have told him everything at once! It turns out that he doesn't care who he falls in love with . . .'

'He's a professor of literature, and you're a poetess – or, if you like, a poet – '

'A poet? I am first and foremost a woman and only after that somebody else!'

'But earlier on you were saying quite the opposite – '

'Earlier on? How can you fail to understand? It's all so easy: everything depends on the specific circumstances.'

Now Lily sat down in the armchair, took a compact out of her bag, and made sure that the elaborate makeup imposed on her face was in order.

'And how did your poetic gift manifest itself?' I asked, not because I was curious but just to change the subject.

'I had to express myself,' she said, calming down. 'I got interested in poetry because they banned striptease shortly after the Revolution. God forbid that you should find yourself in times like that! My first husband, Andrey Bourbon, was a typical bourgeois, absolutely unadjusted to the proletarian lifestyle. I introduced him to literature. Did you ever hear of him?'

'No,' I answered straight away, so as not to establish her guilt in a lie, even though her first husband and I had downed a few drinks together.

And many people knew that the poet Monsieur Bourbon, a Russian nobleman and descendant of French kings whom they had stopped publishing back then, was the one who wrote the poetry for the first-class Soviet poetess, at least up until their divorce. Lily had a surprising ability to turn everything upside down.

'You've set my life on its ear,' she said, after a silence. 'The most terrible thing is that, because of you, I got drawn into harking back to days of yore and danced the Argentine tango with Pete! We're officially a dance couple – he's already paid the entrance fee, and we're getting ready for the competition in Buenos Aires. You've heard about it, I suppose? This is for the Latin American title.'

'Of course I've heard about it!' I said, trying to keep any falseness out of the tone of my voice.

It turned out that she hadn't come to express her indignation but to inform me of her victory.

'My bones are creaking, but he's no boy either,' she continued. 'I went to bed dead on my feet, without a hope of getting up today, but, come morning, I gradually come back to life. I've found a wonderful Japanese masseuse. Massage beforehand – I dance – and massage afterwards. Only she's expensive, the scum. She's fleecing me.'

'Everything has to be paid for,' I sympathized. 'You'll manage, I'm sure . . .'

'Yes, young man, I've found myself dancing yet again. My poetry now pours itself into the tango. Soon I'll be eighteen years old again . . .'

'Congratulations!'

Suddenly she blew out her lips and said resentfully: 'Do you think I couldn't have written better than Tsvetayeva? I had to pretend. Whoever didn't play the part came to a bad end. While I . . . just you wait, I'll create masterpieces that will knock you head over heels. But just now all I have in my head is the tango . . .'

Lord, I thought on the way home, how splendidly a human being is made. She'd just been standing at the coffin of her husband, trying to figure out the best way to survive in a strange country, how to maintain her own self at the verge of death, how to find someone new to lean on. Who would have thought that Pete would turn up with his unexpected hobby? And today the unpredictable Lily was already pouring her Soviet poetry into the Argentine tango and doing it in America with her characteristic energy. Just wait, and a woman like that will get married to some great American poet, and he'll be writing for her. Then you'll see her dancing in world literature, not just in the Russian!

8

The courtship was turning out to be a bit strange. Popping in to the auditorium where Hayter was finishing his lecture, then waiting until he let his students go, I asked him straight up what his purpose had been in getting to know Lily.

'This is the truth,' Pete owned up. 'I told you right off the bat that I needed a partner. I meant for my hobby. I've been a member of a tango-dancing club for thirty years.'

'You mean you're a dancer?'

'Well, what's so surprising about that to you? The tango, my dear colleague, is a drama that only lasts several minutes. In the tango, if you will, there is compressed the entire history of human love – from primordial instincts down to civilization. The tango is a unique blend of tenderness, sorrow, inexorability and love – genuine human passions. Believe me, stronger than in any literature. In the tango the mutual relations of the sexes are more expressive than in life. Two bodies harmoniously merge into one – it's a great art, sticking them together in movement and music. Moreover, mind you, everything is out in the open, as if you and your wife were doing it on the Broadway sidewalk in New York.'

'Who would have thought that you, Hemingway's biographer . . .'

'I've been to Argentina six times to improve my standing and do exhibitions. I even have a diploma for it . . .'

'And nobody knows about it?'

'It's just that I've never advertised it here at the university. But to me this is serious, maybe even more serious than Hemingway. I make my living off him, but the tango is purely a labour of love. Consequently, old man Hem is my means, while the tango is my end. So, then – important competitions are coming up, and my former partner is pregnant.'

'Congratulations!'

'Don't talk nonsense! Not by me. I had an urgent need for a suitable tango partner with an internal passion. I mean for dancing, my dear colleague, since intimate relations get in the way of training. The most important thing is that she have a well-shaped back! The back produces a magical impression on judges. And I've found one!'

It was becoming clear that, once again, I had to take another look at my understanding of the American character, despite the number of years I'd lived here.

'How do you communicate without either language or intimacy?'

'The language of movement in the tango is universal, old man. Music doesn't need any translation, either. Gesture and touch explain everything better than any language.'

Interesting! So they'd gone into a primeval state: they related by gestures.

It was evident that Pete wanted to ask something but was dithering.

'I admit that this is extremely impolite,' he said in embarrassment, 'but how old is she?'

I was at a loss once more: tell him or lie? It's shameful to deceive one's colleagues. I decided to come clean, as if under oath.

'Sorry, she's ninety-six.'

Pete froze, with his mouth open wide enough for a whole hamburger to fit inside. It seemed as if his eyes were coming uncrossed. He regained his composure, but his ears were red.

'She told me that she was younger than me. I'm sixty-four. I'm young enough to be her grandson. Age limits at the competition are going to put us into the seniors' category. What am I going to do now?'

'They don't have a group for the elderly there? Listen, Pete, find yourself another partner, that's all . . .'

'But I've promised her! And I'm not going to find another back like that just anywhere. And, besides . . . generally speaking, I'm . . . in love with her.'

'You've already said that gets in the way. What about your pragmatism?'

'It looked to me like *she* had . . . I couldn't offend her and not respond in kind . . .'

Thus Hayter was revealing himself as a true American. His eyes filled with tears. I stood there next to him, not knowing how to console him.

'Everything will be all right, Pete. It'll all work itself out. They say she was gorgeous when she was young, and she's in great shape still. You know yourself, what a back . . .'

Pete looked at me hopefully, as if making her younger depended on me.

'Would you and your wife,' he asked, 'care to join us?'

The classroom had filled up with students for the following lecture. Affably smiling and nodding his head, the tidily slick-haired Mao Sang, professor of Chinese literature, came in at a light trot, and we had to free up the auditorium for him.

My wife and I discussed Hayter's idea over dinner at home. We live in sort of a rut, without any diversions. We're not very active. We have neither the strength nor the desire for physical exercise.

'Why don't we try dancing the tango?' Valerie enthused. 'It's Argentine, after all.'

I took fright. 'Only not for any competition, naturally! No Buenos Aireses! Tangomania's not for me. We'll just give it a try, that's all.'

We decided to join the tangoists. Purely out of curiosity.

9

Once I'd made it to the American continent in the 1980s, to the state of Texas, I soon discovered that dancing is something they do there eagerly and cheerfully, in what is called a 'honky-tonk'. Some friends dragged us along one night to a honky-tonk mysteriously called the Broken Spoke, and we liked it there a lot.

This honky-tonk was on the outskirts of Austin, the capital of Texas. It was a very simple rural-style building, you could say, looking like a bunkhouse from the outside, although decorated with strings of lights and garlands of flowers inside and out, and with a huge parking lot.

On one wall was a wagon wheel with the eponymous broken spoke. Tickets were cheap. Along the walls were plain wooden benches. The orchestra was on a raised stage: a beat-up piano, two guitars, a double bass and a drummer. Most of the tunes were familiar. People were competing for prizes. From time to time an ageing, vulgar-looking dame would run out and sing, shaking her locomotive-massive hips. Every so often the fellows in the band would have a go at it themselves, in their hoarse voices, to the eager applause of a good hundred of the guests.

The odours of perfume and alcohol, blown around by the air-conditioning, seemed to be coming equally from everyone. People of all ages were partying here: from early-ripened, pimply fifteen-year-old maidens tearing away from home in their mothers' clothes in search of adventure to mauve-haired, silhouetteless old ladies. Men were in cowboy hats, and some of them wore luxurious tooled ostrich-hide boots, the price of which could go as high as a thousand dollars. There were a lot of rednecks among the dancers, sporting the proof of their physical labour under the burning sun. Women wore brightly coloured skirts that flew up with every movement, revealing things you weren't supposed to see.

Some of them were obviously recent immigrants from Mexico, poverty-stricken, normally ready for any sort of work. What they earned during the day they danced and drank away at night. They wore clothes they'd bought at garage sales, only they were clean and close-shaven. They danced until midnight, some with breaks for air, others non-stop.

A bar was set off behind a wooden barrier reminiscent of a porch rail on an old *dacha* somewhere in the Moscow suburbs. The bar had a counter with tall stools, wooden benches and simple picnic-style tables with crossed legs. Here there was an abundance of alcohol – with permission for its sale on the premises tacked up on the wall – and modest snacks. Neighbouring rooms held card-players and pool-shooters; if you really needed to, there were rooms to rent for an hour or two, as you wished: either with your own partner or with their personnel for an additional fee.

Out in the wide world, they might be fighting or celebrating, living through triumph or crisis, but here in the honky-tonk the music rumbles and the ostrich-hide boots stomp, every single night till far past midnight. Drop in and see for yourself.

Now, after recalling that honky-tonk, it occurred to me that Pete was inviting us somewhere analogous. But back there they danced the foxtrot, the swing, the waltz, the two-step, and something else – but no tango. For the tango, you've got to shift your sights upwards a notch. The tango rings out in a different place, a special one.

Beyond a doubt, it was a stupid thing to do, going to an Argentine tango class where the dancers were fanatics, like Pete. Unless you just wanted to pay three dollars for a ticket to come in and gawk at the fervent practitioners. Lonely people of both sexes who don't dance drop by to mix in with the dancers between dances, in the hope of meeting someone. But Valerie and I firmly decided to try to dance ourselves, so Pete told us what we had to do.

'You need a *milonga*,' he said.

If we needed a *milonga*, then by God we'd get one. Without asking him what it was, we agreed and obtained the relevant instructions concerning clothing right there on the spot. We were supposed to put on black costumes, like at a funeral.

'Keep in mind that your shoes have to have leather soles,' Hayter included as his final instructions over the telephone.

He came by for us in his white Honda: it had already been repaired. The mechanics had beaten a heap of money out of the insurance company, which in its turn, of course, had jacked up Pete's insurance premiums. Another half-hour was spent finding and ceremoniously accommodating Lily in the car. She appeared in splendid evening gown. On her breast glittered an enormous medal-like brooch – a golden starfish. Lily froze at the car for a few seconds, giving us an opportunity to convince ourselves of her irresistibility, and then the four of us set off for the *milonga*. On the way Pete got into his stride.

'Do you know what the tango is? The tango is a duel.'

I failed to understand. 'How's that?'

'A socialist competition,' Lily explained in Russian, snatching the familiar word 'duel' from its context.

On the freeway Pete moved into the left lane and stepped on the gas.

'Two men used to dance it, rivals for a single woman,' he continued. 'They would stand in a circle and compete: who's the handsomer, who's better, who's stronger. The loser would even fall to the ground, symbolizing his death. Then the woman would come out to dance, and the man would take her into his arms.'

I read somewhere that the tango was born in the brothels of Buenos Aires, when at the end of the last century immigrants from Europe and Africa rushed to South America in search of happiness. There in the bay of the Rio de la Plata ships would disgorge the homeless in their thousands. Maybe there even were some duels: after all, people brutalized by their lengthy sea voyage had to search out partners for themselves, and it would be hard to think of a better way for people to get acquainted than the tango.

What you do in fact is look around the hall and pick out any woman, even one who's already accompanied. You plaster yourselves together, reducing to nil the laborious process of intimacy, then you get down to groping – and if you feel that she's unsuitable, you invite the next one, until you get to the one who's right.

The word *tango* itself, they say, comes from the Latin *tangere*, meaning 'to touch', hence also the English *tangible* in its meaning of 'palpable, perceptible'. Tangomania spread to the States when hotel owners began organizing dances in their lobbies. On dance nights, the rooms filled up like crazy. The tango became a necessity in Europe in World War I for the same reasons as everywhere else: officers and men alike needed a touch.

'Of course, duelling sounds strange, now,' said Pete.

Lily stayed silent the rest of the trip, even though it was usually hard to stop her talking.

The Argentine tango school in Sacramento threw open its doors for dilettantes on Fridays at eight in the evening. At the entrance you had to stump up your cash, and the fat beer-keg-shaped doorman in his starched shirt and dicky bow stamped 'Paid $15' in brown ink on everyone's hand. If later on you had to go out for some fresh air or a smoke, when you returned you prettily stuck your fist under the doorman's nose.

The schedule indicated that the first hour was styled an 'informal class', after which came dancing till the middle of the night.

Around us in the smallish and rather cosy hall the crowd roaming around was respectable, middle-aged or elderly. The ladies were dressed in expensive, stylish Saks Fifth Avenue frocks. Against their background, it was obviously more difficult for Lily to look as effective as when she had appeared to us just before. The gentlemen moved smoothly, ceremoniously, elegantly. The fancy clothes of both sexes created a mood of imminent ceremony.

The *milonga* is not any kind of honky-tonk for the *hoi polloi*, where they dance whatever they like. The club here was for the chosen few who are devoted to their special, secret union.

I hadn't danced like that since my school days, when they'd organized a dance circle. This was a Moscow boys' school, and for these classes they brought in the opposite sex, all in brown dresses with white pinafores. At the sight of these creatures from another planet a certain languorousness arose within our breasts and spread through our entire bodies. We turned to stone; we even stopped fighting among ourselves.

When they had been seated in chairs along the walls of the assembly hall, my eyes, incapable of resting, chased from one set of clenched knees in nylon stockings – they had just made their appearance on the scene – to the next. Their knees radiated some sort of waves, creating an aura around the girls, turning me into their slave to such an extent that I started stammering as soon as I got as close to them as the length of an outstretched arm.

The teacher was brought in from the neighbouring choreographers' academy. My memory preserves her poisonous violet hair, black grenadier moustache and, most of al,l her unforgettably masculine first name and feminine patronymic: Vadima Vandovna.

'Boys, form up in a line!' she would command us. 'Straighter! Straighter still! Now move slowly in the direction of the girls. Don't grab them; they're not chairs! Place your right hand on their waist. Not any lower! Who do you think I'm talking to? Don't get any closer! Don't get any closer; you haven't come here for that! The distance between your chest and her bust has to be ten centimetres. I'm going to measure it with a ruler, mind!'

A wrinkled, elderly ballroom pianist sat behind her out-of-tune grand piano. It didn't look as though she had the strength to finger the keys, but at Vadima Vandovna's command she would play away, now and again wincing at the out-of-tune notes.

I hate myself for these sorts of recollections, always really stupid and always cropping up for no apparent reason.

The *milonga* started up without any fanfare. Pushing me and Valerie into the middle of the hall, Pete and Lily went and sat modestly in a corner. For an hour we obediently positioned and repositioned our legs under the direction of the slab-shaped instructress, Mrs Martinez, who was nevertheless very elegant in her movements and who was in some way (perhaps through her hoarse bass) reminiscent of the memorable Vadima Vandovna, only she was exceptionally nice and had no ruler.

At first the *milonga* started out without any sort of music, to the clapping of Mrs Martinez's hands high above her head. In the intervening half-century it had got somewhat harder for me to leap around, and the languor in my breast at the sight of female knees, even ones on display to an incomparably more revealing degree than in a Stalin-era school in Moscow, had somehow lessened.

The bar opened. At the counter I felt a lot surer of myself than on the dance floor. After a dose of whisky and soda, the tone of the assembly materially improved.

Now a small orchestra struck up. Two elegant Brazilians with brightly painted bandoneons stepped forward. One of them, drawing wide the bellows of his accordion, launched into a sobbing melody, and then suddenly, almost kissing the microphone, broke into a wonderful tenor in a mixture of Spanish and English:

> 'I want you, *senorita* – with a pa-a-a-assion!
> *El fuego* bl-l-l-lazing in my brai-i-i-in.
> *Amor* to you is just a f-a-a-shion:
> Where is your gladness?
> *Donde esta* rapture?
> Where are you, glad rapture?
> It's like a sum-m-mer rain.'

Or at least that's the way I remember it – but it sounds the same in any country where the cult of the tango exists. And the same conflagration of desire and love, penetrating deep into the consciousness – that's always the same, too. It would be difficult to come up with anything more vulgar, but the passion is being parodied somewhat, and anyway the bit about the rain was strict realism: in these parts the rain stops in April and starts up again in November. The tenor sang out verse after verse, and we, the audience, were mesmerized by the tango.

Everybody paid attention to everyone else here; they studied one another, and that was one of the senses of this event called the *milonga*: a get-together of tango dancers, with amorous-sexual overtones. There weren't a lot of people, the dance floor always had free space, and you could check out every specimen and every couple from all angles, which is almost like being able to see through them. At long last I caught sight of my colleague Professor Hayter and Lily in the process of their religious ritual.

It would be hard to have a figure less appropriate for dancing, but a man, as opposed to a woman, doesn't want to or can't see himself. Even while dancing Pete rocked back and forth like a woodpecker, hitting his partner with his nose on the crown of her head every time. Maybe in Buenos Aires that's what you're supposed to do, and I just wasn't getting it. He'd been saying that he had taken part in contests there on six occasions, but I found out from Lily by accident that he had never actually qualified for the contests, he'd just paid his money for the right to take part. But he showed himself the gallant *caballero*, in every way trying to help his partner demonstrate her provocative femininity, and you couldn't help appreciating that.

In his arms Lily swayed almost gracefully and almost airily. The study of ballet in youth stays with you your whole life. That back that couldn't escape the attention of the tango-dancing Peter Hayter was demonstrably irreproachable. I'm not going to tell any fibs: she didn't look like a girl, despite all her contrivances, but, making allowances for her eternal youth, her tangoing wasn't bad at all.

After taking several turns on the dance floor, Pete was still smiling, as before, only now he was flagging. He came and sat down with us at the bar counter. A drop of sweat was hanging off his nose. Lily looked at him with a certain contempt, or maybe it just seemed that way to me. Her eyes blazed, full of fire; her breast was rising and falling rhythmically. She was killing him, but it wasn't doing a thing to her.

Just then the orchestra struck up something jolly. In the centre of the dance floor some sort of activity began, and the crowd turned its attention towards it.

'What's that over there?' Valerie asked the barman.

'Our new boss,' the barman pronounced, dexterously shaking a cocktail.

It turned out that they were celebrating the birthday of the owner of the establishment. He himself came down from the stage, waddling slightly, in a black dinner-jacket and bow tie, patent-leather shoes and a wide-brimmed Mexican sombrero – a fine young man in sleek good health, in complete disharmony with everything that was going on. He was given a chair, and he sat down on it in the middle of the hall in the broad circle of onlookers.

A girl inconspicuously threaded her way from the circle of the crowd and began doing a belly-dance routine in front of the owner. While she danced she began gradually shedding her clothes. As she took each item of her evening dress off, she tossed it to the birthday-boy in his chair. He held up each one to the audience, kissed it, and dropped it on to the floor. After each successive removal, a part of the audience furiously applauded, spurring the girl on to further exploits, while the rest whispered to one another in amazement and even indignation. The musicians started playing even faster.

'But that's a striptease!' exclaimed Lily suddenly, amazed.

'But what for?' responded Pete. 'We don't do that sort of thing here. This isn't some honky-tonk! That's where they'd hire a professional stripteaser for fifty bucks, to amuse the crowd for a while. But this is a *milonga*! I'll bet the owner himself brought the girl here.'

After getting all her clothes off and spinning around in front of the birthday-boy, the good-looking girl jumped into his lap and hugged him around the neck, then jumped up, snatched her clothes up off the floor and, skilfully threading her way through the crowd, disappeared through a door at the back of the stage.

'Well, what do you find attractive about *her*?' Lily asked.

'Nothing at all, really,' Pete agreed, hugged Lily carefully and turned to us. 'My girlfriend's chastity is outraged.'

Lily shrugged her shoulders.

'I could show that girl a thing or two about how a real striptease should be done,' Lily whispered to me in Russian. 'But Pete wouldn't get it . . .'

She started to laugh, pleased with her own joke. But perhaps she wasn't joking at all? Lily suddenly pushed Hayter's fingers off her, because the owner of the establishment was rushing straight towards her, his huge hands stretched out in front of him.

'Madame, what happiness it is to see you here!' he pronounced in rather good, though accented, Russian, with theatrical emotion.

'Rodrigo!' Lily exclaimed. 'I didn't recognize you from a distance, young man. You'll be rich!'

'Sure, I know that Russian saying!' he answered.

They embraced and kissed like bosom friends, and Lily introduced us.

'Here's that genius Rodrigo Gonzalez from Tijuana. I was telling you about him, remember?'

'Genius – you're exaggerating a little bit, kiddo,' he said.

'He's a charmer, isn't he?' Lily said in delight.

'*Zda-ROH-vuh!*' said Rodrigo to me, totally like a Russian, as if we were already drinking pals, and looked Pete over from head to toe. 'As you can see, I'm now the proprietor of this establishment. A friend of mine got a loan from the bank and for a percentage of the take bought me this tango school off of two dancers from San Francisco, and I hired them back as instructors.'

Rodrigo appeared to be around twenty-eight years of age, or maybe thirty at the most. Hair like Paganini's down to his shoulders and a long moustache hanging down around either side of his large mouth.

His hat with its enormous brim curled up at the sides was tied under his square jaw with laces that squeezed his cheeks forward. I remembered what Lily had told me.

In the little Mexican town of Tijuana, where dubious characters from all over the American continent hang out, Rodrigo worked nominally as a dentist, but he actually 'improved' documents. But now he'd become the owner of this dance-hall property in Sacramento, although it wasn't registered in his name.

'It's never boring in Russia!' Rodrigo mused, not without pleasure.

Rodrigo had showed up in Russia from the Mexican hinterland, where his father had a ranch where he raised riding horses. His son had remained illiterate until he was sixteen years old and had never read a single book. His father bought him a high-school diploma. Rodrigo and a friend decided to travel the world: to see other people, and to show themselves. He wound up in a particular patch of terra firma – Omsk, or maybe it was Tomsk – where he sort of studied a little at a medical institute.

'The Soviet Union still existed then,' he explained to us. 'I wanted them to like me, so I called myself a Trotskyite. That Trotsky – he was a celebrity not just in Mexico but even – what do they call it there? – a builder of Communism in Russia. Isn't that right? But they got scared for some reason. They started interrogating me, even threatened to put me in prison.'

Gonzalez began to neigh like a young stallion just let out of his stall.

'And how!' I grinned. 'They were afraid that you and your Trotskyites would get them sucked into building Communism in the whole wide world, and they'd have to cough up the money for it.'

'So I did the right thing, then, when I told them that I really loved dancing more and I spit on Communism? Then why did they take me to the airport and send me to Paris?'

'So that you wouldn't spit on Communism.'

'Nope, those Russians are a strange crew! They think that 1917 is the year of their revolution. But for the whole of the rest of mankind, that's the year of the Great Tango Revolution that overwhelmed the entire world.'

Rodrigo didn't have to search for words. In rather animated English he gaily told of how a middle-aged woman had recently come – or, more precisely, had rolled in – to see him and expressed a desire to learn the tango. She was in a wheelchair. Rodrigo hadn't wanted to take her on, but there's this federal law that says that you can't deprive citizens of their rights on grounds of a handicap, and she complained to some public organization or another. So he had to enrol her in a class.

At lessons she tried to roll back and forth rhythmically to the music. But that wasn't the end of his human rights problem. When they went straight from learning the rudiments to the dance itself, the *caballeros* were supposed to ask the ladies to dance. But nobody asked her. So this lover of the tango had sued for discrimination. The judge pronounced his verdict: the owner of the establishment was himself obliged, once he'd taken on a student like that, to ask her to dance with him.

'Just think,' complained Rodrigo. 'On the orders of this cretin of a judge I'm obliged to dance the tango with this idiot, holding on to the handles of her wheelchair, you know, pulling her wheelchair all over the place.'

'How romantic!' Lily exclaimed.

'I'd have been better off hiring some stud to do that for five dollars an hour . . . But now you're going to dance with me, kiddo! And without any damned wheelchair.'

This could have been interpreted as an offensive hint at Lily's age, but she either didn't notice or preferred not to. The more so, since Rodrigo had asked her in a tone that brooked no refusal, and barked at the tenor with the bandoneon in his hands: 'Francisco, play a *cumparsita!*'

Francisco nodded to the other musicians and smoothly stretched his bandoneon wide, making a peculiar faltering, tragic signal. The other bandoneonist continued this signal on a higher note and broke off. After a short, deathly pause, the violin joined in with them, the flute sang out, and chords from the grand piano afforded the rhythm. The audience made way, giving the dance floor to the owner and his lady.

I have to confess, it was something to look at: Rodrigo, strapping and at the same time, it seemed, quite graceful in his dancing, and the skinny, straight-as-a-redwood Lily flowed together, as if they had been dancing with one another for an age.

There was no distance at all left between her bust and his chest – everyone noticed *that*. Lily's real age had disappeared somewhere, and the remnants of her bygone ardour were, without a doubt, brimming over. Their sexual *pas de deux* evoked friendly applause: she contrived to lift her leg so that her dress pulled up to her waist, while her heel rested on his tailbone: an equestrienne setting her spurs to her mount.

Although the air-conditioner was chasing the cold air around with all its might, the temperature in the *milonga* increased perceptibly. Probably the energy generated by the two dancers was heating the air. A photographer with an old-fashioned camera appeared out of nowhere and started snapping away from various angles in the hope that the lady – picked out of the crowd by the boss – would shell out for it later.

Pete lounged against the wall, his jaw working.

'She's splendid, Pete!' I whispered, to break the silence.

'She may be splendid,' he responded, 'but not with me.'

He had a sour look on his face. He was hunched over, looking more than ever like a woodpecker.

After the dance Rodrigo gallantly escorted Lily back to us. Her cheeks were blazing. She was radiant.

'My, how he can dance!' she exclaimed loudly, so that Rodrigo would hear. 'He's the best tangoist in Sacramento, a real star! They would take him in Hollywood, only he doesn't need that.'

If you want to get a man hot under the collar, as she had explained before, you have to drown him in flattery. He gets soft and ready for anything. Now she was demonstrating this tactic in action.

Rodrigo guffawed. 'Like we agreed, kiddo!' he tossed her, significantly; then he winked and went off.

Lily lowered her voice and, eyes following Rodrigo, said to Valerie: 'A boy like that makes a woman feel young. He's experienced at breaking wild horses, so it's easy enough for him to deal with me.'

Pete asked Lily to dance with him, but she turned her eyes to him in perplexity and, batting her stuck-on eyelashes, declared that she was tired. But when Rodrigo again set out in her direction, her tiredness vanished.

'There are two kinds of women,' she whispered meaningfully. 'One kind gets indignant when men pester them, the other kind gets indignant when they don't get pestered. I belong to the second category, and that's why I've lived for so long.'

'Let's have another whirl, kiddo,' Rodrigo appealed, coming up right against her.

All things considered, Lily liked that sobriquet. She rewarded Rodrigo with an enchanting smile and placed her hand on his shoulder.

Once again they danced. Inasmuch as he was the owner of the establishment, the musicians pulled out all the stops. The bandoneon sobbed tragically in Francisco's hands. Rodrigo and Lily once more returned to us. Pete looked dismayed. What I mean to say is that it had become clear to everyone: Lily was slipping through his fingers and flowing into Rodrigo's arms.

'See, my poetry is being transformed into the tango,' she winked at me and Valerie, trying to conceal her heavy breathing. 'Just wait, I'll be on everyone's lips.'

'Pete said that your name has been appropriated by a library in Moscow.'

'I'm the one who decided it was high time to do that, but they don't know anything about it yet in Moscow . . .'

Pete sat, gloomy, crestfallen and nervously clenching and unclenching his fingers. Then he slammed his palm down on the table and started trying to talk me into having another drink with him. At first I waved him off: we'd already become decently sozzled. But then I felt sorry for him and nodded. We paid for a pitcher of margaritas thick with crushed ice and poured out a glass apiece.

'This is the second time for me,' he grumbled.

I failed to understand. 'What?'

'The second time a partner has thrown me over. Twenty-seven years ago in Buenos Aires the woman I adored went off with some sort of engineer from Germany. At four o'clock in the morning I was sitting alone in a port restaurant, drinking black coffee and swearing to myself that I'd never get married.'

What could I say to him? We each drank another glass of the margarita, and the remaining six or seven portions flowed from the pitcher into Pete. It occurred to me that his study of Hemingway hadn't been a complete waste for Hayter after all. Today his biographer stood a chance of beating out the biggest alcoholic in America. Pete was quiet for a long time, and then said, his voice all slurred: ''Sall yourf . . . fault.'

'Mine? But why?'

'Wha'd you introduce m-me to this Q-Q-Queen of Spades for?'

He tilted the pitcher with the remnants of the margarita over his glass and waited for the last little chunk of ice to rattle down into it, drank it down, licked off the salt that was sticking to the rim of the pitcher and looked strangely at me. His eyes had become even more crossed.

'Challenge him to a duel,' I suggested.

'But d-duels are against the law in America!'

I've told myself this hundreds of times: think long and hard before giving advice of an unserious nature to an American.

'Take it easy, Pete! If Big Daddy Ernie were you, he would have been delighted with the antics of a creature like Lily.'

'For sure! She and H-Hemingway would have made a w-wonderful pair . . . But Hem used to say, though, that he loved his w-work more than any w-woman or anything else, but I couldn't do that. Do you know what he k-called himself wa-once, in a letter to a g-girlfriend? A g-good son of a b-bitch, whose life was subject to c-cruel c-criticism. I wouldn't mind being as t-talented a scum as he was, but it doesn't w-work that way.'

'You mean you dream of becoming a son of a bitch? Well, that's easier than steamed turnip!'

'How do you know it's easy? Have you t-tried it?'

In his drunken state he'd become a more successful polemicist.

Lily was standing in the middle of the hall with Rodrigo. In the break between dances, the photographer had brought them the finished photos. Animatedly discussing them, they were whispering, periodically stroking and patting each other on various parts of the body, and they were both extremely jolly. Trying not to glance in their direction, Pete set off for the toilet with an unsteady gait. When he came back, Lily, hand in Rodrigo's arm, was standing with us.

'How come?' Pete said, at a loss, when it was his turn to look at the photographs of Rodrigo and Lily.

'You're not looking bad, kiddo!' Gonzalez ladled out his latest compliment.

Suddenly Hayter near-voicelessly squeezed out of himself what should never be said under any circumstances. 'But you're m-m . . . *my* partner!' He stressed the word *my*.

'Zip up your fly' was the simple Russian phrase she riposted with. Rodrigo guffawed in understanding.

'What did she say?' Pete said strainingly, not understanding.

'Translate it for him,' Lily asked. 'He's a real professor: he always forgets to zip his pants up.'

I wouldn't have believed it if I hadn't been witness to what was happening myself. That night Lily Bourbon dumped Pete Hayter, a man as true as a dog.

After midnight Rodrigo bore the Bourbonette off in his sporty Corvette. I invited the half-crashed Pete to come along with us.

'Leave me alone!' he snapped.

We called for a taxi and made our way out. On the way home I fell asleep in the back seat. How Pete, dead drunk, made his way home from the *milonga* without running into the police I don't know. They're very strict about it these days: they drag you out from behind the wheel, put the handcuffs on you, and it's straight to gaol.

That next morning, catching sight of the downcast Hayter from a distance wanly stumbling between the old elm trees on the way to his lecture, I went to my auditorium the long way round.

From that day, every month in the mail I get identical computer-generated invitations to visit the *milonga* once more for Argentinian tango lessons. The yellow-and-violet photograph shows Lily dancing with the owner. She's pressing herself to him with a doglike devotion, something hardly expressible by most women, even ones under the force of passionate desire. Madame Bourbon's long, long, thin-as-a-nail high heel is sticking into her partner's tailbone. The advertisement guarantees romantic adventure and completely access-ible adultery for quite a modest sum.

There just isn't any time to go.

10

Valerie works at a clinic located in downtown Sacramento. There they treat not only Americans but lots of immigrants of various sorts as well, especially a lot of Russians, which is why they hire staff who speak so-called 'ethnic' languages, so they don't have to keep interpreters on hand. Patients who have problems with English are lucky to find themselves there, the more so since the clinic's minibus picks up patients at home and takes them back after their appointment.

Lily turned up at the clinic for the first time and got into trouble right away, because when they took down her medical history she'd called herself Maria Peredelkina, for some reason. But you have to show your medical insurance card, and on her card she was down as Lily Bourbon. Maybe it was true that in her earliest youth she had taken part in the Revolution, as has been stated in several of her Soviet biographies. What if Lenin had personally taught her the art of conspiracy? After all, Lily, if you believe her own tales, was at one time his intimate girlfriend – in between Inessa Armand and his first stroke. The Leader, as she recalled with shame, had overexerted himself.

Doctors at the clinic never have any time to waste on unrelated subjects with their patients, for transparently obvious reasons. However, according to the rules, the doctors first have to establish a certain psychological contact with their patients, asking standard questions about their lives. It's rare, but sometimes people do show up who behave along the lines of the Radio Armenia joke: 'Who is a pain in the neck? Someone who, when asked "How are you?" proceeds to tell you all about it.'

'How are you doing?' Valerie asked. 'How's Pete?'

And Lily was off. She'd already forgotten what she'd come for.

'Oh, sweetie, I haven't seen you since that *milonga* . . . Yes, dear!

Pete gave me a boost up into the world of the tango, but with that, alas, his function ceased to be. You have to talk to me about love and not about Hemingway – because I *am* a Hemingway. He never did anything about getting married, but, since a certain point in my life, I have preferred that they marry me and not just carry on. That's why when Rodrigo invited me to go off with him to the Hawaiian Islands, I agreed, imagining that his intentions were serious.'

'But he's just a boy!' Valerie exclaimed.

'And I'm a girl! We spent a magical week in an expensive hotel in Honolulu with a view over the ocean from the twenty-ninth floor. I almost tried my hand at surfing, even: they have the best waves for that in the world there. Only the fear of breaking a leg stopped me. Despite his low-class origins, my *caballero* was almost as gallant as a French aristocrat. Dear Lord, what a blast that was! I've never had anything of the kind in my life, not with anyone. What nights dancing in restaurants, what days in bed! He even contrived to do it in the ocean under the light of the moon. And what a mutual love . . . He said, too, that it was the first time in his life that he'd had such a passion . . .'

'I'm very happy for you,' Valerie glanced at her watch and tried to get to the matter at hand. 'Where does it hurt?'

'Everywhere! Wait a minute, though, sweetie. We flew back to Sacramento at night, found his Corvette in the parking lot, he drove me home, and carried in my suitcase. I thought he was going to stay, but he said, "And now we'll settle up, kiddo. It's not expensive, madame, a hundred and fifty bucks a pop or three hundred for an all-nighter. I worked for six days and nights."

'It was like being struck by lightning. I was so freaked out I almost forgot to take off my wig. I couldn't utter a word. I thought I was going to pass out. And I should have. But before answering I as usual counted to ten in my head and then asked him: "Do the days of departure and arrival count as one day?"

"As two, madame," he insolently answered. "Plus all expenses for the trip, including airline tickets, the hotel room and the restaurants for the two of us. So in total you owe me $4,100, and I'll take a cheque, but greenbacks would be better."

'The bastard bowed courteously and waited. I dithered a bit, looked into his shameless eyes and then slapped him in the face. Of course he could have killed me. But there's a real man for you: he didn't even flinch.

"That's sadism, Lily," he remarked cold-bloodedly. "According to the tariff, that's double the price now, and if you hit me again, it'll be three times."

'I had to tell him that he'd get his money when I was spinning in my grave. Rodrigo's eyes flashed and he bestowed a magnanimous smile on me: "Calm down, kiddo! A well-born Mexican doesn't take money off women. On the contrary! I'm offering you a job. In the neighbouring state of Nevada there's a chance for me to acquire a massage parlour. The only thing left to do is the paperwork, and I need a figure-head – I don't have American citizenship, and you do! You'll be the owner, OK? And maybe . . . Maybe you'll work there, doll."

'That's me, doll . . . You understand what a massage parlour is in Nevada, where they're more indulgent than they are in California? He's the one who forged my documents for me and knows how old I am.

"Well, I'm not young enough," I tell him, "to . . ."

"You're still al-l-l-l right," he answered. "I'll make up a cool advertisement for you: 'Invigorating grandma with ninety-six years' experience, former Russian poetess, can do things that nobody living today knows how to do.' That's sure to attract lovers of something spicy."

'How do you like that slob? Of course I refused! Then Rodrigo chuckled again. "Don't get excited! I'm just *joking*, again. The girls have already been hired, from Russia. That man from the Russian secret police, the one who was looking after me and fighting Trotskyism in Omsk, he helped me. He brings the girls over here, and you with your perfect Russian are going to be the manager of this massage parlour."'

'That is, like – a madam?' Valerie asked, incautiously.

'Poo! Why so vulgar? I'm just going to Nevada on a long-term business trip. Sometimes, darling, you have to become scum temporarily, otherwise you're not going to live very long.'

Anyway, dear reader, as a schizophrenic acquaintance of mine puts it, love comes and goes, but you're always going to want to eat. Now I recall: Pete Hayter, when Lily was dancing for the first time at the *milonga* with Rodrigo, had asked me if I knew the French word *appâter*.

'Why?' I was surprised. 'It means to lure somebody on.'

'That's the tango style that they're dancing,' Pete grinned crookedly. 'Tango-apate was popular in the twenties. The pimp dances with his prostitute to demonstrate her wares straight to the viewers.'

I failed to understand. 'And so what?'

'Oh, nothing . . .'

Pete had waved a hand and gone over to the bar counter.

But I was just bringing this up right now, by the by.

'So what's wrong with you?' Valerie asked, trying to conceal her impatience, inasmuch as all of the time periods set aside for individual patients had long since been exhausted, and a huge queue was building up in reception, just like in the out-patient clinics of certain other countries.

Only now did Lily finally explain the purpose of her visit. She'd come to the clinic for a cure for the gonorrhoea that *simpatico* Rodrigo had shared with her.

And that, in truth, is the inglorious end of a glorious generation, you will say. However, we won't be jumping to hasty conclusions.

11

Some friends from Australia came for a visit, and that Thanksgiving I decided to show them the famous mountain lake, Tahoe, which is only three hours' drive from our place.

The highway rises along the edges of steep cliffs, and evil tongues say that this is the worst and riskiest road in the States. Ineffable beauty at any time of year but especially dangerous at the sharp turns over the precipices when it's snowing. You have to put snow chains on your tyres, even though this doesn't always insure you against trouble. But, generally speaking, Tahoe is the bluest and cleanest lake in the world. This is what my former student Carolyn asserts – she's the director of the anti-pollution project for this unique site.

The western half of Tahoe is in California, while the eastern one is in the state of Nevada. The town of South Lake Tahoe is similarly divided. Over the border – which you're informed about by a sign on the other side of the road and nothing else – that is, in Nevada, as distinct from in California, casinos and other such diverting establishments are allowed. Parking is free, the hotels cheap, all in expectation that you're going to be leaving your money behind a little bit later, when you start playing.

My guests from Australia had already received the advice of worldly-wise casino-goers: put a definite sum of money in your pocket, one that you're ready to lose, and if it disappears get out at once. As everyone knows, beginners have all the luck. Drop in a one-dollar token and twenty-five of them will come pouring out all of a sudden.

By means of a little artless arithmetic you reckon that if you drop in every one of those twenty-five tokens and get back another twenty-five for each one, that's going to be quite a sum ladled into your lap. But here's where the hitch comes. The one-armed bandit takes your money as readily as the first time but pays out at a more and more miserly rate or doesn't pay out at all. But now you really *want* to win. The best thing is to haul yourself out of there by the scruff of your neck, on to the sunny lakeshore. Otherwise, you'll get in deeper, and . . .

The casino was humming, and lights were glowing with all the colours of the rainbow. The bright roulette wheels spun, enticing you to take a punt. Cards flashed as they were fanned on to the green baize tables. Our Australian guests dispersed through the various rooms, since there were things to gawk at, from the half-naked waitresses to those bizarre machines that promise you millions – just buy a token and drop it in. I myself had given up gambling long since, for a simple reason: whenever I've tried it, five minutes later I'm left without a cent. If only I'd won something, even as a joke. Never once!

Here in the aisle between ranks of slot machines I caught sight of a small group of obvious tourists. There were six of them, all girls, probably students. Although they were a bit too provocatively dressed for students. As they drew level with me I heard Russian being spoken, and then there was a shout from behind them: '*Ee-noff!* Time to go, girls, right now . . .'

Their guide sure is strict, I thought, and in the next instant recognized her. Lily Bourbon in person caught up with the group. She minced along in a striped suit, reminiscent somehow of prisoners' clothing from American action films and, of course, with an improbable quantity of beads wound around her neck from her chest to her ears.

'I never would have thought you capable of showing up here,' Lily sang out, as if her own presence in the casino was something matter-of-fact. 'Girls, wait for me at the elevator! And don't go wandering off!'

Her young charges obeyed unwillingly, darting glances in all directions, halting and then moving on towards the exit.

'So you aren't indifferent to the opportunity of getting rich, either?' There was some irony to be heard in Lily's voice.

I decided it would be better to keep quiet.

I hadn't seen her for a long time. Now I remembered how Pete Hayter, some while ago, at the height of his pairing off with his partner Lily, had dropped in to my office in the middle of the working day, without calling first.

'What am I going to do, my dear colleague?' he asked. 'I took her to South Lake Tahoe to introduce her to a famous tangoist, for him to look at her back while she's dancing and give us some useful advice, but she disappeared into the casino and went nuts over the slot machines.'

Lily had started dragging Pete off to the casino nearly every weekend.

'She doesn't understand that I'm a poor university professor,' he complained. 'My bank account has gotten seriously depleted, while she doesn't give a damn . . .'

'Sure! It's not *her* bank account.'

What did Pete want from me? How was I to know how to behave in circumstances like these?

'And Russians?' Pete glanced over his shoulder for some reason, as if to see if anyone was eavesdropping. 'Are they all gamblers, like Lily?'

What should I have answered him?

'Maybe she should join Gamblers Anonymous?' I'd suggested to him at the time.

'We've got the day off, today,' Lily said, 'and I brought the girls here that Rodrigo signed up from Russia. The kids came here to make a buck, but they have to have fun, too . . . Lord, what an intellectual primitive!'

It would be an exaggeration to say that she'd got younger, but I am ready to swear that she hadn't aged at all: only for you and me does time move on somehow, while for her it had stood still – that was her great advantage. Pete, for all his peckerheadedness and some imbecilities, was right. Lily was definitely a redwood: evergreen, unafraid of climatic changes and living for three hundred years, until the day they cut her down.

'So, have you gotten a feel for your duties?' I asked.

'I've gotten a feel for Rodrigo. What do you think, that I couldn't really get rid of him? I could have dragged him off to the calaboose before he could say boo. But, for starters, my love for him has never run dry. And in the second place, I was curious about what the set-up of his massage parlour was. He's a real mover and shaker for a Mexican. His dream is to buy the presidency of some Latin American country. Soon I'm going to be moving back to Sacramento, to his tango school.'

'The *milonga* keeps drawing you back, after all?'

'And how! I've got to practise up for my centenary.'

'Are you going to be dancing the tango?'

'And how! And do you know who with? With the president of the United States! The whole country listened to my poems, back in the USSR, but now the entire world is going to watch me tangoing on CNN. I'm going to be the first hundred-year-old dancer in the world, and I'm going to get into the Guinness Book of Records.'

'Has the president invited you to the White House?'

'Not yet. But he hasn't got any choice.'

So that was it: Lily Bourbon was already dancing with the president, while the president didn't have the slightest suspicion about it.

'The longer I know you, the more you surprise me. You're a delightful woman!'

I declared this with utter sincerity and affectionately touched her on the shoulder.

'Huh! Do you think you're the first person to discover this America?'

Part Three
MARRIAGE AMERICAN STYLE

'. . . it is something that we, in the full strength of thought,
cannot bring to full clarity.'

– *Arthur Schopenhauer*

Trying not to make too much noise, he stole down the corridor and pressed the button of the lift. The sliding door opened slowly, as if half asleep. Exiting the street door, Kharya craned his neck and ran his eyes along the dark windows. Four o'clock in the morning. It was just about to get light. The place was asleep; only the sign saying '3370 Grant Street' flickered at the corner, and the light over the lobby entrance hadn't yet been turned off.

Kharya prodded with his key, feeling out the driver's door key-hole; he opened it, flung down the bundle that he'd been carrying under his arm and flopped down into the broken-down seat. Holding on to the open door with one hand, he started the engine, wincing at the roar. Without turning his lights on, he drove out on to the road and only then, after once again running his eyes along the windows, did he turn on his low beams and slam shut the heavy door.

Both night and air were like the top bench in a steam bath, as it always was in south Texas at the end of August. His rusting hood stuck out in his gaze; the paint on it had been burned off in patches by the sun. The car's air-conditioner had succumbed long before, but the fan buzzed, creating a weak simulation of freshness.

The cherry-red Chevrolet moved down Bellaire Street, and after several blocks turned on to the ring road. A quarter of an hour later Kharya was merging into the string of cars climbing the flyover on to Highway Ten and sped his wagon to the west. 'Sped' is putting it too strongly, probably.

And he'd scarcely begun putting the tenth mile behind him when the flow slowed, although it wasn't even four thirty yet. Kharya cursed and slapped his hand on the wheel in annoyance. His horn sounded, and the half-awake drivers in the neighbouring cars looked at him askance, perplexed.

It soon became evident that, up ahead, four police Fords were occupying all four lanes of the road, driving parallel to one another, cheek by jowl, keeping their speedometer needles exactly at seventy miles an hour. There's no getting around policemen, so willy-nilly everyone was going at the prescribed speed – that's just how the highway patrol nowadays disciplines drivers. Happily enough, the schooling didn't go on for long. On the outskirts of Houston the cops obligingly slipped off on to a side road. And now a devil got into Kharya.

He cursed again and, in order to make up the time lost because of those idiots, he raced away in the old-but-still-full-of-beans gas-guzzler. A curious word, that – *guzzler*. Originally from the French, supposedly, in Texas the word simply meant a wino, more often than not. It's obvious that the old mid-seventies Chevy was of the dimensions of a good-sized Russian armoured transport vehicle, and with three hundred and fifty horses under the hood was called a gas guzzler because it guzzled down (or swilled, if you like) more gasoline than Kharya's pocket could stand. The car wasn't even Kharya's. Where would he have got the scratch for more up-to-date wheels? So he had to put up with this guzzler, which was just about to be banned by the environmental lobby.

Right now Kharya wasn't into economizing: he had to get through the southern desert as quickly as possible. Early that morning, at home, he hadn't felt like eating, and now he really wanted to slake his thirst and hunger, but he'd told himself he wouldn't stop before he got to San Antonio, halfway to where he was going: and there, without getting out of the car, he was going to get a hamburger, fries and coffee – that would cost three dollars, no more.

Hunger was hurrying him along, the speedometer needle hovering at a hundred and twenty miles an hour. This wasn't Germany, where he'd been not long before in search of a better life; but with their methodical bureaucracy there was nothing doing for him there. On their autobahn you could put the pedal to the metal, squeeze out every last bit of speed, but here going faster than seventy-five was prohibited.

That made Kharya nervous. With his well-developed sense of what was coming, he felt that the success of his life depended on speed, an absurd life up to now, and this feeling made its way all the way down to his right foot in its Mexican *huarache* sandals, pressing hard on the gas pedal.

Apparently nobody had seen him leaving the building. He'd been living there on his own. He had, with difficulty, got a divorce from his last wife, left behind in Russia – he'd had it done in Texas, though, and still owed his lawyer for processing the necessary documents that he'd sent him.

Kharya was living in an eighteen-storey building. As a matter of fact, he lived on the thirteenth floor – but there isn't any such thing, for some reason: Kharya's floor was called the fourteenth, and there are nineteen floors in an eighteen-story building. This phenomenon is called *triskaidekaphobia* – the paranoid fear of the number thirteen. The word is completely absent from Russian dictionaries and encyclopaedias; and I had never heard it until I came to America. It's not easy to find even in English dictionaries.

In ancient times fear of the number thirteen existed, but it wasn't widespread, evidently due to the general numerical illiteracy: what do dangerous numbers matter when you can't count, anyway? But in old England, from where this *triskaidekaphobia* came to America, the number thirteen, falling on a Friday, was considered twice as unlucky: criminals were traditionally hanged in public on that day.

But even today will you look in vain in America for a house number, bus line or train with the number 13. In hotels, Room 12 is followed by Room 14. It's a bad thing to start anything on the thirteenth of the month or invite thirteen guests, and if you have thirteen trees growing around your house one of them has to be chopped down and the stump uprooted as quick as you can.

So we're left to wonder why a nation as rational as the Americans suffers from a mindless superstition – this isn't as widespread as in the old days, but the number thirteen has encroached upon the margins of the minds of those in municipal authority, to say nothing of those cities' inhabitants.

And in this age of high technology there's an endless supply of loafers searching out hidden *triskaidekas* in computer-programming rules, in lottery numbers, in the length of masculine merit, in feminine adornment. If you have to pay seven bucks for something, you don't pay for it with a twenty-dollar bill, because your change is going to be thirteen. If the counter on the gas pump indicates that thirteen gallons of gasoline have flowed into your tank and you don't add more or suck some out, your mood is ruined for the whole day.

Kharya, formerly a practising atheist, wasn't any triskaidekaphobe at all. Why should he have irrational fears when there are quite enough everyday and entirely real troubles? But then why, as soon as Kharya had moved into that subsidized apartment in the building on Grant Street, had his luck changed so grievously for the worse – if it hadn't been for that hidden thirteenth floor, even if it was called the fourteenth?

There in Houston the Social Services Department normally tops up the rental for the subsidized apartments of the Russian and Mexican tenants, mostly unemployed and in receipt of welfare. Kharya was the exception. He wasn't on any sort of welfare and was living from hand to mouth. His apartment held a single bedroom and a sitting-room with a little kitchen section and a hatch between. You wouldn't ask anyone home to dance or set up any billiard tables. But the apartment wasn't Kharya's any more than the Chevrolet, after all.

Newly arrived people were settled in the building. Let me make clear that this meant legal arrivals, with the right of residence. If you wanted to, you could term this settlement a ghetto or a concentration camp. The building was chock full of rubbishy people. The neighbours' every word, every step, was turned over and over, became the subject of condemnation, or jealousy, or even denunciation. There were informers here – former ones or present-day ones, there was nowhere to get away from them. Their spirits burned and thirsted to do a bad turn to one of their own, to rejoice in their neighbours' troubles on the sly.

The area was bad, but it was located right on the edge of a good one. How could class hatred – taken in with the mother's milk of the Pioneer organization, the Soviet Communist version of the Cub Scouts – not develop under such antagonistic conditions of full-fledged imperialism? Out of every window immigrants looked out enviously at the other side of Grant Street, where private villas with their own blue swimming pools were ranked behind tidily mown lawns. All they had here was a pool with enough chlorine in it to burn your eyes out, a single one, free for everyone. And they had no individual garages for their cars, either: just the one common, crowded nose-to-tail (or tail-to-nose, if you prefer) basement parking lot under the building – and even so Kharya had had to wait a long time for a spot to become available for him.

The émigrés themselves, as well, in general and particular, seemed to be human beings – but with their own peculiarities. You can believe me, since I – as you have probably heard already – myself belong to that aforementioned crowd-of-many-colours. Ordinary creatures get born once; émigrés, twice – in two different countries. People tell me that you're born a second time when you get out of the concentration camp; but – I'll tell no lies – such happiness I never managed to experience. But I did survive the émigré muddle: I endured my own woes.

Unfortunately, many of the people in the building on Grant Street were reborn as deaf-mutes. It was as if the first time they realized that another language is spoken here was when they wound up in another hemisphere. It would be all right if it was just English. But you could find yourself in a Spanish or Chinese area, surrounded by people as benighted as yourself and no way to ask for a drop of water.

There's something adventurous in a situation like this, something not to everyone's taste. You can take my word for it; if you don't want to, check it out: a twist of fate like that isn't for everyone. Would you want to risk it, bet your life on a turn of the cards, on the proletarian principle of 'nothing to lose but your chains'?

Turn your attention to the word 'your' in that optimistic Marxist premise. Make sure you don't get into a mess, that you don't wind up in a set of chains belonging to someone else, not knowing which are worse. Certain former comrades, disappointed, dream now of being reborn back again, of returning to their native swamp. Others attempt rebirth a third time, and head for Montreal, Rio or Pretoria.

In the émigré colony on Grant Street, we can boldly amplify on Tolstoy in *Anna Karenina*: all happy families are unhappy in their own way. The newly arrived are dismayed at the abundance in Texas, whose wretched crumbs trickle down to them, and unhappy at their incomprehension of life around them and of themselves. Old-timers are accustomed to benefits and complain about how small the welfare payments are, that they are threatened with the loss of their subsidies because they aren't looking for work, while the jobs on offer aren't anything they would want to take on.

Emigration is a bloody affair, as I heard said by somebody who in his time was a surgeon in the retinue of the Soviet mighty but who couldn't pass the examination to be a doctor in this country and had to become a taxi driver.

Some of the inhabitants of the building moonlighted for cash so that they wouldn't lose their welfare: they would wash windows or babysit other people's children. The pathological loafers among them would wax sarcastic about such people but drink eagerly enough at their expense. Whoever earned less envied those who got more. None of them paid any taxes. And whoever found a real job wasn't about to stick around: he would buy himself a house and be quick to slither out of this snake-pit. The lucky man's new workmates would get invited to his housewarming; his old neighbours, like some outworn material, he would try not to invite.

Thousands of people passed through the apartments of the building at 3370 Grant Street, moving on to every state from Florida to Alaska and Hawaii.

Some time ago, when I was working in Texas, I did happen to look into that building once or twice, although I've forgotten why. At the entrance, on either side of the front door, ran long, never-empty white-painted benches, covered with vulgarities in various languages. The gaze of whoever sat there accompanied you from the door of your car to the entrance, where they would begin to discuss who you might have come to see. Mexicans on the right, Russians on the left, fundamentally divided by an invisible linguistic barrier.

What the Mexicans talked about, I don't know, but the Russians were bragging about which of them occupied what sort of post in their previous lives. Several of them on the bench at the door, despite the appalling Texas heat, had decked themselves out in the full iconostasis: all their Soviet ribbons and medals. Those who had none had decorated their breasts with lapel pins that said 'Prepared for labour and the defence of the USSR', 'Honourable Blood Donor' and 'Go Magnitka!' – which they'd bought at the flea market in Houston.

Here, not all that far from the city centre, the Soviet land had assembled in miniature: there were politically aware vanguard-workers from rocket factories so secret that they were known only by their zip codes, Party organizers, second-hand clothing store opportunists and city-hall chiefs. I met the former commercial director of the Tambov spirituous-liquors plant. He'd had only one professional defect: he didn't drink. He managed to overcome this deficiency only after emigrating to this building on Grant Street.

There was even a former camp boss living there – not a Pioneer camp, of course – who tried to persuade people that he'd developed cancer of the bladder from nerves: he'd strained himself saving prisoners in his Magadan satellite prison from being shot by his superiors who had come for just that purpose. It had been necessary, he said, to defend justice with his own breast, from which he had fallen ill. It wasn't his breast that was ailing, though. It's great that even old NKVD hands can get cured of that sort of cancer in America right now.

The longer the newly arrived live there on Grant Street and splash around in the building's swimming pool, the higher their former Soviet ranks get: lieutenants become majors in their oral recollections, majors become generals; while lowly flatfeet, having read up on their icy blood from crime novels obtained at the nearby Russian shop, become double and triple international agents of influence on whom, apparently, the fate of progressive mankind entirely depended.

One former resident of the Moscow suburb of Mamontovka, who'd come to California from Houston to marry off his daughter (I accidentally crossed his path in casual company), remembered in his cups how he'd passed on orders to Marshal Zhukov, as a result of which they had brought Hitler down.

'But what about Stalin, then?' I asked carefully, so as not to offend him.

'That poxy-face didn't have a thing to do with it!' he explained. 'Stalin never stuck his nose out of his bunker the whole war. Everything was left to me and Zhukov!'

Some of the Grant Streeters (I understand that sounds a bit ambiguous, but what else would you call them?) dash off dispatches to the FBI and CIA in their native Russian, offering their services, while the agencies pay them zero attention; most likely they don't even read them. Talented individuals remain uncalled-upon.

Kharya hated his accommodation but put up with it; his surroundings he despised, and for that, we know, there were certain bases. But he didn't have a chance of getting away from Grant Street for a bunch of reasons, the foremost of which was his illegal occupancy of someone else's subsidized apartment – about which he tried to keep quiet, it goes without saying.

When getting out of the fragmenting superstate got to be relatively easy, an old acquaintance, a drinking pal of his, already a long-time émigré, invited Kharya to come and gawk at America. The guest flew in to Houston and was stunned at what he saw: his friend and all his neighbours did nothing at all, just drank brandy, and when they'd sobered up they drove around among the skyscrapers in their automobiles, as big as in the movies.

Kharya's emotional needs broadened a bit in the air of freedom, and he wrote to his unloved wife that he wasn't coming back. Soon his friend, having saved up the scratch, tore off back to the motherland to demonstrate how he'd become a real American. He'd left Kharya the use of his apartment and his Chevrolet. Most likely his acquaintance had shacked up with someone in Odessa, because months went by and his friend made no move to come back, which suited the abandoned Houstonite just fine.

To achieve legal status, it is a well-known fact that one has to get in touch with an attorney. His first visit to a lawyer began scandalously. Kharya showed up at the office at the appointed time, dressed in his only jacket, a suede one, and his knitted tie. Coming up the marble staircase he caught sight of the secretary, or rather caught sight of the part of her located under her desk.

'My name is Lizzie. How can I help you?' she clattered the standard phrase, felling Kharya with a smile that he interpreted too literally.

Pretty, smart, big-eyed, Lizzie was an actress as well; she'd been in an amateur musical. She was what is called 'burning panties' in Texas – enough said. When clients came out, the attorneys would accompany them on their way back past Lizzie, so that she wouldn't get to take them behind the filing cabinet and brag about the sign on the back of her panties: 'It's unique!'

Kharya was asked to wait. When the attorney came out, he saw his client sitting in his secretary's chair, Lizzie on his lap and the client's hand up her skirt.

The attorney, indignant, said that he was calling the police right now.

'You see this hand?' From under her skirt, Kharya pulled out his hand and raised it. 'This is the Wizard's Hand. I am curing a patient of what ails her in a particular place – and that's all.'

They put a stop to the scene.

Kharya persuaded the lawyer that he was a political refugee who had been persecuted by the authorities all his life and that he'd been thrown out of his native Odessa. He bombarded his defender with anti-Soviet anecdotes, hard to translate and little understood in this remote country. The facts themselves adhered poorly to one another, owing to Kharya's specific profession. In principle, nothing special: according to Soviet officialese he was a 'scientific worker'.

In the sea of sciences permitted in Soviet times, there was one that was a unique, calm, honeyed and, generally speaking, unrestricted backwater, where under no circumstances would you be permitted to engage in research, to carry out any search, make any discoveries or to worry about the failure of any unsupported hypotheses or unsuccessful experiments.

Fundamental theses came down from on high, from the priests who interpreted old idols in terms of their new goals. While you give a course of lectures on the established texts, publish a compilation from theoretical sources approved on high – and you're off. The most important thing was not to go into any thought too deeply, so that no questions of dubious quality might show up and rock the boat.

I won't beat around the bush: in his old life, Doctor of Philosophical Sciences Khariton Lapidar (I completely forgot to give you his full name) was an associate professor at the Odessa Polytechnic Institute, in the Scientific Communism Department.

Easy enough to pronounce in Russian, the surname wasn't made for the American speech apparatus. Texans, practised in the surnames of the whole wide world, after getting their mouths ready to swallow a whole peach together with its pit, then curving their tongues first up, then down and, finally, jutting their lower jaws out first left, then right, even venture to pronounce: 'Mister Leah-PYE-deahr . . . izzat it?'

But the name 'Khariton' turned out to be utter torture.

'Kay-RIGHT-nn? Izzat right? Sound that one out for me, please – I'll try to repeat it. So what'd your momma call you when you were a kid? Maybe it's just a little too hard, huh?'

His momma – peace be unto her ashes in the Odessa cemetery – called her son not just every day but every hour, and she called him 'Kharik'. What could one suggest that would be more immediately comprehensible to Texans? Kharik, Henry, Yorik . . . To cut a long story short, Khariton had to shorten his name for the country he was in either to Gary or, to get closest to the American toponymy, Harry. After that, one day when Harry was getting acquainted with some neighbours, Akop, an Azerbaijani of Georgian extraction, born in Yerevan, now living on the third floor, spoke up in his distinctively accented Russian. 'Why the complexities, my dear? You are just as monumental as the statue of Stalin that, fortunately, they never managed to place on the summit of Mount Ararat. We will call you Kharya! The name Kharya in no way harms your intelligent face!'

So, Kharya it was, at least among the Russian-speakers. He had to resign himself to that, as well. I must note, by the way, that, despite his name, our hero's mug of a face was thoroughly worthy, even pleasant, although maybe slightly swollen from too much food and drink. His eyes (I note for the benefit of potential brides) were dark and kind, his gaze hypnotic but usually dreamily fixed on the distance. The cynics in the Department of Scientific Communism were convinced it was on the radiant future. He had a Mephistophelean profile: a hooked nose, but not so long a one as to fall over his mouth, which had nearly two-thirds of his own teeth. Thanks to Marx and Lenin, Kharya's health had been preserved in tolerable condition.

The impressive Khariton Lapidar was interesting, imposing. His bloom had faded a bit in Texas, but he had grown a square shovel-shaped beard that he looked after every day just like a beloved kitchen garden.

Ultimately his lawyer got him a work visa, but work wasn't anything that Kharya was in a hurry to bring to pass. Not because of his sixty years of age. And not because he wasn't a computer nerd or a taxi driver, for which there was always a demand here. For someone with a résumé as complicated (for America) as Kharya's, it wasn't going to be easy to find a job; and even his adequate English – which he'd learned owing to the abundance of leisure-time in his former life – didn't help.

So, the kind of work that wouldn't offend him wasn't to be found ,and his pride wouldn't let him diminish his social status by delivering pizza. But, most importantly: it wasn't for that that he'd favoured America with his presence. He'd have another five years to wait before he could retire, but, being an illegal, he wasn't going to get any sort of social security. God alone knew what he'd been living on up till now.

Kharya hadn't been badly paid in his previous existence. He had organized group studies for high-school graduates at his own institute with guaranteed placement in it afterwards. Other people trained pupils for examination; others, too, took money for it. Kharya was the middleman, but all the same he nearly wound up in the dock: he hadn't shared properly with his boss, and the people involved squealed on him. Maybe that was something else that kept him from returning. In some sense he really was a political refugee: after all, the political system in which he'd had a place had ceased to exist. He'd become a scientific worker in a science that had disappeared.

There in the time left over to him after Scientific Communism (reality, as he would often say to his friends, was unscientific), Kharya had a good time. His family was no burden. A third of Odessa was familiar with his last wife. She was nicknamed Anka the Scrounge because she was always scrounging things from her neighbours: now bread, now salt, now cigarettes. Following four unsuccessful marriages, Kharya decided simply to collect members of the fairer sex. He got into it, but his enthusiasm was already not what it had been.

At Grant Street they used to say, however, that he was being provided for by lonely well-to-do ladies who would come calling on him. You could consider that a job of sorts. Kharya quickly made contact with former ladyfriends of his who had moved to the States, and he started travelling around to see them (at their expense, understand), as a love-sotted author used to say, 'to collect his arrears'. In the process of collecting one of them in Chicago, Kharya nearly died. The paramedics came to his rescue, healed him and to this day bombarded him with astronomical bills.

Some Odessans who are acquainted with Kharya told me that they try to keep away from him. His notions are always on an exclusively global plan: how to solve the problem of world hunger, how to pioneer the galaxy productively – moreover, not the one we live in – how to travel back and forth in time, stuffing your pockets with money. He remained, as they say here in America, a good-for-nothing – but he looked thoroughly presentable.

He was a big *I-love-me*, or, more precisely, *I-adore-me*. Moreover, he was a very sociable character: in any company he would pick up the thread of conversation, expand on it and not let it go until the very end, falling silent for a moment only to drain yet another glass. I won't say what quantities he drank, neither in gallons nor in litres – just take my word for it: few could drink more than this theoretician of Scientific Communism.

A painful problem for Kharya in his sixty-somethings was his weight or, more accurately, his overweight. Oh, how he did love to eat as well, and, once stuck in to the process, he couldn't stop. Rich food held no fears for him; he sneered at cholesterol. He loathed what in America is called 'fat-free food'. He would buy the cheapest beer and only after waiting for a sale to come along: Budweiser or Miller, beers that even the Americans consider – let's use the medical term here – urine. He kept up to a hundred cans at a time in his otherwise empty bachelor's refrigerator (they disappeared quickly).

So as to lose weight he smoked a pack and a half a day, supporting the tottering finances of the Philip Morris Company, but he never shed any pounds. In his armchair – a wide American one, even big enough for two – Kharya fitted so tight that he wouldn't be able to separate himself from his seat when he stood up, the chair rising with him, and when he would straighten up it would fall to the floor with a crash that would set his downstairs neighbours knocking indignantly on their ceiling with the stick that they had ready for just this occurrence.

The list of Kharya's talents so far is by no means exhaustive. More about them later, when these talents stand him in good stead. In the meanwhile, he'd left the freeway for San Antonio's Old Downtown to fill up his tank and get a hamburger. It was a great place – he'd often made his way there without any purpose in mind, simply out of irrepressibility and an unconcealable interest in full-bosomed Mexican ladies. Of course, the language barrier still divided them, but Kharya hoped sooner or later to overcome it.

At that early hour of the morning the restaurants were empty. Moustachioed waiters, yawning, were lazily putting tablecloths on the tables, no one was importuning the passers-by with passionate guitar music, and the women, of course, were still asleep. Five minutes for refuelling and washing the stuck-on bugs off the windscreen, another three to get his food.

Finishing off his French fries while he drove, Kharya made for Highway 35, hemmed on both sides by skyscrapers. All that was left was to gobble up the remaining half of the way there. Now he was heading south. About two hours later, the stream of cars slowed down. Kharya had started to nod off, but, with a start, he jammed on the brakes. The signs flashing past began indicating 'Laredo' – not far from the border, now. *Don't wind up in Mexico by mistake*: after all, that wasn't where he had to go.

2

The evening before, Kharya had recalled that he hadn't eaten dinner. With melancholy, he had looked into the refrigerator, in which nothing – aside from ten cans of Budweiser – revealed itself; he went out of the building entranceway after deciding to walk to the nearest supermarket and get some supper there.

The illuminated sign over the entrance, pasted over with mosquitoes, was already lit up. On the Russian bench they were discussing the news.

'Did you hear – houses on the coast got wrecked?' asked Akop, tenderly clapping Kharya on the back.

The bench-sitters turned their heads towards him.

'Where?' asked Kharya in incomprehension, his stomach urging him towards the supermarket.

'You haven't heard? Here, in the *Houston Chronicle* – it says a tropical cyclone . . .'

They stuck an open newspaper in Kharya's face, the information in which they had already discussed and worried over. Generally speaking, the folks here were surprised by nothing, even if you stood on your hands and struck up a conversation with your feet. So, if they were discussing something or other, that meant that something extraordinary had happened.

Kharya took the paper. The photographs showed overturned cars, trees down across roads, houses with their roofs carried away. The reporters filed from the spot on how the Rio Grande on the Texas–Mexico border had burst its banks from the rain and the hurricane winds, flooding the environs. A dike had breached, the channel of the river in the region of the city of Laredo had silted up, and the current had split into two, forming an island. The cyclone was moving in mad haste, but its further route still wasn't clear.

Kharya handed back the newspaper.

'Understand? The cyclone, at its speed of 120 miles per hour, like they say, is about two hours from here.'

'Two hours?' Kharya asked. 'Then I'll be totally able to get some grub. It'll be harder to blow me away with a full stomach.'

He hurried off to the store, but, after traversing half a block, he stopped in the middle of the road, on the crosswalk, as if rooted to the spot. The light changed, the pack of cars at the light plunged ahead, and around him everyone began braking sharply. A traffic jam ensued. Nobody honked their horns (that isn't the thing to do), but no one was thrilled by the hold-up. Kharya gazed skywards, slapped himself on the forehead.

'What a — I am!' he barked in Russian, uttering a word that still hasn't made it into the Russian Academy dictionary of literary language.

Paying no attention at all to the stream of cars, he hurried (if that's what you could call his elephantine hulk in motion) to the other side of Grant Street. At the supermarket entrance Kharya forked out three whole silver quarters, dropping them into the slot and taking out a copy of the *Houston Chronicle*. Inside the store, holding the newspaper under his arm, he got himself a box of Chinese sweet-and-sour pork with rice and young green peas and the largest-sized paper cup of coffee and sat down at one of the little tables, where, mechanically stuffing the food into his mouth, he opened the paper up to the page of photos that he'd already seen.

Why hadn't he realized it instantly? Here was the place in the reportage: 'The Rio Grande river channel above Laredo has silted up, and the current split in two,' Kharya mumbled, pressing a chubby finger on the line and translating out loud. 'Split into two . . . forming in mid-river . . . in the middle of the river . . . a large island – no man's land between the USA and Mexico.'

Kharya glanced around him. At the neighbouring table an old lady with red hair was stuffing down a shrimp salad. She hadn't heard anything or, even if she had, wouldn't have understood. Shopping baskets, loaded to the brim with grocery-filled packages, moved past on their way to the exit. Nobody was paying him any attention.

The page piece was torn out, folded in four and stuffed into his pocket. There was sweet-and-sour pork with rice left in the box, but Kharya threw it into the bin next to the table. There went the newspaper, too. Kharya gulped down some more coffee and tramped off home.

Falling into bed, he had set his alarm for four in the morning; but he woke up an instant before and slapped his hand on it to keep it from ringing. He checked his billfold: it was empty. Out of his bedside cabinet he extracted the hidden hundred-dollar bill that he'd been saving for an emergency and put it into his pocket, next to the scrap from the *Houston Chronicle*, and set out for the place the cyclone had hit last night.

Once again I've digressed, but you'll never comprehend Kharya's zigs and zags otherwise.

You've already been told how warning signs had begun to appear before him: the Mexican border was close. So far everything had gone as he intended, but his nerves had been on edge the night before and were still in the same edgy state. He'd been behind the wheel without any breaks – not counting as a break the refuelling stop and double hamburger with French fries, which was starting to give him heartburn.

Kharya allowed his speed to drop a bit, glancing back and forth between his watch and the crumpled map opened out on the passenger's seat to his right.

Here and there the destruction from the cyclone was visible along the road. Trees, torn up by the roots, and overturned cars lay among the homes – the weather, however, was in no way reminiscent of yesterday's catastrophe. The weather forecast turned out to have been an exaggeration. The tropical cyclone hadn't gone north: after covering the environs with floods of rain it had weakened and dissolved, with its remnants turning back over the desert to the Gulf of Mexico, disappearing into the Atlantic. Shreds of cloud were scudding through the sky, but the sun was breaking through them now and again. The heat was mixing with the exhalations from the drying-out earth, and the Texans were gasping like fish out of water.

Pulling the torn-out scrap of newspaper from his pocket, Kharya placed it in front of him on the steering wheel and, shifting his eyes back and forth from the road to the text, read again about the place described by the reporter. There it was, a bit before getting to Laredo, a turn on to Mines Road. Now it was only a little further, but a red light was already on and unblinking: his gas was guzzled, and a road sign was warning him that the next gas station wasn't for a long time. He had to get off.

Kharya had never been here before, but he had no intention of asking the way at the gas station; he just grunted as he counted out the cash to the elderly Mexican. And further on, not straying, he drove as if everything here was familiar, only rarely glancing at his map.

Everywhere around had become monotonous: wretched dun-coloured vegetation along the canals dug out from the river and then, further, all the way to the horizon, fields of cotton and rice. The picture was a peaceful one; scattered houses stood out here and there, untouched. The cyclone mustn't have done any mischief here.

Kharya saw the sign: *Santa Isabel Creek*. His tyres rumbled over the bridge. It was somewhere around here, but if you don't ask, you won't find it.

'Hey, friend!' Kharya braked and waved a hand at a farmer in dirty white overalls who was climbing down from a tractor in front of a small store. 'Where around here's that island that washed up yesterday?'

'Can't see it from here,' the farmer answered, unbuttoning his overalls down to his belly-button and pulling his cap down over his eyes to keep the sun from blinding him. 'But if you keep a-going past the next three crossings, make a turn on to Islitos and afterwards a turn to the left, then another ways to the dead end – the island'll be visible on your left. That's where the place is – the Rio Grande turns sharpish to the north there, and . . . so what's it to you?'

'Just curious. Read about it in the paper.'

'Nothing to be curious about,' the farmer sneered. 'Just an empty spot. Listen, bud. Ain't no beer for sale there!'

Kharya could barely make out the island: it almost merged into the horizon. But his tyres had scarcely left the gravel and moved on to the dried-out earth, raising a column of dust, than there the Rio Grande was, occupying the whole of the landscape in front of him. Two arms of the mighty river merged, forming a single turbid, greyish-yellow expanse, rushing headlong away from where Kharya stood. The branch closest to him was narrow; the one furthest away very wide. Over there was Mexico.

Kharya drove on to the edge of the bank, but he could feel his wheels beginning to slip in the sand and decided not to risk driving any further. He clambered out, still in a half-bent state, and slowly straightened out, as if afraid that his stiffened bones might break.

The weather had altogether improved, and everything looked like Texas once again: a faded sky without a single cloud, sun at the zenith, heat, enough to murder every living thing except the snakes that burrowed into the edge of the bank. A breeze was blowing, but it didn't refresh. The air was hot. Kharya gasped and sprang backwards. Right next to his foot a snake had struck and caught a lizard, cross-ways.

There it was, the island! Flat, with a little hump in the middle, sand and clay. The hurricane had left a fairly large trace. The bank's length was littered with trees torn out by the roots, pieces of sheet metal, broken pieces of boards, rotting palm fronds. Kharya spread his arms wide – he might have been stretching or maybe measuring the area of the island lying in front of him. He mumbled something inarticulate, evidently satisfied with the size of the strip of land.

Once again he looked around. There was no one about. He

opened up the boot of the car and dragged a rubber boat out on to the sand. He began blowing it up with a foot-pump. The boat inflated slowly. Kharya panted and broke into a heavy sweat, struggling with it until its sides finally rose and stiffened.

He thrust the bundle that he had snatched up from home into the front of his shirt, piled the boat on top of his head and stood up, stumbling on the tussocks, to go down to the river. At the edge of the water he threw down the boat. Not taking off his *huaraches*, he stepped in, feeling around on the bottom in the turbid water, heated up like some sort of bath water, and flopped head first into the boat. Turning over with difficulty, he took out two wooden shovels that were going to do duty as oars, and rowed off against the current, somewhat aslant to his course.

He was being carried away; the water around him seethed and the boat spun first to one side and then the other, but Kharya kept on going forward, and the island gradually drew nearer. Finally his hands contrived to grab the roots of an overturned oak tree. In behind its trunk he found a quiet stretch of water and managed to pull the boat into it.

Kharya hauled his little vessel up on to the sand and then fell heavily down on his back, in the shade of the mighty crown of the dead oak, which the merciless watery element had ripped from its native soil and deposited on this island. How old was the tree? Judging by the thickness of the trunk – something that two people couldn't stretch their arms around – it had to be two hundred years old, no less. Where had it been carried from, the poor devil? Now this giant would rise no more.

Kharya's eyes closed by themselves, and he fell into a deep sleep. When he opened them again and glanced at his watch, three hours had flown past. A dragonfly settled on his forehead, and its wings tickled him. Brushing it away, he got to his feet, grunting and swearing; he turned around on his axis and cried out stupidly from a surfeit of emotion: 'Mi-i-i-i-i-i-i-ine!'

'I-i-i-ine!' the echo came back. Kharya was astounded that his cry was repeated, skipping like a pebble skilfully skimmed across the water.

He trudged along the shore, sinking into the sand. Its territory hadn't turned out so small, after all. He made his way slowly to the opposite end of the island and sat there for a long while, gazing at how the two gigantic arms of turbid water flowed together, carrying remnants of yesterday's storm past the island. His own, Kharya's, island! He was here first and no one else!

Kharya stood up once more and began clambering to the highest point of the island. On the way there he bent down and pulled a board longer than him out of the dirt, dragging it up with him.

After making it to the sandy crest Kharya dropped down on all fours and began digging a hole, doglike, with his forepaws. When the sand turned dense and damp it was time for the board. After digging out the hole Kharya, puffing like a locomotive, plunged one end of the board into the hole with all his strength and then started packing and tamping the sand back in around it.

He dragged the bundle back out from the breast of his shirt and unrolled the flag that he'd prepared from a sheet the night before. On the white panel (true, it did have tiny pink flowers on it, as well) he had written in gigantic if crooked letters in blue marker pen, so that no one could have any doubts: *The Property of Harry Lapidar.*

After tying two corners of the sheet to the board, he smoothed it out. The breeze took the sheet, and it began to flap. Now it remained only to step back a few paces so as to have a look at this work of art. Kharya pulled a camera out of his pocket and placed it on top of a tin can that lay not far away, setting the camera in position to capture the flag and a bit of the shoreline and hitting the automatic button. Then he ran back to the flag and stretched it out with one hand so that the writing was visible and put on the smile of a conquistador. The shutter clicked in confirmation: everything had gone as planned.

He had to hurry back to Houston, or otherwise he'd be spending the night here – with neither house nor home. The river water was muddy; you wouldn't drink it. Sinking into the sand, Kharya pushed the boat out from the bank and, holding on to the trunk of the over-turned oak with one hand, walked forward, pulling the boat behind him, in the water up to his knees. Suddenly a green shadow flashed from under the roots. He started. How could he have failed to look into it. What if there were alligators here? There wouldn't be any glory in ending his days in the jaws of a wild beast.

Kharya flopped into the space between the inflated sides. The cur-rent began slowly carrying him away. He turned over, sat up, grabbed his wooden paddles and began hurriedly rowing in the direction of the shore, orienting himself on his Chevrolet.

In any case, he got carried fairly far down with the current to where both of the arms that washed his island flowed together again.

While Kharya was letting the air out of his boat and folding it up, it began to get dark. His wet *huaraches*, full of sand, began to chafe his feet. So as not to get lost he went up to the road that had been made by the tractor traffic and, breathing heavily, made his way down it towards his Chevrolet. It was surprising: he'd been here such a long while and not one other soul had appeared, not on foot, nor on horse-back, nor swimming.

There was a bottle of water in the trunk of the car. Kharya took a long drink, not feeling the warm liquid running from his chin down his shirtfront. He sat behind the wheel and, drunk with all the fresh air, again switched off and dozed awhile. Waking up, he finished drinking the water, chucked the bottle over his shoulder out of the window, started up his engine, turned the car around and headed for home. He had six hours of travel ahead of him, but if he stepped on it, because it was night-time, then he might make it in a little over four hours.

He took a satisfied look out of his window at the flag fluttering in the wind in the distance. The text wasn't visible, but, after all, he knew what was written on it.

3

Now, in so far as I am only recounting the occurrence with the maximum possible accuracy, am hushing up no sort of nonsense and thinking up nothing clever of my own after the fact, while Kharya is heading homewards we'll have to look into the geography tied up with this story. I am fairly familiar with the locale, because I used to have to travel around there a lot.

In general, neither my wife nor I were surprised by the fact of the acquisition of the island by a Russian newcomer. A good friend of ours, Bill, lives in Seattle. We had met by chance in Tbilisi. This happened in the previous century, back in the Soviet era. We were in Tbilisi for the opening of Rezo Gabriadze's Marionette Theatre; during the day we went on a climb of Mount Mtatsminda, and alongside us a bunch of American tourists were making a racket. We passed a few words back and forth.

From the funicular, various slogans on red banners were clearly visible here and there, summoning us to put all our strength into the construction of a shining future. When he asked us to translate what was written on them for him, Bill listened with great seriousness. Then, after glancing around at their tour-leader, he bent towards my ear and said in a whisper: 'Could you possibly tell me in a couple of words what the essence of your Marxism-Leninism is?'

Thinking he was just joking, I came back: 'Well, it's not mine at all. It's theirs.'

'No kidding!'

Bill was absolutely serious and sincerely wanted to understand the sense of the slogan's wisdom. Later, after we had emigrated, my wife and I visited him at his house on Eliot Bay, and I found out that Bill was rich.

His father had showed up in Seattle when it was still a little town on the Pacific Ocean. For $25, his father, an émigré from Belorussia, bought an island from the local Indians, one that was completely useless to them: it was hard to get to it by boat, and there was nothing on the island except clumps of trees and swamps. His father died and left the island as an inheritance for his two sons.

A half-century passed, the city grew apace, and a construction company bought the island from Bill and his brother for, if my memory serves me, three-quarters of a billion dollars. Skyscrapers began crowding one another on the island, bridges joined it to the mainland, workaday life hummed away. Bill gave up his job in a sailmaking factory a long time ago and become a world traveller instead.

I'm mentioning this because if Kharya really gets lucky, then . . . Meanwhile, let's not run ahead and decide for Kharya what he should do. The more so, as Kharya's island isn't in Washington state but in Texas and, even worse, on the Mexican border. If you have a globe handy, you can find the exact place, no problem.

The Rio Grande – or, as it's called on the Mexican side, Rio Bravo del Norte – is a vast river. It rises in the mountains of the state of Colorado, not far from the peak of Mount Uncompahgre, and falls – or, as the Americans say, empties – into the Gulf of Mexico.

In places the river is so wide that you can't see the far shore. There are various landscapes along the banks, but, especially in the lower reaches of the river, they're boring, with no trees at all. It's a large arterial body of water, but it's unnavigable, since it's shallow and in some places even seriously dried up in the heat. On the other hand, though, the environs of the Rio Grande are watered more than enough, with canals covering the entire region like arteries of blood, feeding fields and orchards: rice, cotton, tobacco, fruit – on thousand-kilometre-wide expanses everything lives on the juices of the river.

The border drawn after the end of the war with Mexico goes along the main river channel and in fact is unguarded. It's not the best of people who cross over there into the United States. Whatever is just left around isn't there for long. You shouldn't peer into other people's minds, but it's not impossible that Kharya, tired as he was, on his way home with the pedal to the metal, was thinking along these lines.

The sky had turned dark blue. Green signs with the freeway exit numbers began lighting up over the road. A starry dome that you won't see anywhere in the world but in Texas stretched from horizon to horizon. Cars on the freeway became fewer and fewer.

From time to time Kharya would shake his head or turn the radio on loud enough to deafen him. Or he would suddenly start singing, changing the sense of every song known to him from his student years to his own. His voice was excruciatingly bad, but no one could hear him, and anyway his voice wasn't the problem: the important thing was not to fall asleep at the wheel.

Downtown San Antonio flashed quickly by, with its never-extinguished skyscraper lights. On two occasions Kharya stopped to stretch his numbed back, getting himself a double espresso from the coffee machine at a service station. But then even the coffee stopped helping. The pedal was all the way to the floor, but he wanted to go faster yet, to fly, but he couldn't press down any harder. Something in the rear end was rattling, the motor was roaring, the antiquated Chevrolet was five minutes from its last breath, even though it kept going, the damned thing, like a young bulldog.

The way back took him nearly an hour less. He should always drive at night! There was only some forty miles left to Houston. Now it was getting light. *Step on it just a little bit more, and we're home.* Tomorrow he'd be swamped with things to do, but before anything else he had to register his newly acquired property: there are always people on the prowl ready to make something out of other people's ideas.

The howl of a police siren came from behind him. Flashing red lights glared in his mirror. Kharya dropped his speed and moved into the right lane so as to let the highway patrol car past. But it braked as well and followed close behind Kharya's Chevrolet, almost nudging him with its bumper.

A certain time passed before the exhausted Kharya's brain grasped that the policeman didn't want to overtake him but was commanding him to stop. He had to drive on to the side of the road, his wheels humming as they crossed over the limit line, and the car came to a halt. The police car pulled in behind him and turned off its siren, but its red lights shone iridescently in Kharya's mirror. All he could do was sit and obediently wait.

Traffic on the road still remained light, a few individual cars careered past. Why had they stopped him and not them? The policeman didn't get out as was customary: he was studying Kharya's file on the computer. Then he walked slowly down the right side of the car, tall and thin, with a moustache trimmed from the bottom as if with a ruler. With his flashlight in his hands he hunched over and stuck his head through the window, passing the light over Kharya from head to toe, the beam filling the compartment with light. He found nothing suspicious in the junk on the back seat, and said: 'Mr Leah-Pye-Deahr, excuse me for bothering you . . . '

His intonation was a bit ironic. Kharya nodded his head ingratiatingly.

'Would you be so kind, sir, as to give me your driver's licence?' continued the policeman, attentively following Kharya's hand as it went for the wallet in his trouser-seat pocket.

Shining his flashlight on the card, he again looked at Kharya and said dryly: 'I'll ask you to get out of the car, only carefully. Cross over here, to the less dangerous side.'

Kharya got out. His body was numb, and it moved unsteadily around the hood of the car to the other side.

'Are you coming from Mexico just now?'

'No.'

'If not, then you won't need to open your trunk. People coming from there bring in all sorts of bad things.'

'No, I haven't brought anything in.'

'I hope so. Have you been drinking today?'

'Not a thing but water.'

'Walk down that white line – I'll have a look.'

Kharya took several heavy steps, trying not to stagger.

'I didn't have anything to drink!'

'I see that. Turn and face the automobile and put your hands on the roof.'

He began patting Kharya's clothes, from his armpits down and between his legs as well.

'Maybe you've made a mistake?' Kharya finally squeezed out, completely dismayed.

'Made a mistake? You give any thought to how fast you were going?'

'Approximately seventy-five . . . '

'Approximately? Come on over here, I'll show you: I've got a hundred and nine miles an hour on my radar. I followed you for a long time, and you never even slowed down.'

'Excuse me, sir, generally I always drive at the proper speed . . . '

'Is that so? The computer says you've already gotten two tickets this year for exceeding the speed limit. Under a hundred and it's just a fine. But if you go over a hundred miles an hour I'm obliged to arrest you.'

'Arrest me? But what for?'

'Everyone always asks "What for?" What time is it now?'

This is a well-known little trick that all cops use: in order to look at his watch Kharya automatically held his left hand in his right. A handcuff was latched on to his wrist next to his watch. The policeman pulled on the chain, and his arm was drawn behind his back. His other hand got joined up to it in a flash.

'It'll be more convenient for us to chat this way. Follow me to my car.'

'But what about mine?' The words came out helpless and even pathetic.

No explanation followed, but Kharya understood even without an answer, because the policeman called for a tow-truck and explained where the cherry-red Chevrolet was parked. A yellow receipt was squeezed in under the windscreen wiper. The cop opened the rear door of his black Ford with its white fenders and helped Kharya in, clumsy in his handcuffs. He slammed the door, and there the arrestee was, behind bars. The engine revved, and they drove off.

'So where are you taking me?'

'To gaol,' the policeman said simply, twisting his head to one side, 'since the movie theatres and restaurants are closed at four in the morning.'

'But I'm not some kind of criminal! I want to go home.'

Kharya instantly despised himself for this piece of naivety.

'To gaol first – we'll straighten things out there.'

'Well, in Germany there isn't any speed limit on the autobahn,' Kharya blurted out.

'What are you – German?' the cop said, tearing his eyes off the road and looking round at him.

'No, I'm a Russian, that is, a potential American . . . '

'Permit me to remind you, Mr Potential American: you're not in Germany. And not in Russia, either – don't know what kind of speed limit you have on your freeways over there. We're in Texas. We don't have to do what Germany and Russia do. We've got our own laws.'

Kharya shut up and didn't open his trap again.

In the holding cell at Fort Bend in Houston the policeman took the handcuffs off Kharya. Then they took his fingerprints, and for half an hour two different cops, yawning from their sleepless duty spell, interrogated him, entering every word into their computer. Then they took the hard copy from the printer and gave it to him to sign. There was no mention of the island in the text – Kharya had enough brain- and will-power left to keep quiet about that.

Kharya had no self-respect left: when the steel door of his cell slammed behind him he fell on to the cot and covered his face with his hands.

4

The cold woke Kharya up. He was lying on top of a sheet spread on a hard steel cot. Part of his body, not fitting the space on the narrow surface, hung over into the walkway. Across from him were another two of the same kind of cot, in two tiers. And between them cold was wafting down from the ceiling: on the other side of the window with its mighty bars howled an air-conditioner.

Kharya gradually figured out where and who he was. A blue bruise ached on his left wrist, reminding him of the improperly latched handcuffs. A short Vietnamese was urinating in the toilet in the corner. A long, skinny black man, dressed in multicoloured rags, snored like a tiger on the neighbouring cot, a snore that would now and again outhowl the air-conditioner.

Anguish seized Kharya's heart and would not let go. Get up? Stay lying there? Strike up a conversation with his neighbours? Or keep silent? Go and pound on the steel door? What was he supposed to do now?

He knew a lot about Soviet gaols and camps, about the abyss of cruelty and arbitrariness in them, both from books and from the mouths of those who'd been in them, but the only one he'd ever been in was this one, in free America. The current of his life had been interrupted in a most unpredictable fashion, never mind the loss of that valuable thing that he was just about to acquire.

He was independent no longer. They could do whatever they wanted with him now: keep him from sleeping, starve him, torture him, torment him, pull out his fingernails one by one to make him give up the true goal of his trip. After all, any one of them, as soon as they found out, could just dash off there and occupy his property. And just get rid of Kharya. He wouldn't be able to let out a peep, and not a soul would ever know.

Everything was twisted, hanging by a thread, about to collapse.

His thoughts were interrupted by someone kicking the door. It swung wide, and a young woman in police uniform – fat-assed, her tiny head neckless and hatless – came in, pushing a cart.

'Three of you here?' she asked, in a hoarse, throaty voice.

'As if you didn't know!' said the Vietnamese, stuffing his shirt into his shorts.

Without waiting for an answer, she set out three paper trays on the cots, then as quickly pushed the cart out of the room, the door slamming behind her.

The black giant raked in the contents of his tray with one arm and continued to snore.

In front of Kharya sat a paper box with salad, a hamburger, a box of orange juice and a plastic knife and fork. Always hungry and ready to swill down whatever was going – *just hand it over!* – he indifferently glanced at his breakfast and closed his eyes.

'What did you swipe, tramp?' asked the Vietnamese, who by this time had washed his hands under the tap and, still wet, was tucking briskly into his food. 'What did you shoplift?'

'Why from a shop?'

'You don't have the mug for something serious . . . right?'

Kharya nodded, so as not to get into any confessions.

'Bungler!' the fellow said, starting to lick his ketchupy fingers. 'You should have asked me. I operate smooth for six years, changing the labels on expensive clothes to cheap ones, paying for the cheap stuff, then later on changing the labels back to the ones I hide away. I return the clothes and get my money back but for the expensive ones. And you probably just put 'em on and bugged off? What a jerk!'

'If you're such a smooth operator, what are you in *here* for?'

'Hey, fatso, that's something you don't need to know! They haven't got any proof – why should I give them the rap to pin on me, as well as splitting with you, a competitor of mine? No, I'm going to keep quiet . . . Better just sit out my term. The judge won't send me up for long. And if I get bail – hey, I'll pay . . . '

The door flew open. It was the fat-assed policewoman again:

'Leahp . . . phew, to hell with it! Which one of you?' she said, holding a finger out at Kharya. 'You, most likely? Come on out!'

Kharya cast a melancholy look at his untouched free breakfast, and, rising from the cot, stretched out his hands to Madame Coppette.

'Aren't you going to put handcuffs on me?' he asked, gazing down at her from above.

The Vietnamese behind him shook with laughter.

'What do you need handcuffs for?' she said in surprise. 'What are you, a murderer? If everybody who broke the speed limit got handcuffs slapped on every time, there wouldn't be enough money in the Texas treasury for it. Go on, get out to reception!'

She shoved him in the back with a fist, and he obediently did as he was commanded.

'Hey!' the Vietnamese called to his retreating back. 'I'll finish your breakfast, otherwise it'll go stale.'

It suddenly occurred to Kharya what he had to say. He should have done it yesterday – how could he not have thought of it on the spot?

'I need a lawyer' was the phrase that rose to the surface and burst out of him, a phrase from an English-language textbook.

'You're a Russian, aren't you?'

'You guessed it.'

'Nothing to guess at! All Russians who get arrested say the same thing: "I need a lawyer." Don't know the laws, but they all keep saying that like a bunch of parrots. Go ahead and call your lawyer – there's a phone on the desk over there.'

'But I don't remember his number!'

'Look it up. There's a telephone directory there somewhere.'

The coppette led him into the reception area, pointed a chair out to him and left.

The door was right there, and the daring thought of dashing out on to the street sprang to Kharya's mind. But then, what next? And the revolutionary thought died, unrealized.

He really did need a lawyer, but Kharya didn't have anything to pay for one. Right now he owed a hideous sum for his divorce and for his working visa, and he'd already received three warning letters to the effect that if he didn't immediately pay, then . . . It was better not even to think about that 'then . . . ': they would ruin his credit rating, something everyone was frightened into a panic about, but who in this country would lend him – incomeless as he was – even a penny?

He couldn't see any way out. Leafing through the yellow pages of the phone book, Kharya put his finger on the name 'Robinson, Charlie'. His secretary, as usual, answered that Mr Robinson wasn't there right now, but she was prepared to write down who it was who called. He wasn't that stupid. Kharya painted such a bloody scene of the violation of human rights at the police station that, after the secretary's explanation, he heard Robinson himself say to someone, 'You never get bored with these Russians!' and pick up the phone.

Half an hour later Attorney Robinson burst into the police station. A young, businesslike and black-skinned gentleman with a shaven head, smelling of expensive cologne, in a grey hound's-tooth jacket and blue tie, he signed the desk sergeant's register, plopped his briefcase down on the bare metal table in reception and sat down opposite Kharya. Robinson pulled a box of paper tissues out of his briefcase and spent a while wiping his head and neck, throwing the wet tissues one after another into the bin under the table.

'Mr Leah . . . ' he squeezed out after a pause. 'Mr Pye . . . Oh my God, what a name! No matter how much I practise it, I can never get it . . . '

'Lah-pee-dar,' Kharya said softly, not taking offence.

'No, I'm not in any state to pronounce that! Can I just call you Mr Harry?'

'Call me whatever you want. Just help me get out of here!'

'So then, Mr Harry, I've already wasted a heap of time to get you a licence to work, inasmuch as the social workers looking after immigrants asked me to. And here you are again . . . And on exactly the same day I was getting ready to finally go on holiday with my new girlfriend. After all, I've already explained to you: nothing in America gets done for free . . . I understand your troubles: your ancestors were enslaved by the Russian government and mine by the American. But how long can I go on working for you for free, just for your pretty eyes?'

'I'll pay you, Robinson, I swear! I'll pay you very soon. I just have to get on my feet . . . '

'Get on your feet? What are you standing on right now? I've heard all this a hundred times already, Mr Harry . . . Everyone talks like that. That's probably why my head aches . . . My head is just splitting.'

'Where does it hurt?'

'Everywhere.'

'That doesn't happen. Show me more precisely!'

'It seems like it's here and here. My temples are aching. But what's that to you?'

'I'll try to help you,' Kharya said, getting up from his chair and stretching out his great huge hands. 'Sit up straight. Did you drink beer last night? And not just one bottle, I'll bet . . . Did you have a whisky and soda? Port for dessert? You did, didn't you? Did you have a little brandy in your coffee? Slept poorly . . . '

'How do you know that?' the lawyer said, staring at Kharya.

'I can read minds . . . Close your eyes. Relax . . . Imagine that you've gone to heaven . . .'

'Where?'

'To heaven.'

'That's all I need, to go to heaven!' muttered Robinson, but he closed his eyes.

Straining, Kharya was slowly passing his hands, fingers spread wide, over Charlie's head, when the coppette appeared in the doorway. Catching sight of what was transpiring, she froze in surprise, instinctively putting her hand on her holstered revolver.

'What's going on here?'

'He's giving me treatment,' said the lawyer.

'Treatment? This isn't a police station, it's a funny farm!'

Tossing a folder on to the table, she disappeared, slamming the door savagely.

On the yellow envelope lying on the desk in front of Robinson, Kharya, looking askance, could read his own name and date of birth.

He put one hand on the back of Robinson's head, as if getting ready to unscrew it, and the other, for nearly five minutes, he passed from Charlie's eyebrows up along his forehead and crown to the back of his head, pressing the tips of his middle and index fingers in succession on certain points. His fingernails left dark marks, and Robinson whimpered from time to time. His dark skin became covered with perspiration.

Kharya had mastered this art in Odessa, when he was languishing from boredom those many years at the Department of Scientific Communism; gradually he mastered it and readily subjected his co-workers to the treatment – particularly the female ones – thanks to everyone having at least *something* that ached. You couldn't say that the results were a hundred-per-cent positive, but it did sometimes help, particularly in combination with more orthodox medicaments.

Having finished the procedure, Kharya sat down, panting as if he'd just unloaded a wagonload of watermelons, and folded his arms over his chest in expectation. Robinson blinked his eyes and touched his head, checking to see if it was still there, and pronounced: 'Well, you know, it's sort of better . . . Surprising, but it doesn't hurt . . . What was it you did?'

'That's a professional secret,' grinned Kharya, satisfied with a result that he himself hadn't expected so quickly.

'OK!' The lawyer placed his black hands with their pink palms and manicured nails on the folder with Kharya's name on it. 'Let's have a look at what you're incriminated in, here . . . ' He began leafing through the pages. 'Hmmm . . . Exceeding the speed limit . . . Fine . . .

Again speeding . . . Another fine . . . Speed over a hundred . . . Did that really happen?'

'Unfortunately.'

'Night-time arrest . . . That's serious. An arrest can't be removed from the police computer system. But, generally speaking, they haven't got anything else against you! They don't even know that you've only got a work permit for this country, and don't have a permanent residence permit. I hope you kept quiet about that . . .'

'They didn't ask about anything of the kind!' Just in case, Kharya looked around and up at the ceiling, as if there might be some eavesdropping device there.

'There's zip about you in this police dossier, for the rest of it. By the established rules, they can sentence you to a hundred hours of community service – raking up leaves in the park and putting them into plastic bags. And pull your licence for half a year, inasmuch as you represent a potential danger on the road. But who doesn't drive like a madman these days, except for old ladies – those sweet little airheads?'

'That's what I think, too,' Kharya assented, inspired with hope.

'In principle,' the lawyer continued, 'I could argue the case in court and prove that you never exceeded the speed limit at all. The policeman who stopped you has to appear in court and relate the facts of the case. But cops don't always show up at court when required, while I have my own man in the courtroom.'

'That's greatl!'

'Right. If the policeman shows up – I don't show up, but when he doesn't show, I'm there on the spot, in court. They don't postpone a case more than three times, after which the case is dropped. Only five hundred dollars from you, and I get you off clean. But the police want you to come up with two thousand dollars for the state treasury before you can go free. Can you come up with a sum like that?'

'Does your head still hurt?' Kharya suddenly asked.

'The headache's gone. So what?'

'So, I don't have any money right now, but if your head starts hurting again I'm sure to be around . . .'

'That's what you're on about! OK! But a little friendly advice – don't take up the practice of it for money. You don't have a practitioner's licence, and the first cranky patient you get will sue you for practising illegally. When I started the process of getting you a residence permit, you said that all you wanted was a work permit, and you would agree to any job at all. I got you your work permit, you got your driver's licence. But a job? Did you find one?'

'Not yet.'

'You were saying that you taught that whatchamacallit, that . . . Marxism, mixed together with something else, I forget.'

'Leninism.'

'That's it! You could give private lessons . . . '

Kharya respectfully inclined his head:

'Private lessons in Marxism-Leninism in Texas? There's an idea! Are you going to take lessons from me?'

'Not me, no; I haven't got the time. In principle, though, that sort of thing might be interesting. Americans can be interested in any old thing! I'll ask around my friends . . . '

The fat-assed coppette came in again, rattling a bunch of keys. 'Well, what? Haven't you done enough talking yet?' This time she was minded to be decisive. 'We have to bust up this session with your lawyer. The bus just came to take away all the arrestees.'

'Where to?' asked Robinson, wiping the back of his head with a tissue.

'What do you mean, where to? Not to the casino and not to the cathouse . . . To the city park for some community service.'

'Will you allow me to ask my client just one more confidential question, so I can get straight to court?'

'Get on it. Just be quick.'

Robinson smacked his lips, following the retreating butt of the policewoman with his eyes, paused for a moment, then walked over and pushed the door completely closed. He came back to his place and looked attentively at Kharya: 'Listen, my dear Mr Harry. If you aren't engaged in any sort of business, and you haven't got any family, where were you in such a hurry to get to? There has to be some kind of teensy-weensy valid motive somewhere, doesn't there? What the hell were you driving like that for?'

Kharya took a lungful of air, let it out through his nose, glanced around at the door, and asked in a whisper: 'And do they really not bug conversations in here? You're absolutely certain?'

'C'mon, we aren't in Russia.'

'Then first swear to me, Charlie, that you won't cheat me out of it.'

'I swear,' Robinson said and mechanically raised his right hand the way they always do in court. He grinned.

Everyone knows that there is no greater bunch of liars in America than lawyers. An 'honest lawyer' is an oxymoron, a fable, an absurdity.

'I'll not only make it worth your while financially,' whispered Kharya, 'but make you a major political figure as well.'

'You? Me?'

'Precisely: I'll make *you* somebody. How would you like to be Minister for Justice?'

'That's enough, stop fooling around, Mr Harry. I don't have the time.' Robinson glanced at his watch. 'I've got a plane to catch in an hour and a half.'

'No, not at all – this is dead serious!' The huge Kharya squeezed the lawyer by the shoulders. 'I swear on my mother's memory! I was driving that night because I had a most important task that wasn't going to wait. God Himself sent you to me. Help me get a colossal piece of property registered and I won't leave you a loser!'

'What sort of property?'

'Real! Land, that I was the first to set foot on. It was nobody's and became mine, only I have to stake it down before somebody steals it.'

'But for that you need proof, at least some kind of documentation of your property right . . .'

'Here it is!' Kharya pulled the roll of film out of the back pocket of his trousers. 'It's all here . . .'

Dubiously, Robinson took the film. So as to convince him once and for all, Kharya bent down to Robinson's ear and rasped: 'In all likelihood, there's an oil deposit there.'

That was a flat-out lie, of course. It was just in case, so as to galvanize the lawyer.

But it wasn't any sort of knock-out blow. Robinson shrugged Kharya's hands off him, picked up his briefcase and let out his breath in a sigh only as he skipped out of the police station. These Russians were nothing but nutcases!

5

Kharya really did have a serious reason to be in a hurry, for it's as plain as the nose on your face: a holy place is never empty. The more so, as Kharya wasn't the first to be so clever. There were precedents.

When the glorious third wave of Russian emigration was washing over America from the countries of the Soviet Bloc, yet another inhabitant of Russia came to live in New York, to find himself a soft spot here. He came in a not-very-traditional way, passing up the usual immigration and residence controls. He came in on the sly.

If you're a Russian, perhaps you heard about it at the time through the jamming, over those enemy 'Voices'? A Soviet merchant vessel was passing through the Panama Canal: its captain, Ivan Varvartsev, jumped ship one night, literally landing in the water, and scampered off to the nearest embassy to ask for political asylum. Usually it's supposed to be the captain who abandons ship last, but in this case it was the other way round. Bad examples being contagious, another three or four crewmen jumped ship right behind him. The 'Voices' reported the story and then forgot about it. The jumpers made off whither they could.

Captain Varvartsev turned up in Chile, after being signed on as a seaman aboard a bulk-carrier belonging to God-knows-what country. He led a wretched life as a stevedore in the port, lugging heavy bales for his dinner, then later stowed away on a vessel bound for Florida. There, before the ship had made port, he again jumped into the water and swam off towards the beach, risking feeding the sharks with his footsies – but they spared him. He made his way to New York. He made a living there selling sugar-coated nuts on the street, pouring them out for passing tourists into little paper bags: pay your buck and eat away. But selling sweets isn't sweet work. The desire arises in the passers-by to take pity on the poor salesman, languishing under the hot sun, and this humanitarianism is conducive to the flourishing of the business.

Anyway, everything about Varvartsev's bold leap into the water is something I read in a brochure that he himself had published, complete with his portrait photo and programme for the future, and personally handed to me. It's lying right in front of me on my desk.

My chance acquaintance with him occurred when I was moonlighting at Radio Liberty in New York. He came by to demand that he be given free air time to make an appeal to all the Russians living in America. Characters like that normally put you on your guard straight away. Varvartsev wasn't the least bit troubled by the simple fact that Radio Liberty didn't broadcast to the Russians living in America, just the ones in Russia. And the fact that liberties on Radio Liberty were not taken – except under the strict supervision of the management – never entered his head.

You'd have to say the dude came across as rather disgusting. He smelled of halitosis and a lack of deodorant. When he spoke it seemed as if he was thinking only that everyone underrated him, and he was therefore always offended. A complete egoist and ambitious man. He was certain that he alone had suffered a lot and therefore everyone else was obliged to him. He wouldn't listen to any objections – he would stick to his own notions. His own, though, were something curious.

Naturally, no one was going to give him any air time, but, just to let him let off some steam, a couple of us asked him what he wanted to communicate to the radio listeners.

'I've started a new movement,' he declared. 'An action committee of émigrés is backing me up. We're going to create a brand-new man-made homeland in America. Properly speaking, this struggle of mine is already in full swing.'

The words 'struggle of mine' aroused everyone's attention, and the working populace of the station who weren't engaged in broadcasting at that moment began gathering round Varvartsev. The security officers of the station, unaccustomed to chaos, began getting nervous.

'Well, what are you struggling against, exactly?'

'We're not struggling *against* something, but *for* it,' the former sea captain clarified. 'We've come to a conclusion about the necessity to form an independent Russian nation in America.'

'But you've already dodged out of it.'

'Precisely! And we'll re-create it here on a new basis.'

'What – a country within a country?'

'And why not? Or at worst a Russian fifty-first state . . .'

Quebec, which at that time wanted to secede from Canada, was what inspired Varvartsev.

'But, after all, in America the states are just territorial entities, without any sort of ethnic accents,' someone observed.

'We'll have something unique. Most important is to get ahold of some land, and then later on my confederates and I will figure out what to do . . .'

'What do you mean, "get ahold of"?'

'Like this: seize some territory, fence it off, and set up the necessary guard. I've already earmarked a sort of potential land in the Midwest and came up with a name for it: *Russianland*. Citizenship will be our own, Russianland's, and not some sort of green-card thing that they only hand out if you have connections. And we, the Russianlanders, will feel that we're not some poor relations that the Americans are sheltering but masters in our own land.'

Right there I understood that Varvartsev himself was here willy-nilly, and made an attempt to talk him out of it, laying it on good and thick. 'Are you an American yet?'

'Well, let's say no . . .'

'Then, first off, you're going to have to legalize your status here. Otherwise, if you chop yourself off a piece of land that'll be an act of war. They'll send up a little bomber from the nearest air base, and there won't be anything left of you and your action committee to put into a grave.'

'But we'll buy ourselves radar and some other means of defence,' he objected. 'And if we have to, we'll declare war on the United States!'

'Who's going to be your head of state?'

Varvartsev modestly lowered his eyes: 'Well, there doesn't have to be two opinions on that . . . '

He'd grown a little Führer's moustache under his nose. The fighter for himself and against everyone else seemed even more fatuous than he had at first. It was getting boring, so everyone started quietly drifting off. Varvartsev hastily swung his knapsack off his shoulder, undid the ties and fished out a pack of brochures with red covers. He yelled at their retreating backs: 'Hang on a minute! I have everything set out here! Get acquainted with it . . . Look into it, there'll be enough for everyone. You'll be sorrier still when we take over your radio for ourselves!'

On the cover of the brochure, under his name and self-assured face, was the vivid, optimistic title: 'Our Cause is Just!' Former Captain Varvartsev walked out, dragging his knapsack behind him and slamming the door, like any ordinary crackpot.

His notion, meanwhile, even without any airing over the radio, became widely known in our tight little circle, even a topic of discussion, although more often than not with ironic overtones. 'Why Would Russians Need a Separate Nation of Their Own Inside a Free Country?' enquired a headline in the influential New York Russian-language newspaper *Novaya Russkaya Gazeta*, in the spirit of complete freedom of expression. The article began in intellectual-polemical fashion: 'What does this raggedy-andy Russianlander want, anyway?' The venerable dissident Brunovsky mailed in an op-ed piece from Paris, in which he jeered at Varvartsev with all his might, calling his idea (and I quote) 'the ravings of a thick-as-they-come numbskull'.

As a matter of fact, the multitude of people in America – believers all in God-knows-what – live however they like. Russian *Molokans*, Indian gurus – never mind native Indians! – they all have nearly their own nation within a nation: communes, phalanxes, societies, whatever their hearts desire. There's a whole town that's the personal property of the movie star Kim Basinger – she simply bought all the houses there. And why shouldn't she?

Enthusiasts acquire land, build on it, propagate their notions, prohibit automobiles and ride around on horses, while away their days in candlelight, teach their children their own way in home schools in their own languages, existing from century to century entirely independent of federal and local authorities; they settle their accounts with them, and nobody stands in anyone's way. Except for the American Indians with their lifelong grudge against the European occupation, it is without a doubt that everyone pays their taxes, so that their property and rights will be defended by the police, the National Guard, the army.

But no: partisans of Varvartsev's wanted a specific, completely independent nation and seriously discussed what sort of principal policies their nation would carry out towards Brezhnev's Soviet Union and even towards the United States.

We have no barriers at sea nor on land, in the words of the Soviet song. Some old-timers in San Francisco told me the story of the famous madman of that city, Joshua Norton. Always dressed in a threadbare general's tunic with gold epaulettes – stolen apparently from a theatrical costume rental shop – Norton wore a wide-brimmed hat with a peacock feather, and went around with a sword dangling at his side. The guy had long since proclaimed himself emperor of both Americas, North and South, and the entire city was accustomed to it.

Norton ate for free in restaurants. Everyone everywhere knew that he loved oysters and champagne and would give him a huge platter of them, so that he would be there eating longer. He adored making scenes, too: if someone turned out to be not to his taste Joshua would leap up and reach for his sword. The restaurateurs couldn't help but take delight in the advertising: curious visitors to San Francisco would get to have a look at General Norton and dine in his presence, and, if luck held, crowds would come to treat him to champagne.

Oh Lord, ambition in everyone needs sustenance. I myself, for instance, also sometimes sign friendly letters with a title that I have merely assigned to myself: 'Director, Pacific Ocean'. A plaque hanging over my son's door says 'Manager, Ebb and Flow Tides'. You won't catch up with those who dream big. Imperial instincts are with some of us in our blood, our neurones, our genes. There have been and still are, though, serious aspects to such japes.

Since time immemorial Russians have been trying to provide themselves with property in America. If I remember right, as early as the sixteenth century, after the destruction of Lord Novgorod the Great (as the city was styled) by Ivan the Terrible, several Novgorodian families escaped to Siberia and then made their way across the Bering Sea to settle in Alaska. Anyway, that wasn't the name of the sea back then: that only happened after the expedition of Bering and Chirikov, who sailed to America in two vessels – Peter the Great had envious eyes and itchy fingers.

The sailors sent as emissaries from the ship to the shore in launches were simply put to death by the Indians, who celebrated their victory with a torch-light procession. The survivors' trip back to Kamchatka turned out to be a nightmare. One after another, the trailblazers succumbed to scurvy. On the way home their vessel smashed itself to pieces on some islands. Those who were saved by some miracle buried Bering himself.

Then the Russian-America Company was born. Don't believe the title – it was purely Russian, with colonial dreams. There was even a Viceroy of Russian America, a Mr Baranov.

The conquerors cheated and exploited the Aleuts and Indians, exported the furs, searched out gold and diamonds, introduced orthodoxy for the sake of order in conflict with Catholic missionaries. The charms of New Albion were already beckoning, to which they had extended their activities: they very much wanted to make that land

Russian, too. In 1812 forty Russian river pirates with eighty Aleuts landed on the Pacific shore of what is now the United States and here, in California, constructed the pivotal fortress of Fort Ross.

Napoleon shuffled the cards, bringing into doubt the very existence of the Russian state, and the Russian government was unable to keeps its hands in America. There wasn't enough strength for the realization of imperial plans here. Fort Ross was purchased by the famous John Sutter, whose activities resulted in the Gold Rush starting up, not very far from where I now live.

When Alexander II sold Alaska to the American government, the greater part of the Russian settlers stayed on. Before sailing off, some of the sailors jumped from the departing ships, so as not to go back. In the language of the Soviets (I've just looked into the Great Soviet Encyclopaedia), 'American capitalists began their predatory exploitation', while 'the native populace was subjected to cruel oppression and doomed to gradual extinction'. But why, I wonder, are things so good for the native populace of Alaska and so awful for the native populace of Siberia, left unsold, so far?

The trouble for all of us Russian émigrés in America is that, unlike immigrants from many other countries, we have nowhere to return to. In Ireland, for instance, they start affirming to tiny little children, scarcely able to go off to school: 'Do well at your studies, because we're a small country, and not everyone is going to find work here. A lot of people have to emigrate. You'll most probably work in America until you get your pension, and then, if you want to, you'll come back to your homeland.'

Irish communities are very strong in the USA. Parades of Irish-sprung people gather millions of viewers. 'Kiss me – I'm Irish!' is practically the most popular motto on the breasts of thousands of Americans. The Kennedy family is from there, to say nothing of various others. But the Irish don't go around setting up any nations or phalanxes in America. On the contrary, after saving up their fortune and retiring, many of them go back to their homeland.

Returned emigrants in Dublin are welcomed home as their own, and helped to re-acclimatize. Their American social-security payments are neatly lodged in their bank accounts at the beginning of every month. They buy themselves homes and, like a knife through butter, enter into their new-old full-to-the-brim life.

A sensible system of societies for returned Irishmen has been created to accept them, warm them, gladden them, entertain them. I have an Irish friend, a professor of medieval French literature who works in California and who has raised two daughters there. Every summer they go to Ireland for their holiday. He dreams of returning for good with his family. He's already looked into the price of a cottage there. But he definitely wants to work here in America until he retires.

Writers, however, have no need to leave their home in Ireland, for another instance. I know of no other country where poets can breathe so free. Books of magnificent quality (step inside any bookstore in Dublin!) are published at government expense. In the basement of the Dublin Literary Museum and Writers' Union there's a restaurant called (get this!) Chapter One, where you can sit and chat with fellow writers, who in Ireland are excused by the government from income taxes. 'Everyone in Ireland is a writer – in his own mind,' an Irish colleague said to me, even though he himself is thoroughly professional.

In contrast to many other immigrants, Russians in America lack any communities of their own. Clubs, if they're ever formed, have a pathetic aspect and soon disintegrate. Calls to unite fade away into thin air. It's possible that the collectivist ideals of our radiant past have knocked out any will to flock together, while leaders along the lines of Varvartsev scare off normal people. And we can't go back: there's no one waiting for us back in Russia with open arms.

A friend of mine who went back to Moscow after selling his home in the state of Ohio and buying himself a country *dacha* in the hinterlands of the capital was tracked down and twice robbed, after he had gone to the police for the necessary registrations. It wasn't anyone else but the cops who set the bandits on the former American. Friends and non-friends alike told him the same thing, whether seriously or in jest: 'You're all we're waiting for, here, sunshine. Now get on back to where you came from!' He had to give up the little *dacha*, go back to Cincinnati and start all over from zero.

But now I too have to return to the main plot.

Khariton Lapidar, formerly without a care, someone who had lived out the end of the Soviet era among the obedient Party member-propagandists of the foremost doctrines in the world, who, when it was safe, quietly slipped off to America, had never heard jot or tittle of those Varvartsevisms. Never a single distinct patriotic Russian notion had Kharya ever had, he'd never fought for anything or even intended doing so – the only thing he ever could recognize was crisp-folding material well-being.

If someone of Varvartsev's partisans ever heard that there was a no man's land somewhere to be had, on which they could set up their own state, that someone would be off there at the speed of light. But Kharya was the first to secure himself some land on the shores of the Rio Grande. All that was left to do was hold on to the land with his own two hands and in the meantime ponder what to do with it. For example, in its capacity as personal property, it might be advantageous to sell it off.

However, almost everyone who makes moolah is at heart certain that he's a benefactor of mankind. In certain circumstances that might be true but not always, by a long shot. Various suchlike amorphous happy thoughts on his account were rolling around Kharya's mind while he was driving to the spot, and especially on his way back. His breath was taken clean away by all the opportunities presenting themselves. And now all his schemes were fettered by those damned handcuffs.

It was the Devil who'd speeded him on, on that freeway!

6

'Lizzie, my sweet, I'm free of that idiot with the unpronounceable name and I'm on my way to the airport. Where are you? Oh, you're already there . . . Get ready! In fifteen minutes I'll be kissing you, my little pussycat!'

Robinson stuck the telephone back into his pocket and stepped harder on the gas.

Lizzie had become his new girlfriend a week earlier. That is, properly speaking; he'd had his eye on her for a long time. As we've already related, there was something there to hanker after and something to get your hands on – it wasn't any accident that Charlie had wanted to take strips out of Kharya. But Lizzie had been his office secretary at the time, and it had been better not to have her on his mind. Feeling Robinson's fixed and serious gaze on herself, probably, she had moved to another job, in an insurance company twenty storeys further up from his office, so he could phone her on something other than business.

She was a dark and scrumptious little Mexican girl – wasp-waisted, a near-perfect figure with an ample bosom and long black hair now and again mysteriously covering sometimes an ear, sometimes half her face – she would flip her hair back with a finger, but then it would fall back again.

Best of all would have been to get her home as fast as possible after taking her to dinner, but Lizzie so aroused Charlie's whole being that he wanted to make it a lengthy affair. And for that it was desirable to impart a striking tone to it, a more romantic beginning. As everyone knows, you have to pay more for romance, so he'd booked two places in Puerto Vallarta.

A new woman, particularly one as striking as her, was someone to brag about. But not in front of her co-workers, who had known her for so long already! Robinson phoned Tony Gobetti, an old friend of his, together with whom (as it became clear when I met both of them later on) he'd rattled around from bell to bell in the law school of UC Berkeley. Right next door there, in Sacramento, Tony had arranged himself a job in a small law office. And shortly after had married there Jennifer, a college student, whom he'd met a year or two before in the line at the post office.

Tony Gobetti, who looked like Marcello Mastroianni, with his fat wife, her hair cropped like a boy's and slightly pregnant, had left their car at the airport and flown to where Charlie and Lizzie were going, the resort town of Puerto Vallarta, to spend a long weekend there, from Thursday to Sunday.

The flight from Houston was delayed by thunderstorms somewhere on the way to Mexico. The sun was already setting into the ocean when Robinson and Lizzie, after quickly changing into their bathing suits, found their friends between the fountain and the swimming pool on recliners under a gigantic thatch umbrella. Charlie and Tony had continued explaining to one another on their cell phones who was where, until Jennifer grabbed the phone out of her husband's hand. Turning it off, she pointed her finger at the approaching Charlie for Tony's benefit.

'Don't be surprised,' Jennifer said to Lizzie. 'My husband is on the phone even when he's having sex. Let's get acquainted. You're a marvel, sweetheart! Wherever did Charlie find such a lovely creature? Right, Tony?'

'My girl's all right,' agreed Charlie and hugged the giggling Lizzie, kissing her neck in emphasis of his property rights.

'We'll have to drink to us!' exclaimed Tony, combing his fingers back through the hair that had fallen in front of his eyes. 'Hey, waiter! Bring us some champagne and something to snack on!'

While the four of them await their champagne, I will allow myself to note that the normal Mexican squalor, altogether reminiscent of the Russian, ends at the gates of this reservation for foreign tourists.

The bay around which the town of Puerto Vallarta is situated, with its view of the Pacific Ocean clear to the horizon, is quiet and sunny the year round, something that especially attracts northerners. The lighthouse at the edge of the bay, exchanging its winks with the moon by night, is not so much something needed by ships in our satellite era as it is an important romantic accessory. The beach is clean as a whistle, even though the majority of visitors prefer the sea-water swimming pools, of which there are three here. The hotel is an ideal of cleanliness and comfort, you can drink the water without fear of ruining your stomach, the food is excellent and the well-schooled staff try to anticipate your every desire.

A little table on wheels appeared between the recliners, covered in a snow-white cloth, the champagne fizzing away in the glasses.

'Charlie Robinson, old buddy!' exclaimed Tony, after a sip of champagne. 'We haven't seen each other for ages, have we?'

The bubbles tickled his nose, and he hiccupped.

'Yeah,' said Charlie, smirking, 'and we wouldn't be seeing each other right now, Mr Tony Gobetti, if . . .'

'If you hadn't decided to trot out your new girlfriend.'

'Exactly! I've been running around like a squirrel in a cage. Guess where I was before I made the plane.'

'In court or at the gaol – where else is there?'

'Second guess is right on. I have a client there, a strange Russian dude from Odessa, it seems.'

'Whoa, my grandmother is from Odessa, too!' said Tony delightedly. 'My Italian grandfather, Gobetti, met her on board a ship from Europe, and married her first thing as soon as they got to New York.'

'What, can you speak Russian, too?'

'Well, as they say, I can't *razz-moh-vlyatch*, but I do remember a bit:

> Smell-ah . . . meev . . . boy . . . pah-yeddum
> Zahv . . . last . . . sah-vettuf
> Chee . . . cock . . . ah-deen . . . oom-roam
> Vvv . . . bar-bay . . . za-ettuf!

He sang in Russian, a little out of tune, in a sort of Italian-Ukrainian accent, and added: 'My grandmother would sing that to my grandfather, but he'd just laugh. But as far as I knew he didn't understand squat.'

'I didn't understand anything, either, of course,' said Robinson, frowning.

'How to explain it to you? Generally, all Russians are ready to fight for socialism and die for it *en masse*, get it? Everybody as one. It sounds like a satirical song to me. If all the socialists get killed, who needs their socialism? It smells a little like necrophilia to me . . . Anyway, let's drink us some more of this stuff instead.'

Tony poured everyone some cham pagne, except his wife. So they had another drink.

'By the way,' Charlie recalled, 'this poor guy from Odessa, who wants me to represent his interests – he's an expert in that stuff.'

Tony failed to understand. 'In what stuff?'

'Back home in Odessa he was a professor of socialism. Something like your grandmother.'

'Maybe your criminal and I are related, back in Odessa.'

'Hey, he's no kind of criminal! Not yet, at least. He'd been arrested for speeding. And he asked me to help him register some property.'

'What sort of property?'

'Some land . . . There might be some good money in it, but he hasn't got his green card yet, just a working visa.'

Jennifer was getting ready to go for a swim but stopped right there. 'So is he married?' she butted in.

Robinson didn't understand. 'What significance does that have? He's divorced. So what?'

'You remember, Tony,' Jennifer said, poking a finger into her husband's hairy chest, 'we have a widow in Sacramento who needs real bad to get married? Well, her husband left her such a weird will . . . You introduced me to her, you said she was some kind of Byron in a skirt. Spry old lady!'

Gobetti stared at his wife. His eyes screwed up tight. He set his glass quietly on the table and studied it for a long time in silence, as if there were something written on the bottom of it. Deep in thought he stuck his thumb into his mouth and gummed it with his lips. After the pause, Gobetti shifted his gaze to his colleague Robinson. The latter sat silently on his recliner, a white towel with orange stripes thrown over his shoulders, holding his unfinished glass in his hand.

'What are you staring at me for?' Charlie asked.

'Think, Charlie!' Tony insisted. 'Strain your brain!'

Robinson shrugged. 'Wedding bells, surely?'

'Exactly! As a result, two birds with one stone.'

'Once lawyers get their tongues stuck into their business,' said Jennifer, 'you'll never get them apart. Let's go for a swim, Lizzie.'

The women detached themselves from them and, chattering about their own stuff, dived into the pool. The water boiled around Lizzie, a skilled aquanaut, and the other hotel residents around the pool, or walking around the pathways enjoying their conversations, immediately turned their gaze on her. Lizzie did a nifty racing turn at the far end of the pool and came back, nearly a third of the way under-water.

'It's hard for me to swim,' complained Jennifer. 'My tummy drags me down to the bottom.'

'What's it going to be?' Lizzie sat up on the edge of the pool, managing to make eyes at everyone passing.

'The ultrasound showed a boy. But I haven't told Tony. He wants a girl.'

'Maybe the doctor made a mistake.'

'That's why I don't tell him . . . But, you know, that Russian widow, the one I remembered about, as a matter of fact, she's something else. She's ninety-seven. She looked at my tummy and said to Tony: "In our game, the most important thing is to know whose it is!"'

The women laughed.

'Since you're all mysterious over here, that means you're getting along,' said Tony, sneaking up on the women. 'That's reeee-ally nice . . .'

'What's so special about it?' asked Jennifer.

'Special, because we have to leave you here.'

'And Charlie?' Lizzie said, raising a shoulder.

'Are you serious?' asked Jennifer.

She wrapped her arms around her belly, and tears came into her eyes.

'Sorry, kid, but Charlie and I just discussed the situation. This business smells like money, and only a total idiot would miss this chance. Thursday's on its way out, and we've only got Friday for all the things we have to do. Any later and we'll miss our chance. You two stay here and finish your vacation, OK?'

'What a fool I am! Why did I ever put this idea in your head?'

'No, you're a good girl, smarty pants!'

'You're just bullying us,' Lizzie said, turning her back on him and looking far and wide.

'Don't get mad, pussycat. We'll do it all a little later, OK? Absolutely everything! Right now I'm going back to Houston, and Tony's going back to his place in Sacramento. If we can get them married, then . . .'

They hurried off to change.

'Our guys can go to hell, Jennifer!' Lizzie yelled, loud enough for them to hear. 'We'll find ourselves something even better here . . .'

Jennifer didn't answer, just put her hands on her protruding belly.

'And that's no obstacle,' giggled Lizzie.

7

Kharya had avoided physical labour since childhood, and now it was an utter torment for him. Who would have thought that there was such an incalculable quantity of leaves in a city park that you could never rake them all up? Rake and rake, and they just keep on falling. It had never even entered his head before that evergreen trees drop their leaves as well – only, unlike the regular ones, not just once in the autumn but the whole year round.

It was morning on Friday when Attorney Robinson, having returned on a night flight to Houston, rolled up to Hermann Park. After looking around a bit, he caught sight of the arrestees in their red overalls. Charlie knew the policeman who was guarding them, and he let the lawyer have a word with Kharya.

'I had the photographs of the island printed,' said Robinson, 'and I talked it over with a judge I know. In principle, the judge thinks that the property rights are untrammelled and that generally your chances are good. But the contract has to be materially remunerative for the attorneys: a third of the value of your property plus payment of all overhead expenses.'

'Agreed,' Kharya nodded hurriedly.

'OK! Now there's just one little hitch,' Robinson said, coming to a halt. 'The case will drag on for months, taking into account the bureaucratic system we have here in America . . .'

'But then some scumbag will take over my land!'

The lawyer glanced around and leaned in towards Kharya's ear: 'So that nobody'll scoop you, you should register your property in Mexico, quick as you can. Not because the operation is illegal – I wouldn't ever do something like that in my life! – but exclusively to speed things up.'

'Great idea!'

'But there's a problem. Americans have the right to acquire property in Mexico, but you're not an American, after all. That's the trouble. So there's no chance for you to do that.'

Kharya's look clouded over.

Charlie licked his dry lips. 'There is a way out, sort of, though . . .'

'What, precisely?'

Robinson hummed and hawed.

'Well, speak up, man, damn you!' Kharya said, getting nervy. 'They're about to take me back.'

'You have to get married. You can register the property only in your wife's name.'

Kharya fastened his eyes on the lawyer in silence, taking him in, as if it wasn't him but Kharya's inevitable bride standing before him here. He scratched the back of his head. 'So I've got to get married,' he grinned. 'And why not?'

'But I have to tell you fair and square.' Robinson in his turn looked Kharya over searchingly. 'She's not that young.'

'That is?'

Robinson fell into thought. Did he have any right to say how old the bride was? But, on the other hand, this wasn't a case where he could just blow some smoke – it would come clear anyway.

'Just don't get scared, Harry. Because, as my friend Tony Gobetti, her lawyer, said, there's a whole set of factors going for it.'

'Well?' Kharya roared in irritation.

'She's . . . ninety-seven.'

Kharya burst out laughing. 'Ninety-seven?' He couldn't stop for a long time, until, having laughed himself out, he remarked, wiping the tears from his eyes: 'I haven't got one of those in my collection yet . . . Does she have a green card?'

'My colleague, Attorney Gobetti, says that she has not only her green card but passports from three or four different countries. Is that good enough for you?'

'Oho! What is she – a con artist?'

'No more than you, my dear man!'

The policeman walked up to them and politely hinted that there was a time and place for everything. The prisoners had been brought to the park to work.

'Do me a favour, officer. Give me another three minutes or so,' Robinson said, clapping him on the shoulder.

'Three – and not one minute longer.' The cop walked away.

'What's more important to you right now, Mr Harry, romance or material well-being?'

'A ridiculous question!'

'Then get married in as rational a fashion as you would enter any legal transaction advantageous to both sides.'

'And what's she getting out of this? You couldn't expect a cocks-man like me to make her less lonely.'

The lawyer grinned. 'I would guess that that's not a priority with her. The deal is that her late husband left her a huge inheritance that she's unable to collect.'

'Wow. And I can help her?'

'If everything works out the way Attorney Gobetti and I are planning.'

'Hey, Charlie, you're hot today!' Kharya shouldered his rake in pretence of going back to work. 'You know, though, I sometimes have trouble expressing myself in English. Somehow I still don't quite get it.'

'It's all simple! So, we'll get you married, then!'

'Maybe I could just get a peek at the old lady, first?'

'Listen up, Mr Harry! This is a *biz-in-niss* marriage!'

'What – don't you even have a snapshot of her?'

Men have become very sentimental in this day and age: they want to have a look at their brides before they get married. But Robinson just ignored it.

'We have to be quick, Harry . . . Here's the judge's leave to go. He said, "Marriage is a serious business," and signed a 48-hour release for you in connection with personal circumstances. On Saturday night you're obliged to go back to gaol until your trial. If you're late, that automatically adds time on to your sentence.'

'So you should have said that right away! When are we getting married?'

'Immediately!'

The policeman, displeased, had come back and was already standing there in readiness to take Kharya away, but the lawyer handed him the court order. Then Robinson dragged his cell phone out of his pocket, fingered the buttons and was connected to Gobetti in Sacramento. 'My client's ready, Tony. Get to work!'

8

I've already bored the reader with my tales of lectures and students. It's nothing new: everyone in the world lectures people, if not in the university, then in the kitchen. It's better to get it in the kitchen because they'll wine and dine you. But I'll take that risk one more time – no escape.

A student of mine, Maximus Tibb, half Mexican, half something else, a former soldier, comes to lectures by day while working at night at the Kaiser (which is to say, in a hospital) as an assistant pharmacist. The hospital pharmacist mixes the potions that they give internally to their seriously ill patients, while Maximus takes them around the various wards on a trolley, helping the nurses hang the solution-filled bags on the IV stands. Tibb speaks all known languages, apparently, and mixes them all up the way potions get mixed for the patients.

'And when do you sleep?' I asked him, one day.

'I got enough sleep in the army' was his answer.

'How's that?'

'I slept in the barracks for two solid years when I was serving in the Mexican army. But a soldier's pay there isn't very much at all, so I transferred to the American army. There I slept for another three years in an armoured transport vehicle during my training, so during the time of my army service I slept enough for the rest of my life.'

Stern reality, however, didn't support his claim to have slept enough: having worked the night through at Kaiser, Tibb would sit sleepily in class, fixing a rabbity gaze on me, since he was getting only three or four hours of sleep a day. Most likely he was dozing with his eyes open. It wasn't so awful that he was sleeping in class: the army pays for the education of all their ex-soldiers but not for their lodging, food, textbooks or amusements – they have to earn that money for themselves.

I was lecturing on Karamzin's *Poor Liza* one Friday morning, gazing on my dozing student with dissatisfaction. Even in a good translation, it's hard for Americans to understand the exceedingly simple point of it: 'Even peasant women know how to love.'

In this thought lies an entire stratum of the history and culture of an unknown country. And the living subtext slips away. It's better not to get involved in a discussion of it – I know this from experience: everything reduces down to the notion that city women have more access to information and know more methods. One can, though, as my students suggest, substitute for the peasant woman a queen, a prostitute or a dog, and the formula remains correct, eternal and valid for any circumstance.

After the lecture, evidently out of association with it, Maximus walked up to me and said: 'One of our female patients sends you greetings. Her name is Lily Bourbon.'

'She's in hospital?'

'In Kaiser, where I work.'

'What's wrong with her?'

'Nothing serious. She's just had a pacemaker put in. She's a great poetess, for all times and peoples, and I'm helping her. I translate the thoughts that she utters . . .'

That should have been expected! Like all self-confident personages, Lily had an ability to use people, to make them work for her – a trait typical of all leaders and celebrities. In the meantime, people don't think that they're doing good for her but that she's doing good for them. Thus she'd roped in Maximus to run errands for her, and he took great pride in her trust.

Want it or not, Lily had become a presence in my life. As a friend of mine said, among émigrés you don't make friends with whom you want but with whoever is around. I went back to my office, as always buying a paper cup of coffee on the way. Some students sat waiting at my door, but first I got the number of the hospital from the directory and dialled it. The operator, after asking for her name, put me through to the ward.

'Who told you that I was in here?' Lily said sternly.

'A student of mine passed on your greetings.'

'I never asked him to do that! On the contrary, I forbade him to say a word to anyone at all about my being in this hospital. Bear this in mind: I am never ill!'

'Understood. If you're well, then – goodbye!'

'Stop! Since you were so quick to ask after me, I have a little request for you. Could you come visit me at the hospital, dear heart? My lawyer is coming, and he always puts me out of sorts. And last night he left a message on my answering machine: "Madame, I have some news that could turn out to be a very welcome surprise."'

'But what does this have to do with me, Lily?'

'The lawyer assures me that he understands a bit of Russian, says his grandmother was from Odessa, but I don't trust him . . . This business is vitally important. Don't leave me in the lurch!'

I was intending to resist, but the Bourbon lady begged so hard I had to give in.

Through the crack of the partly open door I could see Lily putting lipstick on with a finger, so I waited to let her finish this important procedure. In the ward I was greeted by the joyful barking of a white fluffy little dog with protuberant eyes.

'An American woman has everything: a husband and a dog and a computer,' Lily explained. 'But I didn't have any of that – not a husband or a computer or a dog. That's why I acquired Poopsik.'

In hospital – with a dog? Only Lily Bourbon could have talked the doctors into letting her Poopsik stay with her. All the rules are against such a thing, but an exception always gets made for Lily for some reason.

She pressed a button on the control, and her bed turned into an armchair. The beds in American hospitals! They carry you around, shift you from one side to another; they're ready to turn on the television for you, to give you a telephone or a table for your food. You're surrounded with sensors like a cosmonaut, and in order to operate a bed like that you have to undergo minimum instruction at a cot-riding school, so to speak.

'See that? I couldn't get to drive a car, but at least I'm really confident at driving this bed.'

If Lily could joke around, it meant that she was still alive, at least.

'What happened?' I asked. 'How are you feeling?'

'Don't ask a woman untactful questions. Terrible! Now, instead of saying "I love you with all my heart," I have to say "I love you with all my pacemaker." How could I be feeling? Nothing but the aged all around me, while I want to be with the youngsters . . . You'd be better telling me this, though. Didn't you once live in Texas? What's the weather like there?'

Had she called me in just to talk about the weather in Texas?

'The weather there's fine,' I answered. 'It's the people who have trouble with the heat.' And I had opened my mouth to begin my explanation of the sensation of being beef on the barbecue when Lily interrupted:

'What an awful lot I've had to settle for in my life! I never had any luck in the Silver Age. I came into my own only in the Soviet one. Not long ago I was insulted in the *Literary Gazette*; they called me the "grandmother of socialist realism". A while ago I would have just made a phone call and the editor would have been taken away. But what now – am I supposed to just take it? Or sue them?'

Despite her illness, Lily was on her hobbyhorse. So many people of her generation would have been proud of that title – but not her. It was hardly the phrase 'socialist realism' that was rousing her ire, though: most likely it was the word 'grandmother'.

'To hell with them, Lily! Why should you have to spend your life in court, feeding lawyers?'

She seized on my words: 'Right, right! My lawyer's coming right now; I'll introduce you as my oldest friend. Help me figure out what it is he wants. He called me here, in the ward, and was talking about something hairy.'

Tony Gobetti walked into the ward, plopped his briefcase down on the floor next to the bed and pronounced in his ridiculously accented Russian: '*Zdoh-roh-ven-kee boo-lee*! But of course mine Russian expressivenesses has its limits.'

'You see?' Madame Bourbon remarked delightedly. 'How glibly he slings our bat!'

'Sling what where?' said the lawyer in confusion.

'Let's speak English,' I suggested.

Red already from the exertion of his attempts to remember his Russian expressivenesses, Tony was overjoyed: he let out his breath in a rush and firmly shook my hand.

I don't want to say anything negative about the likeable Gobetti, but lawyers put me off. The American system of jurisprudence has achieved perfection – and seems to be the chief pursuit of the populace. One half of Americans are either constantly or periodically suing the other half for major or minor causes, so business in the legal profession is plentiful.

And the lawyers themselves are out looking energetically for reasons to sue whomever they can. For example, in a respectable department store, an automatic door closed too quickly and whacked a lawyer somewhere lower than his back but higher than his legs. As a result, he had a pain in the region. No sort of the most modern medical apparatus could prove that he didn't have a pain there. That meant that he did have a pain there, and consequently the store had to pay out a million and a half dollars to the victim as compensation for his discomfort.

It would seem that there's nothing so efficacious as a lawsuit. The lawyer wrangles for 30 per cent of your future money. I once met an attorney who said that he would sue himself if there was any big money in it. On one occasion I tried suing someone, too, but I've promised myself never to do it again in my life.

The new house that we'd just moved into filled up with water. Out of spite, a construction worker who'd been fired for lack of conscientiousness sneaked into our nearly completed house and hammered a nail into the water main in between the ground floor and the first storey. The insurance company messed me around for a long time with their own mighty lawyers, outwitted me and never paid a thing. I gave up. God forbid you ever get stuck in a lawsuit and spend the rest of your life in it. Surely Lily wasn't going willingly into the mousetrap for a piece of cheese?

Gobetti's tale of Kharya took nearly twenty minutes to relate, while I translated precisely for Lily. It was clear that Kharya was a true hero of all times and climes.

'I don't quite understand what this has to do with me,' said Lily.

'His aim is to marry you,' the lawyer summed up artlessly and, winking at me, added: 'He's read every one of your books and considers you the greatest poetess of our age.'

Wow, what a compliment! No mistake. Madame Bourbon stayed silent for a long while, her eyes and evidently the cogs of her brain as well spinning around.

'Is this fellow divorced or a widower? Ah, divorced! That's even better. Usually men are so lazy that they're too lazy to leave the women who are patently unsuited for them and just call that family life. If God had made me a man, I'd be changing my woman every day. But what good is this fellow to me? I'm not a girl, after all, to jump on the neck of the first man to come along, much less when he's not even in front of me!'

'He's already swapped around enough women to have beggared himself,' said Tony. 'Madame, this marriage, putting it more precisely, would be a business one. A partnership to your mutual advantage.'

Her eyebrows rose. 'What in heaven's name does that mean?'

Gobetti looked at her in some surprise: 'After all, your husband, Ken Stemp, left you his money for the construction of socialism, didn't he? A client of a colleague of mine in Texas has some property which he is unable to realize, and you have money that you are unable to obtain. And Mr Leah-Peed-Air – I hope I'm pronouncing his name correctly – is a major Soviet theoretician of that very same socialism. He knows everything there is to know about where, how, and with what aim it is to be constructed . . . Do you catch my drift?'

'Curious,' Lily pronounced, deep in thought. 'Nobody on earth has a clue about it, but he's an expert . . .'

'But you aren't actually going to be constructing socialism,' I muttered to her as fast as I could in Russian, so the lawyer wouldn't pick up on it. 'You've said so before . . .'

'Shhh . . .' she pressed her finger against her lips. 'You're missing the point, dummy. Some Russian Communists have already been on to me here, promising posthumous glory and even a plaque on the Kremlin wall if I aid them with money. But I'm alive and well! If I got any money, I'd be able to buy myself a plot alongside the Lenin Mausoleum myself, without them. Let my lawyer explain to his Leahpeedair, Leapeedore or whatever it is: no money of any kind until he's married to me!'

The lawyer waited patiently while I translated for him what she'd said and merely nodded as a sign of agreement.

'But, once we're married,' she asked unexpectedly, 'I won't lose the right to my husband's money? You're certain?'

So Lily was even more practical than one could have expected.

'Of course not!' Tony said, soothing her. There's nothing about any subsequent marriage in your late spouse's will. You're entirely free in your choice of a new partner.'

She hesitated for a moment.

'OK. To hell with it! I'll risk it.'

'With your eyes closed?' ripped out of me.

'My heart!' said Lily, smiling condescendingly, 'You mustn't fail to understand a woman to such a degree. Everything is separate for me: I was always able to be wife to one man, to love another one, and to have sex with yet a third. But that's not everything. My greatest pleasure comes not from men – only trouble from them – but from the satisfaction of my own ambition.'

I scrutinized her with admiration. 'So what about your plans to dance with the president at your hundredth birthday?'

'Eh, young man! What nonsense is that – a pensioner dancing with the president? Anyway, as I discovered, hundred-year-olds have gotten so common in America that they've stopped inviting them to the White House. The most important thing is that I'm not forgotten. In order to do that, I have constantly to attract attention to myself. In the given situation I will be realizing certain hopes, and after that I can meet with presidents. There's lots of them and just one of me.'

'My Texas colleague, Charlie Robinson, suggests that it's easier to register the property of his client in Mexico,' said Tony. 'But it won't be easy to find the necessary people there.'

'I've got the necessary person, in fact,' said Lily, stroking Tony's elbow.

'Really? Who?'

'A businesslike fellow from Mexico. He's called Rodrigo Gonzalez. He can do everything there!'

'Hmmm. Put me in touch with him,' requested Tony.

Gonzalez came tearing into the hospital almost as soon as Lily phoned him. You could only admire his nose for money. His ostrich-skin cowboy boots scuffed along the quiet ward, a wide smile spread his moustache. Rodrigo knocked back his huge white sombrero with a jerk, and it hung on his back. His long black hair was tied back with a rubber band.

After hearing all about the impending wedding, Gonzalez got excited and, to the amazement of the lawyer, immediately turned to Lily and switched from English to Russian without any problem: 'Congratulations, kid! You've caught this one on the hop. I've always said you're irresistible; there's not a randy man who can resist you.'

He guffawed, pleased with his witticism. Gobetti explained the situation to him.

'I'm catching your thoughts on the hop. An ownerless island was born in the Rio Bravo? Brilliant! A gift from Daddy Nature . . . That is, in Russian I'd have to say "Mommy", ha ha. Double congratulations, madame. Such affairs should be taken care of exclusively in my homeland! I know some folks in Nuevo Laredo. But since the affair smells like big money, it'll be necessary to dig deep for the property registration. Nothing for me – I'm an absolutely unselfish man. You're going to have to slip something to the local bureaucrats, though – OK?'

'I'm afraid of illegalities,' Tony said, his face contorted.

'What other way out is there?' Lily stared at him in expectation, while I translated. 'Don't stop when you're halfway there!'

Rodrigo nodded at this sign of support.

'So here's how it is,' he pronounced gravely. 'Amity is the most important thing on earth. Lily's the sort of creature that only a terrible swine would not give help to. I'll fly there with you – you won't get anywhere there without me. In Mexico they'll just fleece you, be sure of that, and you'll be left with nothing at all. Now I'll explain to the lawyer how it's done there.'

Rodrigo put his arm round Tony and herded him into a corner of the ward, sitting him down on a chair, where he began to expound a strategy for the operation. Tony listened and nodded in silence.

My student Maximus loomed in the doorway in his white smock, and asked: 'Lily, how can I help you?'

'Maxik,' she entreated. 'I need to get out of this hospital lickety-split. Could you run along and take care of my release form?'

Maximus nodded and, like a well-schooled butler, hurtled away to carry out her instruction.

Madame Bourbon turned her gaze on me and asked: 'Well, sceptic, what are you so gloomy about?'

'This isn't my affair, at all,' I mouthed to Lily in a whisper. 'But aren't you afraid that you'll get caught up in something illegal? Here in the States they take a dim view of . . .'

'My dear! I have gone through fire, water, trumpets of sounding brass, and Soviet life. What do I have to fear, at my age? A life without risk is like soup without salt. You have to go for it!'

That was the moment of Lily's return to health. Unlike men, who perish under the wheels of life as simply as a dog, women (I noticed this a long time ago) have nine lives, like a cat. They might be dying that night, but next morning they're ready to clamber up Mount Everest. Even with a pacemaker stitched in next to their heart.

9

In California they tell a story about how a fellow is walking on the beach, praying, and he blurts out: 'O God, could you at least grant me one of my wishes!'

Suddenly the clouds open up over his head, and God pronounces in a thunderous voice: 'I know that you try to believe in me and follow my commandments. So, in order for you not to have any doubts about Me, I will grant you one of your requests. What do you need?'

The man thinks, and then says: 'Build me a bridge from California to Hawaii, so I can drive to the Hawaiian Islands in my car whenever I want.'

God frowns, and says: 'A bridge to Honolulu? Huh! Your wish is way too materialistic. Just think what kind of overhead that would be – how much concrete, how much metal would go into it! And how much labour! Do you have any idea of the length of a bridge like that? Yes, it's within my power to do that, but surely you have a request that's more spiritual, more important for a human being?'

The guy scratches his head for a bit. 'Lord,' he utters at last, 'I would like to understand women. What do they feel? What do they think about when they're not talking? Why do they cry? What does it mean when they don't say anything? Explain to me how I can make them happy!'

God splutters and chokes, rocks back and forth for a bit on his cloud, sighs heavily, and asks: 'You want two-lane or four-lane traffic on that bridge?'

Whenever I think about Lily, that joke hits me in the head like a nail. Madame Bourbon somehow talked my wife Valerie and me into being witnesses at her wedding. And she'd talked God around, too: he was building her a bridge to Mexico.

So now we were flying with Lily and her lawyer, Tony Gobetti, on a Southwest Airlines flight to Laredo, that place where so recently Kharya had driven in such a hurry in his old Chevy. Tony had phoned his wife in Puerto Vallarta to tell her and Lizzie to fold their tents and fly there, too, at once.

We sat next to each other in the plane, and it was evident that Lily, despite her invariable external self-assurance, was agitated. On the way she kept elaborating on how I was to introduce her.

'Just don't forget! Everything could get spoiled if you let things slide.'

'I swear I won't forget! I'm to say: "Here before you is the foremost poet of modern times" – all right?'

'After that add "world famous", "incomparable" and then – since it's completely appropriate as well – "charming". You won't get that all mixed up?'

'I'll remember it for the rest of my life.'

'You're probably thinking: How prudent she is!'

'Not a bit! You're being carried along by circumstances. The émigré life is a complex thing . . .'

'What do you think,' she said, looking up at the sloping ceiling for some reason. 'Will Ken be mad at me for cheating on him?'

Ken Stemp had been a nice, kind and naive man. It hadn't been a year since he'd died. But now I got the strange feeling that Ken was here somewhere. Could he be flying with us? I even looked out of a porthole at the pink clouds, as if the spirit of my ex-student could have been accompanying us in some materialized way. Stupid? But the fact that the late Ken was distressing Lily was making me think.

'If he can hear,' I said, 'then he'll forgive you and even approve of this step. Surely he wants you to be settled down.'

'I'm not so sure. God forbid that you turn out to be wrong.'

'Lily, how come you've never had any children?' asked Valerie, to change the subject.

'You don't need a lot of brains to have children,' answered

Madame Bourbon, smirking. 'But never once in your life to get pregnant and never get a single abortion – that's already legendary, there's a whiff of bronze monument about that.'

I was seized with laughter, and Valerie jammed her fist into my side. 'Pay no attention,' she apologized. 'All men are tactless . . .'

Lily frowned. Was she really offended, in truth? It occurred to me that she wanted somehow to justify herself. But in what?

'I have always wanted to build my nest only at the top of the tree,' she said. 'But up there it sways, and watch out you don't get blown off. There was glory there, yes, but my family life was neither good nor bad, ever . . . Maybe it'll work out, now.'

Wow! Had all the grandiose fulfilment of her ambition really come down to a nest on a branch, as with any normal woman? She was being modest, coming down to the level of us poor sinners . . . She wanted to be understood and supported.

'I have a feeling,' I said, 'that your opportunities are limitless.'

'Nonsense, my friend! Old age isn't fashionable now. Even for women like me there are limits to dreams. You can't live on the third floor of a two-storey building . . .'

Thus, in peaceable discussion, we landed at the airport in Laredo, Texas. Attorney Gobetti, sitting in the row ahead of us – I couldn't tell if he understood any of our conversation in Russian – glanced around at us occasionally, as if to see whether Madame Bourbon had vanished into thin air or not. The plane's engines had scarcely fallen silent when Gobetti whipped his cell phone out of a pocket and dialled Robinson.

'Our plans have gotten somewhat more detailed,' said Tony, switching off from Robinson. 'We'll take a taxi and head from the airport to a hotel over in Nuevo Laredo. It's real close to here, in Mexico. Robinson and Mr Harry are already waiting for us there.'

'But there's no way I can go straight there!' Lily resisted. 'I have to fix myself up.'

'Oh, don't worry!' agreed Tony. 'The best room in the place has already been booked for you.'

At the baggage carousel they brought her the cage with Poopsik, who was whimpering, and, as soon as they let him out of it, he jumped up and licked her on the cheek.

It was getting dark, but the stuffy heat hadn't decreased. The Mexican taxi-driver skilfully wound through the streets and rolled out on to Highway 35, heading for the border.

Laredo turned out to be a slovenly little border town, built without rhyme or reason and similar to all the other settlements on both sides of the Mexican border. Right now, as I write down the details of our adventure, I'm looking at a Funk and Wagnall's encyclopaedia, from which I understand that Laredo is an industrial centre; they make mattresses there.

We looked out of the windows in silence; sitting in Lily's lap, even Poopsik's eyes were darting everywhere – it looked as though the dog was reading the advertising along the road.

Highway 35 came to an end, and the road came to a huge bridge across the Rio Grande. Fleeting warnings to reduce our speed at the border flashed past. The driver asked for three dollars to pay the toll. The wheels whickered for a long time on the seams of the bridge. Because of the concrete walls we couldn't see the river. Some empty border-control booths – and there we were in Mexico.

The oncoming lane was full of vehicles, mostly trucks: the American customs service inspected them unhurriedly on their way in.

The Mexican town of Nuevo Laredo isn't much different from the old Laredo on the Texas side of the border, which is not surprising, since they're divided by the river but joined up by the bridge, across which streams of vehicles and pedestrians move hither and thither twenty-four hours a day.

Again outside the window arose a picture as familiar as in the Russian provinces: people just sitting around their houses, looking at the passers-by and idly talking. In this sense, the loafers who spend the entire day on the benches on Grant Street are just a reflection of morals acquired genetically. You don't see anything like that among native-born Americans – or Yankees, at least. A day off is sheer idleness; do-nothingness is a life's goal that's unacceptable to the Yankee. He drives his car into his garage, spares his neighbour a word or two – 'Hi, how's it going?' – and, sometimes not even waiting to hear the pat response, goes straight into his house.

Even an American who's exhausted by physical labour, after coming home and having dinner, will mow the lawn (so his house doesn't look any worse than anyone else's), fly a kite with the children, or maybe watch baseball on television while he sternly pedals away on his exercise bike. No benches around outside to lounge on. There's nothing to bite off and spit out, either: sunflower seeds are sold shelled; they put them straight into their salads. Old ladies chewing the fat with their neighbours – that's the way it is in Russia and here among the Mexicans. We love to envy others and bemoan our own fate.

An American is not simply a resident of his own home, that he will sooner or later sell, most likely, either moving away or retiring – because his house is his financial capital for his old age. This capital stands on a street, and when somebody buys a house they pay close attention to the street and to the neighbouring houses. The English word 'neighbourhood' has all the meaning of a whole range of words in Russian: 'surroundings', 'locality', 'district', 'vicinity' – and all of them can be translated as 'neighbourhood', too. So this word in America is a quality of the medium of residence, in other words, your level, status – that is, what your value is in the milieu of other people.

If your house has a bad appearance, an unpainted façade, for instance, or an unmown lawn and untrimmed hedge or an absence of flowering plants – you're going to lower the value of your neighbours' homes, of the whole neighbourhood. In certain American cities, if the local authorities notice any sort of mess in front of your house, you get a letter requesting you to cut your grass; if you can't do it yourself, they'll send a gardener and a bill for his services.

Striking, I thought, looking at the streets of Nuevo Laredo: these same untidy Mexicans are the very ones who work in America as gardeners, where they introduce beauty. In truth, cobblers without a shoe . . .

The taxi came to a stop in front of a hotel with a somewhat twisted but ornate red sign, gleaming in the twilight: *La Hacienda*.

In the half-lit lobby Rodrigo Gonzalez was already sitting on a sofa in front of a dim orange floor lamp, sucking on a margarita through a straw and artlessly, almost childishly, smiling. It turned out that he wore the Mexican sombrero only in America; here, it had disappeared. Catching sight of us, he jumped up and gallantly kissed Lily's hand.

'Congratulations once again!' There wasn't the slightest innuendo to be heard in his voice. 'Today's your big day, kid. I've already acquainted myself with your bridegroom-to-be. He's an extraordinary personage, a great talent. In Mexico he could become the leader of the Trotskyites. He and I downed a bottle of tequila, and he stole away to his room for a snooze before the wedding. His attorney also went off to his room, with his beauty.'

Rodrigo lit up a thin cigar. This *nouveau* Mexican (what else could you call him?) felt himself to be in complete charge here.

'Tony, my boy,' commanded Lily dryly, as if she had already received her inheritance, 'take care of this business – it's your parish.'

'I've already made arrangements for your marriage ceremony,' Rodrigo hurried to inform her. 'You're not Catholics, either of you. An official from the municipality will come here for the beginning of the wedding, in a couple of hours.'

'Two hours is enough for us to put ourselves in order, isn't that so, girls?'

Having said this, Madame Bourbon, Poopsik gathered into her arms, headed off for the stairway, while Valerie explained the situation to the Russianless Jennifer. She and Lizzie had flown in before us. Everyone had assembled now at Hotel La Hacienda, and we were gradually gravitating to our own rooms.

'Well, and how about that other issue?' Tony asked Gonzalez.

'Everything has already been explained to your colleague, Robinson. He and Mr Harry think that the issue can be considered taken care of. Only one obstacle came up at the municipality.'

'What, exactly?'

'The border between Mexico and the USA goes down the middle of the river. Thus, formally one half of the island is ours, the other half American. Only our half of the island can be registered here.'

'And the other?'

'Fortunately, the border is not very definite, and the Americans don't pay any attention to such minor details; so Madame Bourbon – with her husband, naturally – can have the use of the entire territory of the island. But for the registration of the deal, the money has to be in advance and only cash, preferably in new banknotes. Robinson has already paid.'

Gobetti, disconcerted, let out a little grunt. 'Hmmph.'

'You settle it with him yourself – he's your friend, after all. My end is entirely friendly service, for free.'

Rodrigo smiled amicably and clapped Tony on the shoulder. 'I'll get to the restaurant and see if they've forgotten anything. Mexicans are absent-minded people,' he added, winking at me. 'Like the Russians . . .'

Tony opened his briefcase and starting looking over some sort of documents. I waved a hand at him and went up to my room.

Valerie was sleeping. All I had left to do was arrange myself alongside for a snooze before the night's revelry.

10

I was awakened by the orchestra playing at a deafening level in the courtyard. My wife, as it happened, had already arisen and was sprucing herself up. I opened the window a bit. The smell of grilling meat and spices was carrying into the room on the light breeze. Downstairs, in the square of the courtyard, the party was gathering steam.

The sky had turned dark blue, stars had come out. Garlands of coloured lights played in the trees. A pianist and a drummer were madly rumbling on a tiny stage. Guitarists were strolling around the little tables, wooing the first guests with the sobbing of their strings, extorting recompense. It was time to go downstairs.

Everything would have been top class if it hadn't been for the stuffy heat that made you gasp open-mouthed like a fish washed ashore. Women were in evening clothes. Gold gleamed on their necks and wrists. Tony introduced me to his colleague Robinson and the latter to his cheery girlfriend Lizzie. Lizzie shone in a black outfit, open at the back all the way down, and in front – I'm too embarrassed to say down to what. In short, eye-catching. Diamonds gleamed on Jennifer, drawing attention away from her protruding belly.

Decked out in a snow-white suit with a raspberry handkerchief in his breast pocket, Rodrigo was reminiscent of a soap-opera star. For the ritual occasion, both attorneys, Robinson and Gobetti, were arrayed in similar dark-grey suits and even identical black shoes, of the type that a friend of mine calls 'accountants''. They resembled secret-service agents, lending significance to the undertaking. About myself and my wife I won't say anything; we were there just as witnesses.

Rodrigo began circling around Lizzie, suggesting that a Mexican was better for a Mexican girl than any black man from Texas. But Robinson threatened him with a finger, and Gonzalez had to back off.

Only one person was mooching around without finding himself a mooring. His corpulent body was suffering from the heat; it was arrayed in a coat and tails, rented overnight from a neighbouring shop. The suit had seen numerous clients already. The coat sat on Kharya like a saddle on a cow. Kharya was trying to smile, but that was reminiscent of a grimace – one that he would wipe off his face now and again along with streams of sweat, with a huge handkerchief like a beach towel. But the grimace would reappear. He was walking up to one person after another: they would greet him and then continue their conversations among themselves. He made as if to force himself on Lizzie, but she pretended not to recognize him.

So now I introduced myself to this Superfluous Man.

'Listen,' said Kharya. 'Let's not stand on idiotic formalities.'

He did in fact appear to be an interesting conversationalist, and right off the bat he was looking for a like mind in me. Only a single defect of his came to light, one that I, even with all my patience acquired over the years, find it hard to endure. Kharya was a skilful conversationalist, but he was devoid of any ability to stop. He was already in his cups, fountaining out ideas with the endlessness of a Möbius strip.

All that was missing was the leading lady. Giggling, everyone waited for Lily to appear.

At Rodrigo's command the orchestra struck up a march. I was sure that it was Madame Bourbon herself who had instigated that – who else? She appeared at the top of the stairs, her back as ceremoniously straight as a guitar fingerboard, and everyone fell silent. Her bosom in the enormous décolletage of her white wedding gown towered higher than a sex-bomb's, supported by God-only-knows what. Around her neck was the obligatory unbelievable quantity of beads. Now and again she would stumble on the carpeting on her inconceivably high heels; but she walked with her left hip thrust forward, like a model on the best of Parisian catwalks.

The female form has an aura, a sort of call-sign signal or radiation.

Magnetism hides in every woman (I'm not sure where), although certain of them don't sense its presence in them, are not able to manage it and don't at all use it in any way, losing out on a lot in life. But then others do know how to manipulate this radiation, focusing it in a definite direction, usually on an individual of the opposite sex.

Evidently some women use this magnetism on men more strongly, others less so, but in contradiction to widespread opinion I think that this magnetism is unconnected with any beauty of the face, figure or soul. A pimply young airhead can turn out a dozen times more talented than a cold doll with legs up to her armpits who's just been made a Playboy centrefold.

And I'm even more certain that the magnetism that's given to every woman by nature, even though it might change its wavelength with age, never goes away. The unpractised girl or the old woman who has forgotten how it's done – they both carry in them a charge of mystery, and on them alone does it depend whether or not that charge is manifested. It's preserved in the body until the last gasp – maybe it extinguishes gradually as the body cools, or maybe even the magnetic soul floats off into space and after death calls men after it.

Maybe an exception will soon be made on this earth, if it hasn't already been made, by American women, the majority of them impetuously losing their feminine essence and more and more often now making themselves out to be manlike robots, smiling their white-toothed smiles. Flirtation and courting are now termed sexual harassment. The difference between the sexes is preserved only in that American men shave their faces, while the women shave their legs.

Lily Bourbon, despite the zigzaggings of her destiny, had remained a real woman her entire life, and now all eyes were magnetically attracted to her.

'There sure is something in that broad!' Kharya said to my surprise, rousing himself alongside me and whispering: 'I was thinking that even an old lady is a godsend in foreign parts. But she's in great shape.'

'And how!' I agreed, and immediately queried: 'But have you already met her?'

'I popped in on her as soon as you flew in. She had a headache, and I got rid of the pain for her. I'll try to rejuvenate her with sheer willpower – I know a couple of ways. She's agreed to it.'

That was something! The bride and groom had already hit it off. So our madame had already charmed him! We were being idiots to worry about it – this was all just put on; they were PR people.

'Here before you,' I started gabbling, remembering that I had a promise to carry out, 'is the foremost poet of modern times, world famous, incomparable . . .'

'Where were you earlier on?' Lily remarked calmly. 'This is already clear to everyone now.'

When and where had I been supposed to appear earlier?

A brisk grey little official of the Nuevo Laredo town municipality took Kharya by the hand like a backward child and led him over to Lily. Mr Khariton Lapidar began breathing heavily through his nose, like a bear stuck between two aspens. Where had his wits and determination gone all of a sudden?

If you like, the long and skinny bride and her groom, fat as Falstaff, made an entirely harmonious couple. The official made the newlyweds put their signatures in a heavy brown book with a coat of arms in relief and the legend 'Estados Unidos Mexicanos' on the cover. All that was left was for me and Valerie to sign in our capacity as witnesses.

And so the wedding feast began buzzing, in the courtyard of La Hacienda.

Nothing so loosens the tongue and takes away tension like tequila. And if you alternate it with lemonade and young red wine – don't forget the champagne – then life gets better right in front of your very eyes. You know yourself what's going to happen to you later on, but in the meanwhile – toasts to the bride, to the groom, to the both of them. Someone tactlessly proposed a toast to the not-so-distant hundred years of life of one of those present.

196

'Why limit it to that?' countered the bride.

The familiar invocatory tones of the bandoneon summoned us to the highlight of the programme – a *cumparsita* tango. Rodrigo, jack-of-all-trades that he was, had thrust himself forward with the intention of demonstrating his prowess with Lily; but Kharya, raising his bulk in front of him, said tenderly: 'Keep your seat here, little fella. We'll manage by ourselves.'

And he led Lily off to dance. No spectacle was to be beheld, though – although the orchestra was trying with all its might and everyone was clapping encouragingly. Out of tiredness, or from the heat, they stopped after scarcely getting into it, and, standing in the middle of the dance floor, they were discussing something, maybe a five-year plan for the construction of socialism on an independent little island surrounded by capitalistic monsters. People started yelling 'Kiss! Kiss!' at them, but Lily just waved them off.

'Cut it out!'

And, after shedding a few tears, she went back to her seat.

As she walked past, Valerie handed her a tissue.

Noticing that we were watching out for her, Lily said: 'I've gotten a bit susceptible as I come up to a hundred.'

I recalled that she had also been crazy about Ken Stemp, saying at the time that she had just fallen in love for real for the first time in her life. After everything that she'd lived through, why not have another 'first-in-my-life' love?

That's the truth, though, surely: even old ladies know how to love. It only takes . . . Well, what does it take? A neighbour of mine had to put herself in an old folks' home, but even there she dressed and dolled herself up every night, telling everyone she was going off to do some dancing, even though she hadn't been anywhere for a long time, since she hadn't had the use of her legs in over ten years. What was most important in the life of Madame Bourbon?

'I'm all over impatient,' she whispered to me. 'After all, Khariton has told me that the island could be an independent country – do you know what that smells of? Of course, the issue is who's to be its leader. Oooh, that is something to dream about!'

Lily's ability to enter into a role and instantly take up a privileged place in any given situation continued to astonish me, possibly because I am entirely lacking in self-confidence. And then it occurred to me – with surprise but not a trace of envy – that I had never had a wedding ceremony of my own. This was already Lily's second wedding in just this one year, not counting any hanky-panky of hers on the side.

The groom had scored tolerably well, which was inspiring him to new verbal feats. Kharya's corpulent body was moving slower, his cheeks flushed and chubby – it seemed he was eating, drinking and talking simultaneously. He rose, hanging on to the back of Lily's chair with one hand, a champagne glass full of tequila in the other.

'G-g-guss-pah-DAH!' he bellowed in Russian.

No one paid him any attention, and he had to tap on his glass with a knife to get the orchestra and the chatter all around to quieten down.

'GEN-tle-mennnnn! Al-looo-wwww meeee to pro-pooooohse a tooo-ooast.'

Kharya rocked back but kept his balance. A pause ensued. But now – professional lecturer and experienced scientific demagogue that he was – he gathered himself together and began to orate in Russian as if he'd had only the tiniest bit to drink and that only for Dutch courage.

'An elderly couple, man and wife, lived long and happily and died within hours of each other. And because these were good people, they went to heaven. God greeted them and took them to a palace: "This shall be where you dwell." "And how much do we have to pay per month for this palace?" said the husband. "You don't pay anything – you're in heaven, after all." They came out of the palace, and at the grand entrance was parked a brand-new Cadillac. "This is your car," said God. "And the price?" asked the husband. "Free of charge." Then God took them to eat in a chic restaurant. After dining, the husband asked how much he was to pay for the meal, and God again answered: "Nothing, I tell you! Haven't I already explained: everything in heaven is for free." The husband turned to his wife: "There, see! If it hadn't been for your damned diet we would have fetched up here ten years ago!" '

'Bravo!' Lily was the first to say and clapped her hands.

Those who spoke Russian were amused and buzzed away at translation for those who didn't. Kharya raised his glass on high to signal that he hadn't finished yet. Waiting till the laughter died, he said: 'You have already understood what I want to say, hopefully. I haven't got a clue what's going to happen to me after I die, whether I'll go to heaven or hell; but you have all gathered together here to be assured of this: I – that is, Lily and I – are going to build a little heaven here on earth. I give you my word! Let's drink to that!'

The gathering applauded feebly. Kharya kissed his wife. She was radiant. Then he knocked back a glassful of vodka, which Lily followed sadly with her eyes.

Another pause ensued. It was broken by a strange, shrill sound, as if a string had broken somewhere in the square of sky over the restaurant or the wind had begun to howl in a loft. The lights went out, came on again and began blinking the way they do in a strong wind; the bulbs glowed at half-power. I felt a pain in my ears, like when a car is driving high up in the mountains or a plane climbs sharply. It continued for a minute or maybe two.

'Oh Lord – Ken has appeared . . .' Lily muttered in prayer. Her face had turned deathly pale.

'You're not well? You're just tired. You're imagining it . . .'

'No! It's him, Ken! I saw him! He glowed in the dark, right over there – I recognized him right away! He shook his finger at me and disappeared . . .'

Meanwhile the lights had come back to full power and weren't blinking any more.

Everyone had fallen silent or simply become hoarse from their exchanges, had drunk their fill and were beginning to disperse to their lodgings.

'Attention, please!' yelled Attorney Robinson to the entire group. 'We're meeting tomorrow morning in the lobby, at ten o'clock. We've rented a launch, and we're going to the island.'

The newlyweds were led off by the hand. To Kharya's honour, he managed on his legs better than I did.

Rodrigo flung a witticism after them: 'We aren't going to check the sheets in the morning!' His white jacket was stained in front with red wine.

I'm not going to relate how a 97-year-old woman did in bed. Kharya is an intelligent man and kept his own counsel, they hadn't needed any translator under the bed, and it would be hard for me to make anything up, owing to my own lack of experience in such alliances.

About two o'clock in the morning, Valerie dragged some man into our room. Me, apparently. She pulled off one of my shoes and left it on the nightstand. I declared that I could take off the other one myself, but the shoe had gone missing somewhere along the way. The sheet pulled over my head, I was asleep in an instant.

11

Nobody got much sleep. The impending trip dragged us to our feet early.

The morning, sunny and cool, began with a press conference. In the lobby young kids in orange T-shirts were uncoiling cables and fooling around. The local television station had heard of the event and was weighing in with all its ammunition.

The floodlights went on. The television camera passed over Lily from head to toe in the armchair where the producer had sat her. In her bright red dress Madame Bourbon looked altogether like a young woman – well, maybe a somewhat tired one.

She began talking, and I was going to translate, forgetting that the language here was Spanish. Rodrigo sprang to help. He hadn't studied in Tomsk – or was it Omsk? – in vain.

'It's a delusion,' Lily declared, 'that man produced woman from his own rib. God was just joking. As a matter of fact, it's well known to every person older than six years of age that woman produced man, and not at all from some rib but from a different place entirely.'

Off camera, the television people laughed soundlessly. It seemed like she was going to be a feminist theoretician, it occurred to me.

'At the age of thirty,' she continued, looking into the camera, 'I felt like an old woman. I looked at myself in the mirror and considered my life at an end. But now I'm ninety-seven, and life goes on, albeit with encumbrances. In contrast to the sluggish male, a woman just shrugs it off and can do this many times.'

'Lily, wouldn't you like to write a bestseller – *Secrets of Victory Over Men*?' enquired Jennifer. 'The American public just *adores* books like that. You'll sell a million . . .'

'Tell my secrets to everyone?' said Lily, shocked. 'No way! In my second youth I've become more selfish. Egoists, they say, are people who love themselves more than other egoists do. I talk nonsense out loud. But the secrets of victory over men – those are like the brand name of my perfume: they will depart this life together with me. I'm not about to head off to that world, however. A new life is starting for me, as you know . . .'

I don't know what sense any Mexican television viewers were making of the sight of Lily, but the idlers gathered in the lobby of the Hotel La Hacienda weren't going away.

The camera turned to Kharya, squeezed with difficulty into a narrow armchair next to Lily. Attorney Charlie Robinson introduced him to the estimable public.

'In front of you is Mr Leya-Pye-Der-der-der . . . I've finally learned how to pronounce his name right! He's a courageous Russian Columbus, the discoverer of a new island in the Rio Grande–Rio Bravo valley.'

Khariton Lapidar modestly inclined his head and added, pointing a finger first at one lawyer and then the other: 'Mr Charlie Robinson will be our Minister for Justice and Mr Tony Gobetti, our Attorney General.'

Charlie grinned, and Lizzie pressed herself against him, happy with the career of her boyfriend. Meanwhile she was making eyes at Tony – with his Marcello Mastroianni looks – whom she liked as well.

'Listen, little buddy: what kind of system are you going to have in your country?' asked Rodrigo, who had picked up a little something in his Soviet higher education.

'A republic, possibly,' Kharya came back swiftly. 'A republic in which full democracy will establish its absolute dictatorship.'

What a formula – streamlined and soft, like a drop of stearic acid that gets hard when it cools.

'No republics of any kind!' reacted Lily just as swiftly. 'I wish to be a queen.'

'Her Highness Lily the First,' one of the people in the crowd pronounced softly. But everyone heard it, and the buzzing began.

'Maybe it would be better anyway to have simply a democratic republic?' suggested the future Minister for Justice timidly.

'No sort of democracy; I'm already fed up to my back teeth with that. I need a throne. You just wait: I could still give birth to a prince.'

'But you're nearly a hundred!' Rodrigo blurted.

'Well, so what? Why do you think women get married? Life expectancy in America is growing; within ten years there'll be a million people here older than a hundred. If the medical techniques get perfected I'll be the first woman to give birth at that age. I'll bear an heir to the throne.'

'And its name? What are you going to call your country?'

'Very simple!' Kharya said, laying down his cards: 'It's a new island between two banks of the river, after all. Consequently, we will be the Kingdom of Grande-Bravo.'

'A socialist kingdom,' elaborated Attorney Gobetti. 'Otherwise nothing will be gained.'

'Without fail!' nodded Madame Bourbon, smiling.

Kharya thought quickly: 'We guarantee socialism,' he said, glancing at his new wife and theatrically slapping himself on the forehead. 'How could I forget? A crown of pure gold for my spouse.'

Out of his pocket he fetched a collapsible golden crown, like an oriental skullcap, that he'd surely purchased in a children's toy shop, put it on Lily's head and slipped the rubber band under her chin.

The assembly applauded.

'It really suits you,' I said.

'And how!' said Lily, with a smile.

Her golden crown, in which the camera lights were reflected, somewhat resembled the knob on top of a samovar, where you keep the pot with the brewed tea.

The camera lights went out. The station had ended the broadcast. The boys in their orange T-shirts started winding up the cables. The people who had just happened by dispersed. This didn't stop Kharya. He continued to develop his project but to me now. I liked everything that Kharya wanted to accomplish. Yes – he'd become even more fanatic than the addled Varvartsev who I mentioned. But, after all, the notion was coming to pass. The island was already there!

'All this dilatoriness is just trumpery,' he said, squeezing my elbow confidentially. 'Few are able to think on the level of the whole of humanity. My island is opening up broad horizons, touch wood. I've thought everything out. This land is nobody's. Do you remember the fighting with the Chinese for Damansky Island on the Amur River? I hope that everything goes peacefully here. We're not in Chechnya or Tartary. Not *inside* any country, so it's logical to be independent. Money is going to flow in fast. We'll start building; we'll look for oil. I'll declare us a Free Port – a free trading zone, like in Odessa back in the nineteenth century. Trade will take off.'

'And your start-up capital?' I asked, recalling the phrase, which had wandered into my lexicon from God alone knew where.

Kharya was ready with an answer. 'One American businessman has already promised me a hundred thousand dollars for development on the condition that he be the prime minister. You understand, everyone wants a ministership; nobody wants to dig in the dirt. There aren't enough to go around. I'm going to be prime minister and minister for defence. For now, my army consists of seven men, six of them generals and one of them a marshal. You have to promise your friends high rank, otherwise they won't come along, and after all an army is extremely necessary. Barbed wire – you and I know that – before anything else. The environs all around us are bourgeois.' The prime minister grinned.

'But it's an island, after all,' I said. 'That means water is what's all around it.'

'So what? My wife, you could say, is a yachtswoman by her former husband. We'll set up a navy.'

'And what kind of a uniform will you have done up as minister of defence? Are you going to be a marshal? Maybe you'd be better off a generalissimo?'

'I was thinking that,' Kharya admitted. 'But I haven't finally decided as yet. A uniform is necessary. Perhaps powder blue, with a wide sash across the shoulder – red.'

'Better the other way around,' I suggested. 'Jacket red, sash blue.'

'Not under any circumstances!' he cried in agitation.

So we nearly came to blows over the colour of his uniform. But it was made clear that I was very necessary to him.

'What for?' I enquired, cautiously curious.

'Get this,' said Kharya, embracing me around the shoulders. 'It'll take a long time to get the economy going. Tourism? You have to have something to show, and, except for the muddy river and garbage that's washed up out of it, there's nothing there, yet. Our revenue will come from educating foreigners. There'll be an international university. You'll give the lectures and write about the new country. What do you think?'

'I like it. I'll get to be the Keeper of the Court Annals – I'll have a high rank and maybe a uniform with a sash.'

'That's it! And when you're on top of things I'll appoint you the president of the Academy of Sciences. Or Minister for Culture . . .'

There we were, talking along those lines about the near future, when Lily plugged in to us.

'I've always dreamed of becoming a real queen!'

How could I have forgotten? Lily was, in numerological terms, a number seven. That made her a purposeful woman, making for her goal even through a briar patch. I only now paid attention to the fact that on her bosom dangled the tarnished medals of a laureate of the Stalin and Lenin prizes, the Order of Lenin and still more Soviet baubles of various kinds. Of course, in America they're sold at any flea market (I myself bought some for peanuts for some students), but those awards were her very own.

'I have a friend, a noteworthy artist,' recalled Kharya. 'He can paint canvases like Rembrandt, like the *Peredvizhniks*, like the Impressionists. It's only his own style that he doesn't have – after all, in his entire life in the USSR he painted only Lenin, and his imagination atrophied.'

'That's what I need!' Lily exclaimed. 'Call him up. Have him come at once. He'll do my portraits. For starters, he can paint me prancing on horseback – I dreamed I was doing that not long ago. If he's painted Lenin, then he could manage a horse, I dare say.'

I wanted to suggest something intelligent, to sound interesting in my capacity as the future president of the Academy of Sciences of the Kingdom of Grande-Bravo, but absolutely nothing came into my still-unsobered brain.

'And have you forgotten about me?' said Gonzalez, using the pause to insinuate himself into the debate.

'Rodrigo, my boy!' Lily said, turning to him. 'You're entitled to a nice little position, too.'

Rodrigo ran with it: 'Let's open a House of Culture – of completely ill repute, huh, kid? We'll bring in girls from Russia. All of South America will come charging up here to us . . . But if you want to hang on to power' – here he prodded Kharya in the chest with a finger – 'you, guy, are going to be needing a secret police. You won't find a better man than me to head it!'

'Have to think it over,' Kharya said, at a bit of a loss.

And now Gonzalez played his knight's gambit. 'I've prepared something for the assembly,' he said, and his eyes flashed. 'In Mexico we can do this – no problem.' He opened a black case with cipher locks and began passing out small green booklets to everyone assembled there.

I turned over what was handed to me and saw my own physiognomy on the photo; I read that I, a citizen of the Kingdom of Grande-Bravo, was a subject of Her Majesty Queen Lily the First. The stamp in the passport attesting to the incontrovertibility of this fact had a royal coat of arms that consisted of the profile of Queen Lily in a crown, enclosed in a laurel wreath.

'Everyone present,' announced the chief of the secret police, 'can freely come to the Kingdom of Grande-Bravo on this passport, without any visa. The visa fee is payable on site.'

He gave a command to two servitors, and they began raising a scarlet panel on the wall. Soon the Hotel La Hacienda was decorated with the slogan *Long Live Lily the First – the Mother of Her Kingdom, Grande-Bravo!*

The restaurant orchestra struck up the national anthem of the Kingdom of Grande-Bravo. It was a famous Mexican hit tune. Everyone began standing up. Faces turned to Lily.

'Long live Queen Lily the First!' cried Rodrigo. 'Hurray!'

'Hur-ra-a-a-y!' yelled everyone who was in the lobby, including the doorman.

They yelled so loud that the crystal pendants on the chandelier in the middle of the hall began tinkling.

'Hur-ra-a-a-a-a-a-a-y!' I bawled.

But then I heard Valerie's voice asking: 'What are you yelling hurray for? Let me sleep for another half-hour at least.'

12

After waking up, for real this time, I caught sight of my shoe on the night-stand. All I had to do was find the other. It awaited me in the corridor – moreover, it had been polished. The porter had found it and hauled it up.

In the crack under the door someone had thrust two little green booklets. Again I opened my new passport – this time in a waking state – but now I noticed a typographical error. In place of the Russian word *poddannym*, or 'subject' in the phrase 'is a subject of Her Majesty', there was now the word *poddatym*, meaning 'tipsy'. What he'd written was what Rodrigo had been taught in his youth in the Soviet Union.

It was a pity that they hadn't slipped us some of the currency of the new kingdom together with the passports, even a few hundred 'bourbons'. I could have exchanged the bourbons for dollars, the dollars for roubles and made my fortune.

Valerie and I went down to the lobby. Rain poured down outside the windows.

'You see what's getting up,' said the doorman to a departing hotel guest. 'They said on the radio that a cyclone is coming in from the Atlantic again.'

The Hotel La Hacienda had been plunged into gloom. There wasn't even a whiff of any sort of press conference. Who needed any damned television, anyway – hardly anybody could stand on their own two legs after the all the drinking. Some were crashed, some (I won't point any fingers) sullenly wandering in search of some hair of the dog, and some were fussily putting salad on their plates, hurrying to get some breakfast before they closed the buffet.

Two men were spruce in their ties and briefcases. Sitting in arm-chairs in the lobby, they were in patient expectation of a third. Robinson and Gobetti had long before discussed everything and were looking now at the entrance, now at their watches. The third man, that is, Rodrigo Gonzalez, had not yet appeared.

The driver of a little minibus at the entrance had opened his doors in expectation of clientele, but not a soul was sticking his nose out of the hotel.

Rodrigo appeared, not from off the street but from the courtyard where the rain was pouring down on stage and tables. He closed his umbrella, under which a puddle immediately formed, and took a seat across from the lawyers. He was dressed in a new denim suit and cowboy boots. Radiating a smile, he lit a cigarette and spoke after blowing a smoke ring.

'Everything is arranged, gentlemen.' He twirled his moustache with two fingers, to keep it out of his mouth. 'As proposed, it's better to do this without any witnesses. Here's the document from the municipality, to the effect that the property – the dimensions are not filled in – belongs to the spouse of Mr Harry, Madame Lily Bourbon. This is a Xerox copy; the original hasn't been issued yet.'

A pause set in. Both lawyers were deep in perusal of the document.

'The clincher, gentlemen,' Rodrigo resumed in the meanwhile, 'lies in the need to grease the palms of our benefactors.'

'Grease them with what?' asked Robinson.

Gonzales laughed loudly. 'This isn't America, here. Without the grease, no deal can be processed.'

It was Gobetti's turn first.

'How much more grease do they want?'

'Fifty thousand dollars . . . to give to the necessary people upstairs. The bureaucracy here isn't the same as in the States or Russia, but they've got to get theirs, too!'

'What, have they gone crazy?' Robinson said indignantly.

'Let me finish the thought,' said Rodrigo. 'They want fifty, but they're agreeable to ten, if it's cash and quick.'

'Where is he, this Mr Chapped Hands?'

'Here, around the corner.'

'I'll have a talk with them!' Gobetti said, getting out of his arm-chair.

'You'll ruin the whole deal! They fear American lawyers like fire, and they sent their clerk for the grease. Trust me, don't blow the whole deal this way. That sort of money is infinitesimal compared with the profits from this property. Isn't that right?'

Robinson waited for Gobetti to decide. The latter vacillated.

Lizzie and Jennifer were sitting on a couch facing them, not inter-fering in the men's debate.

'We'll risk it!' Gobetti's eyes flashed excitedly, and he got up from his armchair. 'I got this deal going – I'll get the ten thousand out of the nearest bank.'

'Good idea!' said Rodrigo, approvingly.

Gobetti took Gonzalez's umbrella and walked out.

Tony came back about twenty minutes later and handed a fat envelope to Rodrigo. The latter nodded in satisfaction and disap-peared. Back he soon came, solemnly bearing a document. Behind him came a small-statured, greying Mexican.

'They've sent him with us,' said Rodrigo.

The official in his worn shirt was carefully shaven; he smiled throughout and spoke tolerable English.

'What size is your land?' he asked.

Kharya was at a loss: 'In what sense?'

'Well, how many acres?'

'I don't know yet – but so what?'

'I've been ordered to measure the property and fill in the form for my boss. He said there wouldn't be any problems.'

The travellers began making their way outside and seating them-selves in the bus. Queen Lily the First sat in state on the first seat, next to the driver. She didn't look young, but she did look hearty. Kharya dragged along a hamper from the kitchen, with champagne and *hors d'oeuvres* for the picnic. When everyone had taken a seat he crammed the hamper into the aisle of the bus and arranged himself on it, next to Lily.

'Well, newlyweds, how did your first wedding night go?' shouted Rodrigo, who had seated himself in the very back. 'The people want to know the truth.'

Lily cut him off: 'I beg you not to be vulgar.'

The bus moved off. Tailing along behind came a little truck with a trailer, on which bobbed the launch.

They soon made their way out of Nuevo Laredo, and between the cornfields and orange orchards the cortege moved towards its cherished goal.

The rain suddenly stopped, the sun came out, the road was wreathed in steam. To the right a rainbow hung over the fields. Soon the heat began to overcome them all. Someone asked about the air-conditioning, but there was none to be had in a bus that old.

Kharya pulled two maps out of his pocket, one American and one local, purchased at the hotel kiosk. He compared one to the other, back and forth – after all, he'd got to his island by the opposite bank of the river. Road No. 2 (this time on the Mexican side) dodged around somewhere close to the river on its way towards the little town of Colombia.

Before they got to Colombia Kharya ordered the driver to turn off. The bus slid down the track. Outside the window, a possum, frightened by the noise, came out of the grass and took to its heels. They drove past a tobacco field, and then bare earth began. Conversation in the bus fell off; everyone looked to both sides in search of the prime cause of our journey. Here was the little village of Blas-Maria: it shouldn't be far from it, although ahead of us was still nothing but bare earth, slippery after the rain.

'Stop, stop!' cried Kharya.

He leaped out first, lit up a cigarette and nervously drew on it.

'That's your last one, Khariton,' Lily warned him sternly. 'I want you to live for a long time.'

'Agreed,' he said, obediently throwing his whole pack away under a bush, but he kept on sucking on the one he had.

Madame Bourbon pulled a golden crown out of her handbag and

put it on. Noticing it, Kharya nodded with a smile, even though he wasn't into crowns himself.

Our strange gypsy caravan, like some scene from some never-seen film, approached the river. The festive clothing didn't suit either the place or the time in any way. In front stomped Kharya with the two maps in his hands, behind came Lily in her golden crown. Poopsik ran alongside at her feet, whimpering and trying to sit down for a rest.

The land had dried out a bit, but puddles glistened here and there. The hot wind made breathing difficult. No one knew how much further there was to go.

Kharya now and again stopped, looking now at the sun, now at the road left behind us. Behind him minced the official, with measured tread. The attorneys manfully hauled their heavy briefcases. Provident Jennifer had brought along with her a bottle of water, from which she drank now and again. Lizzie was a bit down – it was evident that this trip wasn't her style at all. Valerie and I were sorry that we'd got mixed up in this affair, but meanwhile there was nothing we could do. Rodrigo was stomping along in the distance, whistling something that sounded like a tango and looking from side to side.

The only good thing was that the promised cyclone was either late or had changed direction.

'When? When are we going to get there?' asked Jennifer, not for the first time. 'Otherwise I'm going to have my baby right here . . .'

'Don't make jokes like that,' Tony implored.

'My strength is failing,' complained Lily. 'I'm not prepared to go all the way around the globe on foot.'

We had to stop. Gobetti turned out to have some foresight. He asked us to wait, threw his briefcase to his colleague Robinson and ran back to the bus, returning in a little while pushing in front of him a collapsible wheelchair that he'd borrowed from the hotel. The wheelchair bumped merrily over the hummocks. But Lily flatly refused to sit down in it.

'It would be better if I died on my feet, rather than go around in a wheelchair!'

They wheeled the chair along, just in case. They weren't going to just chuck it into an empty field.

'Hey, look over there,' Lizzie said. 'A sail!'

Far off, on the yet-invisible river, a sailboat was being noiselessly driven by the wind. So the river was already very near.

'Just a little bit more,' muttered Kharya, panting. 'My landmark has to be somewhere around here . . .' There was a look of dismay on Kharya's face.

'Well, where is your property, then?' asked the official.

Again we came to a halt. The sailboat, drawn by the current, was getting larger. It became evident that the sails were heeling over in the wind, now to one side, now to the other.

'Soon, soon,' asserted Kharya. 'We'll get across this embankment, and . . .'

We marched another hundred paces, no more.

'There it is. My island!' the prime minister suddenly bawled out, pointing both hands at a bend of the river. 'There!'

'Glory be to God!' prayed the queen. 'Finally!'

Kharya ran ahead. Came to a halt. Started running again. Once again came to a stop. Sat down on the ground.

There was no way to go any further: at his feet, washing away the shoreline, swirled spouts of turbid water. Everyone stared ahead, gathering in a tight clump around Kharya.

But he was frozen to the spot; he'd lost the gift of speech.

In the midst of the river lay a narrow brown strip of land. Here it was, the island! The flag with its sign in English, 'Property of Harry Lapidar', still stood on the little ridge, but the shaft had heeled over and the wet standard was being pulled at by the current.

The island was being quickly washed away by the rising water from last night's rain, and it was melting before our eyes.

We stood as silently as at a funeral. The sandy ridge was crumbling away, becoming narrower and narrower. Finally it was entirely licked away by the tiny waves. The flag – the board with Kharya's sheet – fell into the water, swelled up in a bubble and floated off, the last memento of the Kingdom of Grande-Bravo.

Kharya cursed vilely.

'What's he saying?' Lizzie asked.

'Primarily things about your mother,' guessed Tony.

'He doesn't know her, does he?'

Nobody answered Lizzie.

'Uh-huh!' drawled Attorney Robinson. 'I suspected this . . .'

'Suspected and didn't say anything!' yelled the indignant Attorney Gobetti.

'From the start I had a foreboding about this,' Robinson gloomily continued. 'I closed my eyes to the fact that your client, Lily Bourbon, is from the state of California. And here you are . . .'

'What does California have to do with this?' said Gobetti in surprise.

'What do you think? California, in the official enumeration, is the thirty-first state of the USA. Switch the digits' places and what do you get?'

'Thirteen,' pronounced Gobetti, his voice sinking. 'I never thought about that . . .'

'Thirteen,' Robinson repeated in a whisper and crossed himself. 'Forgive me, Lord, for pronouncing that word out loud.'

Tony swore at him: 'You're a goddamned triskaidekaphobe!'

'Yes, I am one,' admitted Charlie. 'And you don't have any superstitions – so you go and swallow this crock of shit!'

'But on the other hand, we did have a good time,' objected Tony. 'Only bringing the launch was a waste.'

On the far – American – side, two police cars silently drove down to the river and came to a stop with their front ends to the water. The cops climbed out, stood up and, talking between themselves, observed what was going on over on the Mexican side. One of the policemen was talking on the telephone. A little later a third car drove up to them – highway patrol. They took turns checking us out with binoculars.

'What nonsense this is!' exclaimed Lily, hands clasped in emotion, hurting Kharya's feelings. 'The Kingdom of Grande-Bravo!'

'Why nonsense?' he asked forlornly, sitting on the ground and pressing his head between his hands.

'Don't you get it? After all, the acronym for that is KGB! All my hopes washed away . . .'

She stood, her lips tightly compressed, ready to sob.

'Now I know what size your island was,' the official – who'd stayed quiet up to now – pronounced sympathetically.

'How?' asked Robinson.

'Its size was thirteen acres. There's a bend in the river here, and periodically an island gets deposited – always thirteen acres of land. Then the water rises, and . . . I've been working here for twenty-four years . . .'

'Hey, Rodrigo!' bellowed Robinson with all his might.

'*Go-go-go!*' came back the echo from all around. Nobody responded to it.

'Who saw where Rodrigo went to?' remembered Gobetti suddenly. 'He's probably aware of these little things, too!'

Everyone started looking around them. The kingdom's chief of secret police had secretly disappeared.

'Where's our money, sir?' Robinson demanded of the official. 'Where's Rodrigo, that son of a bitch!'

'Who's that – Rodrigo?' The official went pale with fright. 'That fellow who brought me to you? He was somewhere here . . . But I don't know anything, sir! The head of our office sent me with him to measure the island – I came along . . . I swear nobody has given me money of any kind!'

I was thinking that Rodrigo was probably hurrying off to South America to buy himself the presidency of Nigilesia. They'd said on

CNN that morning that the president had died there yesterday – I caught that on the television in my room. Rodrigo had probably heard it, too, and decided not to lose any more time with us poor fools.

A jeep with two Mexican policemen in it had driven up to our bus. They climbed out, waved to their colleagues on the other shore and began questioning the driver.

'We have to go back to the hotel – there's nothing doing, here!' decided Gobetti and added in the great and mighty Italian language: '*Finita la commedia!*'

Nobody budged from the spot, though. Kharya, fat and ungainly, got up from the ground and stood there, gloomier than a storm cloud. With a queenly gesture Lily got her handkerchief from her sleeve and wiped the dust from her cheeks.

'Hey, Mr Harry!' yelled Robinson, glancing at his watch. 'Don't forget that you have to get straight to the gaol at Fort Bend.'

Phantoms have a hypnotic effect on me. I kept on looking fascinatedly at the water, where, according to all the tales that had so inspired me to various contradictory thoughts, last night and even this morning there still existed the grand Kingdom of Grande-Bravo.

Lily was trying to tear the golden crown off her head, but it had caught in her hair. In a rage Madame Bourbon tore at it even more fiercely, and the crown came off together with her wig.

Even in the scariest of dreams I wouldn't have been able to imagine Her Highness totally bald. She frenziedly tore the crown from the hair and tossed it into the river. The wig she stretched back on to its old place, but it was on crooked, like a cap with ear flaps on her drunken lover Yesenin, back in ancient times.

The crown floated in the water and turned over, with no intention of sinking. The gold foil came unstuck from it and turned into a long, curling strip. The current carried it off. Coming to a whirlpool, the gold glittered one last time and dwindled into the deep.

The queen sobbed. Valerie began weeping too, either from the tragicomic happenings or out of feminine solidarity.

Unexpectedly Poopsik, who had been getting tangled underfoot everywhere, froze. He stretched his nose into the air, snarled more in fright than threateningly and then whimpered.

'What's wrong with you, my sweetie?' asked his mistress, sobbing.

'Be quiet. Right now I haven't got time for you . . .'

But the dog barked, pressing himself against her legs as if defending his mistress from something.

'Lily, darling!' A hoarse voice rang out from God knows where. 'Pardon me for dying . . . Don't be afraid of me!'

We all looked around, not understanding what was happening.

'Good Lord – Ken!' Lily's eyes widened. 'See, it's Ken! He saw how much I'm hurting, and he came back to me . . .'

The spectre said, in abominable Russian: 'I want you been happiness. Do *toap-toap* on me . . .'

We stood as if paralysed, not even breathing.

The sailboat came closer to the shore, so that its name became visible: it was the *Lily*. Ken Stemp, in white shorts and a T-shirt with the legend *Non-fat only!*, keeping his balance with one hand on the mast, dropped his sail and threw his anchor into the water. The yacht turned its nose into the current and was still.

Weightlessly stepping along the water, sockless in sandals, spreading his arms wide as if to embrace someone, Ken came to the shore and slowly, solemnly paced straight towards us, his goatee trembling.

The sun reflected from his bald spot, as if a golden nimbus were shining around his skull. Several paces away from us Ken came to a halt. His chest expanded, taking in air with a whistle, greedily, and he began to sing boomingly:

'Lay on my breast your head so tender,
And to your love I will surrender,
Until the day begins anew,
And nightly shades envelop you . . .
Nightly shades enve-e-e-lop you.'

O my righteous God! My former student had translated the old Russian *romance* all the way to its end. When had Ken done it? Had he managed it in this life or in the next one, unbeknownst to us?

Finishing his song, Ken came ever closer. We stood around Lily as if under a spell. Ken, however, paid not the slightest attention to us. Only Lily existed for him, and the distance between him and her slowly diminished. Why had he appeared? Maybe yesterday he hadn't latched on to the fact that his wife had found herself another worthy gentleman. And yet they say that everything is visible from on high . . .

But, I won't lie, I thought of this afterwards: at the time fright had seized us, deprived us of the gift of thought, bound us all fast.

Ken's face, formerly burned by wind and sun like a redskin, had lost all colour. You would scarcely have been able to guess at his nose and lips by their contours, as feeble as if drawn by a sketching pencil. He opened his mouth, as if to say something, but no sound came out. Then Ken strained with all his might. Two tears like unpolished diamonds welled slowly out of his eyes and ran down his cheeks. Suddenly he uttered in a hoarse voice: 'You don't have to be afraid of me, Lily! Make *toap-toap* on the yacht! Go there . . . There you will be really queen. It's nice there!'

His Russian had perceptibly improved. He blinked his eyes and made something like a smile. Taking a smooth and weightless step forward, Ken tried to embrace Lily.

'No, no! No-o-o-o!' she shrieked hysterically. She stepped back a pace, tripped and fell flat on her back. And lying there continued to yell: 'No! I won't go there for anything! Disappear! I want to live . . .'

Ken blinked, waved his arms like a conductor, began swallowing air and, sighing, became so transparent that you could see the shore and the river through him. Another instant and he was at rest, serene. A true knight of love, turned in the light of day into a night-time shade, he evaporated, as if he'd never appeared at all.

The sails on the yacht spread in the wind, she parted from her anchor, and, solemnly rocking from starboard to port and back again, she sailed off downstream. We followed it a long time with our eyes. The sailboat began to decrease in size and faded in the fog, finally disappearing over the horizon.

Poopsik whimpered a bit, shivered a little and calmed down. He began to lick Lily's face. Valerie and I came to ourselves at the same moment and hurried to help her get up. Her chic dress was covered with mud. The queen hung on us like a mannequin, came to her senses and again began sobbing; she couldn't calm down for a long time. The paint was running off her face and neck, revealing the cracks there, as deep as canals on Mars. One whole eyelash fell off, sticking itself to my shoulder and blinking in the wind. We sat Lily with difficulty in the wheelchair.

We had to calm her down; we were supposed to say and repeat the sort of necessary banalities that are always pronounced in situations like that, but – nothing doing, suitable words evaporated, nothing came to my mind. I squeezed out something intended to comfort her, anyway.

'What are you, a psychotherapist?' she exclaimed in the middle of a sob. 'This is the first time in my life I've ever suffered total defeat. I wish I was dead.'

'Why dead, when you've got a new husband and Ken has left you his whole fortune? It didn't work this time, it will next time.'

'Fortune!' She screwed up her red, wept-out eyes. 'I kept quiet, counting on the island. There's only beans in my stupid late husband's account – that's all. Beavered away all his life and put crumbs away. How could he have the nerve to summon me to him?'

'Maybe he loves you? And summoned you because there's no need for money there?'

'How do you know that? Money's necessary everywhere.'

'They say there's no happiness in money . . .'

'Quit cranking out nonsense! You'd do better to stop talking altogether!'

So I have to shut up. Not write any Chapter 13. What can you do when such a woman demands it?

As Voltaire used to say in days of old – I kiss your wingtips.